NO COINCIDENCE

No Coincidence
A Morgan McGhee Novel

Ann Baker

Avanti Books
Tampa, FL

NO COINCIDENCE

A Morgan McGhee Novel

PUBLISHED BY AVANTI BOOKS
P.O. BOX 13681
Tampa, FL 33681-3681
www.avantibookpublishing@yahoo.com

This book is a work of fiction. The events and characters in this novel are a product of the author's imagination. Entities and locations mentioned are included only for authenticity and are not intended to indicate any events occurred at or within any entity or location mentioned. Any resemblance to actual events and/or persons, living or dead is purely coincidental.

LCCN: 2005920029
ISBN: 0-9764315-0-5
Printed in the United States of America
August 2005

This book is dedicated to my mother. She has never ceased to support me in every way possible.

Special thanks to all of those who assisted and encouraged me during the production of this work. While there are too many to mention, you know who you are. Your kindness will not be forgotten.

PROLOGUE

SEPTEMBER COLD FRONT

Short bursts of hot, moist air with a faint scent of wet dog, drifted into her nostrils. A wet tongue lapped at her cheek as someone in the distance yelled. Long past the shivering stage, she felt numb and could not find the energy to move. A feeble attempt to open her eyes was all she could manage.

Believing she must be dreaming she tried to disregard her seeming delusion and drift back off into sweet unconsciousness. The pain in her shoulder was still searing, and she knew the warm moistness she felt on her back was her own blood.

If she could just go back to sleep, it would all be over. There were worse things that could happen to you than dying. She didn't want to think about how the man she thought she would be with for life was gone forever. Nor did she want to remember how easy it had been to betray him with another less than two weeks after he was gone.

She felt something cover her face as the sound of a distant engine approaching faded in and out. *Oh, God, I must be dead*, she thought. *This would be a good time to ask for forgiveness.*

Warm hands touched her neck and she felt a face brush against hers. She could have sworn it was his voice she heard shouting. The words escaped her as she hoped against hope it was him. What a fool she had been to run from him. He was the only one that could protect her, and at the same time the only one that could utterly destroy her.

It was hard to tell how long she had been there. The night had fallen and the wind was howling as the cold air that followed the rain had begun to set in. Already the temperatures had fallen a good twenty degrees since she left the cabin. Her wet clothes clung to her rapidly diffusing what little body heat she had left.

People seemed to be around her, as the sounds ebbed and flowed, but never stayed long enough to get a handle on. The sweet seduction of oblivion drew her like a warm fire, as she paused suspended between one world and the next.

A faint smile began to form as she thought she heard him whisper, "Morgan, Morgan, I can't live without you. You've got to pull through this. I do love you."

As the helicopter set down in the field and the paramedics ran to her she realized her angel had come for her. Dream or no, he was here with her. She could die in peace now. Surely God would understand why she had been so foolish.

ANN BAKER

ONE

This year's roses were superb, the best she had grown so far. The garden had taken years to mature, but every effort had been worth it. Nothing made a house feel like home more than fresh cut flowers.

She placed the vase in the center of the table and stood back to survey her work. Everything was perfect, but if Greg didn't get home soon the steaks would dry out. He was already forty-five minutes late.

Nervously, she popped the cork and poured herself another glass of wine. All day she had tried to find some magic phrase that would make her news more palatable to him. Nothing had come to her, and she doubted it would in the next few minutes.

At last, she heard him at the front door. She began putting the food in serving dishes as he came into the kitchen, tossing his keys on the counter.

"Hey there, pretty lady."

"Hey yourself," she said smiling.

"Would you like a glass of wine?" she asked. "I made all your favorites."

"Sure, it looks great."

He took his place at the table and began serving himself as she poured his wine.

"You have any rolls to go with this?" he asked.

"They're almost done. You go ahead and start."

Morgan held her tongue as they ate. Greg never liked conversation when he ate dinner. It had taken her years to get used to it. She gulped the last of her wine as Greg belched loudly, signaling he was finished eating.

"That was great. You're the only one

that can cook a steak the way I like it."

"Thanks," Morgan said, clearing the table.

"You want to have your wine in the spa? I got some of your favorite cigars in Ybor City this morning."

The offer was too good for him to pass up. Within minutes he was savoring his cigar and sipping his wine. Morgan, seated in the spa next to him, was anything but relaxed as she gathered her courage.

"I got some good news today," she began.

"What's that?" he asked casually.

"I was accepted for a job I applied for."

Greg dropped his cigar in the spa as he sat bolt upright. "You applied for a job?"

There was no turning back now. "Yes, I did. About six months ago. I thought it'd be fun, just to see if I got hired. I couldn't believe they called me. I almost forgot about it"

She was rambling on nervously as he sat staring at her. His cigar circled wildly in the bubbling water.

"You told them you were joking, right?" he finally managed to say.

"No, I didn't. Greg, I can't stand sitting at home all the time. It's been years now. There's nothing for me to do."

"You're not going to start up on the baby thing again, are you?"

"That's not fair. It's not about that. I'm wasting my life sitting here."

"You call taking care of me wasting your life?"

"No, it's not that," she said, already becoming weary of the argument.

"Then what is it? You know, Morgan, I'd hoped you'd have been better at socializing. My position is pretty important, and the promotion to Director of Finance meant something, whether you know it or not. I'd have a good shot at something better if you'd just play the game."

"Is that why you married me? I feel like a classic trophy wife without the pedigree."

Greg had no answer for that. That wasn't why he had married her. Her long blond curls and emerald green eyes had taken his breath the first time he had seen her. For years he had felt incredibly lucky to have married her, but since his last promotion he had begun to wonder if she was really right for him at all.

"Was it that friend of yours from the gym that put you up to this?"

"Who, Felicia?" Morgan asked.

"Yeah, that's the one. Was it her?"

"She mentioned they were accepting applications. I asked her how to go about applying."

"Great, I guess you can chase cops like she does. Mark my words Morgan, this'll lead to divorce."

"I think you're overreacting. It's the 90's, Greg. Women are allowed to leave the kitchen from time to time."

TWO

This break was only twenty minutes, so Morgan raced down the stairs as fast as she could. The smell of the new oil-based paint on the banister was still pungent, and it burned in her nose. Turning left sharply, she hit the release bar on the door and shoved it open. The metallic snap echoed down the long, empty hall. There were very few people in the building this time of night. Again, turning left, and then taking a quick right, she arrived at the women's restroom.

This was the nicest restroom in the building, used by the Sheriff's and his colonels' secretaries. It was the only bathroom with decent lighting. Snatching the handle of the first entry door downward, she lowered her shoulder to push open the second.

The handicapped stall had the best mirror. It was low enough to see if your shirt was tucked in smoothly. The dark green polyester pants were standard issue for dispatchers and they showed every line or wrinkle with absolute clarity.

Removing her toothbrush from her purse, she put some toothpaste onto the dampened brush that waited. Hurriedly she scrubbed away hours of bad taste. She found it impossible to go through the whole twelve-hour shift without brushing at least once. Feeling refreshed, she quickly fixed her eyeliner and grabbing her lavender plum lipstick from her purse, hastily smearing it over pursed lips. Then turning on the water she dampened her fingers and ran them through her blond curls to freshen them. Satisfied with her appearance, she left, still rushing as she glanced at her watch. It was just about time for the "Tonight Show" to begin. The monologue was all she cared to hear, but if she didn't hurry, she would miss it.

Hurrying from the rest room, she slipped into the back entrance of the break room that was just across the hall. As she hurried past the tall refrigerated display cases, she noticed a low murmur of voices in the room just on the other side. Rounding the end of the counter she discovered the room, which was normally empty at this hour, filled with deputies in dark green jump suits.

There seemed to be about twenty-five of them, sitting at tables talking. From the looks of things, there wasn't a woman among them, but she wasn't looking around to find out.

It only took a few seconds for Morgan to figure out who they were - Tango Units, Street Crimes. Working mostly against illegal drugs at the street level, they were a light cover squad, able to perform several types of tasks at the whim of their major. One squad was assigned to each district.

There was a momentary pause in the conversation, as the startled men adjusted to a female violating their domain. Recovering quickly they resumed talking. The pause was so brief it was barely noticeable. Morgan felt her cheeks warming as the blood rushed to her face. She was embarrassed for having trespassed on this gathering of the testosterone rich.

As a fair-skinned blond, she had been plagued with a curse of turning bright red whenever embarrassed. Today was no exception. Looking down at the floor, she hoped her hair would conceal her face and went straight over to the vending machines.

Out of the corner of her eye, she could see a tall man to her right at the soda machine. She fumbled with her change, and finally got the sixty-five cents into the slot. She pressed the button to make her selection and stepped over to get a snack. She could see the deputies behind her through the reflective Plexiglas panel. It was clear that the majority of them were watching her at the machine. She told herself it was normal, after all she seemed to be the only female in the room.

Crawling to the door seemed like a good idea at this point, but she forced herself to feign composure. Feeding a crisp dollar bill into the snack machine, she pushed the button for a peanut bar. The change dropped down, and she leaned over to remove it. At the same time, she noticed her candy was stuck on the metal coil that held it. Cursing under her breath, she turned and hit the machine as best she could with her hip, facing away from the tall man, still standing off to the right. After several futile attempts to budge the machine, someone yelled, "Hey, help her get her candy, it's stuck."

Now even more humiliated than before - if it was possible - she was too embarrassed to turn around. The tall man by the soda machine sauntered over, and she stepped aside. He placed one large hand on each side of the snack dispenser, as she held her breath. When he shook the machine, like a box of Cracker Jacks, the candy bar fell to the slot at the bottom. She had just enough courage to look up, as he lowered his impressive body to get the candy bar for her.

His eyes were a dark khaki color, and caught her attention immediately. Feeling her pulse quicken she was sure she would faint or have a stroke at any moment. His blond hair was cut high and tight, and was very becoming. He smiled revealing a brilliant flawless smile. *God, he was gorgeous.*

She noticed that his face seemed a bit too red, and wondered if he too, was plagued with involuntary blushing. She felt as though he was reading her thoughts as she stood there breathlessly, swallowing hard trying hard to maintain composure. Somehow, she managed a small gasped thank-you. Nevertheless, as she looked into his eyes, she hesitated a moment too long, allowing him to look into her eyes a little too deeply.

She remained there frozen, as if a terrified animal cornered in a hunt, unsure what to do next. With his free hand, he opened the flap of her right breast pocket, the Velcro closure that held it fast made the characteristic sharp sound. He then slid the candy bar into her pocket with an exaggerated slowness. Then taking her hand in his, he shook it, as if in the way of introduction. However, to her surprise, he never spoke. He just grinned a sly, sensuous, knowing grin, as he continued to watch her intently. As he released her hand, he slid his palm slowly over hers, fingers following. Morgan was acutely aware of the unusual electricity this man exuded, and the seductive aspect of the whole chance meeting had just increased exponentially.

The other men in the room watched as the miniature melodrama played itself out before them. They would be sure to have a good laugh as soon as she was out of earshot. Armed with this knowledge, she gathered her wits about her, and she tore her wayward eyes from this large gorgeous man. Turning for the back door of the break room, she raced out of there and up the stairs that led back to the hall to Communications.

At the top of the stairwell, she paused to catch her breath. Her hands were trembling, and she was panting like a rabbit that had just outrun a pack of wild dogs. It was so unlike her to have such a ridiculous response to such a simple encounter. How could she have allowed herself to act so foolishly? Ordinarily she didn't even find blond men attractive, couldn't even remember one that struck her as good looking. Well, she had certainly seen one now. And he wasn't just good looking; there was something else that went way beyond looks. It was a base animal type of attraction, electric and alive. It was like nothing she had experienced before, and certainly she hoped she wouldn't ever again.

Down at the other end of the hall Esther was making her way toward her. Her ever inquisitive eye gave Morgan the once over. Finding nothing out of the ordinary in her cursory scan, she passed her by. She mumbled some vague greeting as she entered the door, and Morgan breathed a sigh of relief. She followed Esther in, catching the door just before it locked behind her.

Morgan ran to the restroom to make sure she didn't bear any physical signs of what had just occurred. Sure enough, she gazed in the mirror, and she looked just the same as she had moments before. Little did she know; she would never be the same again. A small seed, planted moments before, would grow to enormous proportions in her life.

THREE

Returning to her position at 911 in the Communications Center, Morgan picked up her book and tried to look normal. After reading over the same page, several times she realized she had not comprehended a single word. Giving up, she put the book down, and closed her eyes, and leaned back in her chair. Why had this stranger had such an effect on her? Who was he? Something about him seemed familiar - like she had known him forever - and yet she was certain she had never seen this man before.

She had all but forgotten the candy bar in her pocket. Just remembering it was there brought a fresh blush to her face. Breaking it into pieces first, she opened the package and began nibbling on the chunks of peanuts coated with candy.

It was a sweet daydream as she allowed her thoughts to drift. Oddly, she remembered every detail of the muscles that were so very apparent. She could feel her pulse increase as she thought of him. Even her breathing changed in response.

With her eyes still closed, she didn't see Randy coming up behind her. He was equipped with a large rubber band, and snapped her with it on the upper arm as he passed by.

"Ouch!" she protested loudly. "That was a cheap shot. My eyes were closed."

"Hey, you know when you close your eyes around me, you're just setting yourself up. You could have taken a seat anywhere else, but you just had to be near me."

"Thanks for reminding me. Now I owe you one. Just don't close your eyes around me, or even blink, Mr. Conceited," she joked, rubbing the now reddened spot on her arm.

Randy was the office gigolo and clown rolled into one, and he was excellent at both. Tall and slim with dark chestnut hair, worn to one side and layered, he was strikingly colored. His deep azure eyes had drawn in more than one unsuspecting lady. He was a very handsome man and he knew it.

By far his most outstanding characteristic was his overwhelming charm. Women fell all over him, young women, old women, it made no difference. He worked the room like a professional, breezing past one after the next. He would drop one disingenuous but believable compliment after the other as he passed through his female admirers. Truly, he was a work of art in motion.

From the beginning Randy and Morgan had disagreements, and they were always very heated. It was usually over some matter of moral principle. Although they enjoyed each other's company, it was difficult to solve the many major philosophical differences. At just the wrong time, those differences would surface, and the clash of wills would begin. Soon after words that cut deeply were exchanged, and then one of them would do something to make the other laugh and the friendship would resume.

He sat down at the position next to hers and logged onto 911. As he leaned way back in his chair a loud "Ahhhhh," escaped. Turning his gaze slowly and directly toward her, he stared for a moment. She tried desperately to look busy, but she wasn't fooling him for one minute. He leaned over in her direction, and then in a deliberate, slow, exceedingly sly tone asked, "Soooo... what's up?"

"Nothing," Morgan responded, looking away. Both actions came a little too quickly.

"Reeeealy?" he asked, moving closer to observe any visible reaction, like a cat watching a mouse.

She hated his uncanny ability to sense

when she didn't want him to know something. Eventually, she had learned to go ahead and tell him everything to begin with. He was, after all, trustworthy if nothing else. Many times, she had begged him for information about someone else, but to no avail. He always remained silent, refusing to surrender even one small detail.

"Your face is... uhhhh... looking... uhhh... a little flushed there Goldielocks. You sure you are okay? And look at that little grin there."

"Randy!!! Really!" she stalled.

"Hummmmmm?" he leaned closer.

"911-what is your emergency?" she was saved by the bell. But, the call didn't take long enough. Randy picked right back up where he had left off.

"So, what's going on?"

"Randy, you drive me crazy."

"I know that," he purred. "You might as well tell me, you know you will anyway."

She sighed long and deep, giving him a sideways grin. "Okay, I'll tell you, if you'll just stop interrogating me."

"That's more like it," he gloated. His expression turned to one of disappointment as he received a call.

"911-what is your emergency?" He let her know the reprieve was only temporary by holding up his index finger while talking. "Where is he now?" he paused as the caller answered, and he typed furiously. "Does he have any weapons?" He called out to the District One radio operator, "Event 2037, the male is signal zero with a gun." Talking again to the caller, "I'm going to get an ambulance rolling to you. Stay on the line."

The call Randy had received lasted a long time and Morgan took two more calls while he stayed on the phone with his complainant. She was hoping that he would forget his inquisition of her he had begun by the time he disconnected, but that was not the case.

So, she told him the whole story from the beginning. He relished each detail, asking more questions than she had thought possible along the way. Since he had gotten married, he seemed to live vicariously through the experiences of others. Perhaps that was part of his charm; he really seemed interested in what was being said. He seemed so genuine, almost convincing you that he really cared.

"I just ran into the most exciting man I've ever seen in my life," she confessed.

"Oh, yeah. Who was it?" Randy countered now intent on the conversation.

"I don't know who it was. I've never seen him before, and hope I never see him again," she said honestly.

"Why would you say that? Temptation a little too much for you?" Randy taunted malevolently, as he laughed aloud.

Morgan hesitated in her response, knowing he had hit the nail right on the top of the proverbial head. Squirming in her chair was enough of a response to indicate to Randy that he was right, so he continued.

"Come on, come on, admit it. You're human. There's nothing wrong with that. You see a good looking guy, and you want him."

"All right, Randy! That's enough. You're right. Isn't that enough for you? Do you have to rub it in?"

"Why, yes!" he replied, shamelessly. I love rubbing it in. It is one of my favorite things to do.

"What did he look like?" Randy continued.

"Well, he was tall, really tall. I'd say about six feet five. He had blond hair and was built like a Scandinavian god. Oh, yes, and he was gorgeous. Did I mention that?" she gushed.

"Yes, you mentioned it about five times

21

already. I think I have that part of the description down now."

"Don't get smart with me, mister. You're the one that asked. I'm simply answering your prying questions the best I can."

"I can't believe you didn't even get his name or anything," Randy continued relentlessly.

"Why would I need his name? I'm married, and that means something to me, even if it doesn't to most of the people that you know."

"That still doesn't make you blind, quite obviously," he said attempting to have the last word.

"I never pretended to be blind. I just find it better to avoid temptations," Morgan defended.

"So then you're admitting you were tempted."

Morgan gasped in exasperation. "I hardly had time to become what I would term as tempted, but I can tell you this."

"Yessss," Randy hissed. "Do tell."

"I hope I never see that man again."

"Why in the hell would you say something like that?" he asked genuinely interested.

"Because, I don't like feeling like that. It's a little too rich for me. He's way out of my league… You know."

"At least you admit you are a weenie."

"If it makes you happy to think of it like that, then you have my permission."

Satisfied that he had gathered all the details that he was going to, he now teased her mercilessly about what he had learned for the better part of an hour. Then without warning, he dropped the matter without further comment. Morgan was relieved for the moment; but knew without any doubt, that Randy had only filed the matter away in memory for use against her at some future date.

FOUR

The rain was coming down hard as Morgan made her way through Ybor City to the Sheriff's Operations Center parking lot. Her umbrella was in the trunk, as usual, and would be of no help. The parking lot just west of the building was rapidly becoming what she affectionately referred to as beautiful Lake Ybor. The wipers on her poor old Toyota were slapping wildly and inefficiently as she pulled into the parking lot. As she located a parking space, she surveyed the area for the best way to make a dash for it.

Across the street in the flooded dirt parking lot, an older red Firebird was parked. It was a beautifully kept 70's model. A large, burly, cop-looking guy in a muscle shirt was sitting in the driver's seat. She felt a little shiver, as he kept looking in her direction, his eyes disguised with dark, wrap-around sunglasses. It was strange to be wearing such dark glasses in the pouring rain.

Gathering her bags, she shrugged off the ominous feeling he provoked and ran to the porch. She was completely drenched during the short sprint. The rain actually felt good at the moment, but she knew it would be very cold upstairs until she dried off.

The roll call room was almost empty. People were probably running late because of the rain. The Interstate would be backed up for miles, a normal each time it rained.

Supervisor Johnson conducted the roll call. "The day shift doesn't really have much to pass on to us. They're working a suicide on the east side, Echo zone. A thirteen year old female was successful. She cut her wrists.

It's raining out there, so there will be lots of wrecks. Don't forget to give the ones on the Interstate and state roads to Florida Highway Patrol. If they can't work it let them give it back to us. As usual, when it rains the alarm calls will be coming in large numbers. Those of you working dispatch positions be sure to check with the street supervisors on what they want to do about canceling them. Does anybody have anything?"

Randy was unwilling to let an opportunity to speak pass him by. "Don't forget to put call back numbers in the calls. Yesterday several calls held for more than thirty minutes and I couldn't call them back."

"Okay, everyone try to get call back numbers," Supervisor Johnson reiterated. "Does anyone else have anything?"

He paused and no one responded. "Let's do it then. Remember to watch each other's backs and work as a team."

They all got up and filed out to their assigned positions. Morgan was still in radio training, the last phase of her dispatcher training. Her trainer Penny was assigned to dispatch. Penny signed on typing at warp speed. Morgan jumped in at her position, sitting down where Sandy had just been working.

"There are oodles of alarm calls holding, and 1B3 just got in a wreck, but he's not injured," Rhonda briefed hurriedly. "The Sergeant has been notified, and legal, but the Public Information Officer hasn't been yet. See ya, I'm outta here."

"Bye," Morgan called quickly.

"Station 10-75, Dispatcher 276, 1852 hours," Morgan began. "One Lima Two, 10-4 your 10-20?"

"I'm 10-4, thank-you ma'am," was the reply.

The "thank-you ma'ams" were all that made the job bearable at times. Some of the depu-

24

ties appreciated a competent radio dispatcher. Their attitude could make the difference in whether a day went well or not.

The radio traffic was non-stop from that point on for the next three hours. It was then that Morgan noticed she was tired and badly needed a break.

"Penny, when do you think I'll get a chance for lunch?"

"God! Who knows, it's wild over here. Send out a message and see if you can get anyone to relieve you."

The message was sent with no response. "No one is stupid enough to come over here right now, Penny."

"Go ahead and go then, I'll double."

"I can't do that to you. What are you crazy?"

"No, you won't get to go if I don't. Go ahead, I promise I'll call someone over if it gets to be too much for me," Penny promised.

"Okay then, I'm not gonna wait for you to say it twice. Units 10-23 for 10-37 change."

Morgan logged off and flew out the door, running down the steps and through the building to the gym. It was very convenient to have a rest room with showers in the building. She kept clothes for working out and emergency cosmetics in her locker. Changing quickly, she hurried into the gym, wanting to get as much as she could from her forty-five minute lunch.

There was a man in the gym. She had seen him many times before. He always said hello, and carried on some small talk, none of which she ever remembered. She still didn't know his name, nor had she ever cared to ask. As he continued to chatter, she selected the equipment farthest away from him to use first. Trying to be polite in her disinterested answers, Morgan wished he would stop talking.

Morgan had been there about ten minutes,

when the door opened from the men's dressing room rather abruptly. In stepped a man in blue jeans and a black muscle shirt, covered by an open button-down shirt.

He looked like a cop, built big, with a very large neck. Actually, he could easily been mistaken for a football player, a big back type. Immediately she recognized him as the man she had seen earlier in the Firebird. He was scanning her in one of the many mirrors, and quickly averted his eyes as they met hers.

"Hey, Chuck," the rambling talker said.

"How's it hanging, and on which side?" was the reply.

How rude, Morgan thought - an obvious sexual innuendo.

"Oh, you know, it's hanging, but I never tell to which side. I try to keep myself busy after the divorce. You still working out?" queried the rambler.

"Yeah, every now and then, not as regular as I would like though," Chuck answered, barely concealing his boredom. "Things still the same down at the courthouse, Mark?"

"Yeah, nothing ever changes there. The life of the lowly bailiff is always dull."

Mark watched himself overtly in the mirror while he performed hammer curls with twenty-five pound dumbbells. He should have been able to see that his form was very sloppy. It appeared that the weights were too heavy for him. He swung them wildly, without control.

"So, Chuck, what do the chicks like now? I've been working out for that big upper body. Isn't that what's in now?"

Morgan was so appalled by the stupidity of the conversation, she couldn't help herself. "I really like fat guys myself," she blurted out.

There was an awkward silence before Chuck started laughing. However, Mark wasn't deterred.

"What do chicks look at first?" he asked Chuck, ignoring her.

Perhaps she was just feeling mischievous, but she couldn't resist. "Its been my experience that women tend to notice the wallet first, and the rest is only secondary."

Chuck directed his gaze straight at Morgan. She noticed he had brilliant powder blue eyes that smiled naturally. He flashed a charming, little boy grin, and excused himself from the blond.

Walking over to where she sat at the leg press, he extended his right hand to her. "Hi, I'm Chuck James. I don't believe I've seen you around here before."

"Nice to meet you. I'm Morgan, Morgan McGhee."

He winked as he shook her hand. "Beautiful name for a beautiful lady. Nice to meet you."

"Likewise," she said, looking away quickly.

"And how long have you worked for the Sheriff's Office?"

"Only about five months now."

"That'd explain why I haven't seen you before. I know if I had, I'd have remembered."

"Oh, really, and why is that?"

His only response was a backward glance and grin. He was already headed to the door. Boyish and shy was the impression he had given, but her intuition screamed *Wolf*, loudly. Somehow, she was quite sure she would see Chuck James again.

FIVE

When she had finished her work out and showered, she returned to her position at the radio. It was only two more hours before she was to be relieved. The radio had slowed considerably, and was much easier to manage.

Joe relieved her for the second half of the shift, and she was scheduled to work 911 for the next six hours. Felicia Langston had the seat next to her. She was an attractive petite woman in her late thirties.

Felicia set her gym bag on the floor at her position. She was a few years older than Morgan was, trim with a muscular build. She wore her chestnut hair in a long layered style that curved to frame her face.

"Your uniform always looks like it just came from the cleaners. I'm wrinkled before I leave the house," Morgan said.

"Thanks," Felicia replied. "How was the radio today?"

"It was crazy busy, but I like it that way. The time goes faster. Penny is so funny. She makes me laugh all the time."

"That's great. I'm glad you're having fun. Work is too big a part of your life not to enjoy what you're doing."

"I went to the gym on my lunch break," Morgan ventured.

She told her the story of the men talking in the gym while she was there. Felicia listened between calls, amazing Morgan with her ability to keep track of the conversation with all the distraction.

"So, who was the guy that wanted to know what 'chicks' like?" she asked.

"You know him I'm sure, he's down there all the time. He's the guy with the brown crew cut, short and stocky, drives the orange Corvette. He said his name is Mark."

"Oh, yes!" She laughed, snorting as she tried to gain composure. "I know exactly who you are talking about. I didn't know his name. I think he works downtown though."

Morgan loved to hear her laugh. She didn't care about being dignified she just really enjoyed herself. Everyone teased her about it, and she took the teasing good-naturedly.

"He said he's a bailiff."

"Well, who was the other guy?" she asked.

"He said his name is Chuck James."

"*Chuck James*!!!" she said exaggeratedly. "Oh, honey. You've just met the most licentious man in the agency. You'd better watch out for that one."

"There was a dispatcher up here that went out with him a few times. She didn't know he was married."

"How could she miss that little detail?" Morgan asked.

"I guess she was too stupid to look him up in the personnel file in the computer. Anyway, she told me that he was quite a twisted kind of guy."

"Twisted - in what way?"

"Well, it seems he is kind of.... well... let's just use the word kinky. It seems he got her into quite a situation, and she had a hard time getting herself out of it. Then she found out he was married. He told her he didn't think it was any of her business."

"Let me get this right. He didn't think she needed to know that he was married?"

"That's right. He said that his marriage was his business, and didn't concern her."

"Sounds like a real nice kinda guy."

"There are a lot of them out there just like him, honey. Trust me I know."

"I guess I've got a lot to learn."

"That's an understatement. I never tell anyone my business, except maybe Randy. If someone happens to find out by chance... oh well. People are going to talk. I'd rather leave them guessing."

"I'll have to learn not to care what people think. That's Greg's first priority."

"To hell with them all," Felicia said. "As long as you feel right about what you do, don't let it bother you."

Morgan got a tone in her headset signaling an incoming call. "911, what is your emergency?"

"This is Janice Eversol, I need the police."

Morgan verified her address and phone number and asked what the nature of emergncy was.

"I need to be arrested. I killed my baby."

Horrified, Morgan motioned to Felicia to listen in, continuing to type furiously. "Janice, can you tell me what happened?

"She wouldn't stop crying. I just wanted her to stop."

Felicia ran to the radio operator's position and told him what was going on. As she passed Bill Johnson she told him to listen in from the supervisor console. As soon as he heard he called for a medical rescue unit to be enroute.

"I put her in the dryer," Janice said, losing her surreal calm and becoming hysterical. "I closed the door. I didn't mean to hurt her. Please hurry," she screamed.

In spite of her revulsion, Morgan tried to calm her. "Janice, is your door unlocked?"

"Yes, it's open," she sobbed.

"Who's there with you?"

"Only Marcie," she whispered.

Felicia yelled across the room to Morgan. "See if she has any weapons. A deputy is rolling up now."

Janice said she didn't. Morgan yelled across the room so Joe could tell the deputy.

"Janice I want you to go to the front door and step outside. Keep your hands out in front of you so the deputy can see you are unarmed."

Janice agreed and put the phone down. When Morgan heard the deputy talking to her she put down the phone. Immediately she logged off the console and ran to the break room.

Bill Johnson followed her. Felicia was right behind him. Had it not been for their consoling her, Morgan would have left that day and never come back.

It was almost a full hour before she came back to her position to work. She could feel everyone's eyes follow her across the room. Her eyes were red and she was embarrassed. A closer look around the room confirmed her suspicions that she wasn't the only one that had been crying. For the first time she felt as though she belonged.

SIX

The parking garage was dimly lit and at first Greg didn't see the Taurus parked next to his car. When the passenger window rolled down he was startled.

"Get in," the driver said.

"Doug, you scared the shit out of me. What are you doing here?"

"Get in," he repeated.

"I've got to get home. My wife has dinner cooking," Greg stalled.

"Who the hell do you think you're talking to? Get in the goddamned car," the driver ordered.

Against his better judgement, Greg got in. The Taurus backed out of the parking space and headed up the ramp to the upper floors.

"What's going on?" Greg asked.

"We've got trouble. Did a county commissioner ask you for some financial records recently?"

"Yes, he did."

"Who was it?" Doug demanded.

"You know who it was."

"Under no circumstances are you to give him those records."

"I don't have a choice. They're public record. Besides, he already has them."

"Oh good God, it's worse than I thought. How long ago did he get them?"

Doug stopped at the top of the parking garage. There wasn't a single other car up there, and no witnesses to see them together.

"His clerk picked them up early last week."

"You're going to have to do something about this," Doug demanded.

"What do you think I can do?"

"College boy, you're the one with the fancy education. I'd say you'd better start figuring. Anybody with half a brain could see what's been going on."

"I thought you said you had it covered. No one would ever question it."

"Did I now? Well let me tell you a new one. When they do figure it out, it'll all come back to you. If anyone hangs over this, you'll be the one that goes down."

"Now that's loyalty for you. I guess since my dad's gone now there's no need to protect me anymore. So much for the brother-hood of Masons."

"You're expendable. At the very least you should have contacted me before you gave those documents up." Doug lit a cigar.

Greg had hear enough. He got out of the car and walked toward the stairwell.

"Take care of it," Doug yelled as he drove away. "Take care of that pretty wife of yours too."

The last comment made Greg livid. A few more months and he would have been out of this mess. He planned on bailing out of the game and focusing on his political carreer. Hank Wright's inquiry was sure to put an end to that.

Wright had been elected to the county commission three years ago. Coming out of nowhere he had made a big splash when he jumped in the pool. He was determined to make a name for himself.

First he sponsored a penny gas tax to build a new museum. Private financing paid for his urban renewal project. He was constantly making the front pages of the local newspapers with one ambitious venture after the next. Of late he was lobbying for the Democratic National Convention to hold their convention in Tampa.

No one minded the efforts to modernize what was essentially a one-horse city, despite the large population. Now he was looking into where millions of taxpayer dollars were slipping through the cracks. More than a few eyebrows were raised, and somehow it was all falling on Greg's shoulders.

SEVEN

As time passed, Morgan became very good at her job. It took at least a year to really understand the big picture. There were so many things to learn, so many computer programs. In addition, the ten-codes, signal codes, and radio procedures had been like learning another language. Then there was the general knowledge you needed to answer the phones. People called the police when there was no one else they could think of. They wanted help with everything from complex legal problems to how to get their cat out of a tree.

Dispatchers answered the non-emergency and 911 phones, and worked the police radio. The radio was divided into three positions. The variety of the work made the night go much faster. Moving around also allowed you to sit with different groups of people and get to know them better. Each one seemed to have unique and interesting background.

There was a certain type of personality that was required to be a dispatcher. More than anything else, you had to have a sharp mind, able to do three to four things at one time. Fast typing ability, especially speed with numbers was essential. Above all, a thick skin and an ability to work with difficult people was the most important. Not only were coworkers hard to deal with, but the public that called on the phone could be totally obnoxious. Then the deputies would get mad at you sometimes. If everything came together just right on a given day, suddenly the job could become unbearable.

One of the hardest things for Morgan to understand was the lack of knowledge most depu-

ties had of the job of dispatcher. It would
seem that with the level of interaction required that they would have wanted to understand as well as be understood. Nevertheless,
there was a pervasive attitude that communications was a demeaning job, and therefore unim-
portant. At least that was the "old school"
mind set.

There were many obstacles to overcome
just to do the job, but Morgan always enjoyed a
good fight. And fight she did, with many of
the people there. Most had similar personality types, there were bound to be clashes. New
people were tested and pushed by the more se-
nior, to see what they were made of. Any hint
of weakness, or the slightest retreat, was
viewed as a signal to move in on the vacillat-
ing victim. And sometimes it was a whole pack
that shared the kill.

Friendship was a fragile thing in the
Comm. Center. Anyone willing to talk to you
was just as willing to discuss everything you
told them with anyone and everyone else. Not
that Morgan minded, it was just the little
twists and bends they added to the story that
were maddening.

The only person Morgan really trusted
was Felicia. They worked out together in the
gym downstairs instead of eating most nights.
She told Felicia all of her secrets, knowing
she would understand without being judgmental.
It was unusual to find female friend that was
that accepting without being competitive.

Felicia and Morgan had been in the gym
workng out - on lunch break late one night -
when Morgan began to realize what the term den
of iniquity really meant. They had all but
finished working out when the door from the
men's room opened. Morgan wasn't familiar
with the man who came in, but she later learned
Felicia was.

He was a good-looking guy and it was more

than obvious he was no stranger to the gym with his well defined muscular build. It was almost as if he was the only one in the room as he slowly made his way around the three walls that were covered in full-length mirrors. Admiring himself in each one, he flexed his arms and then his legs before taking off his shirt. Discarding his shirt on the squat rack, he moved on to flexing his chest muscles, shamelessly staring at his own image.

It was then that the door from the women's room opened into the gym and a bleached blonde fitting the "rode hard and put up wet" description sauntered in. Her eyes met the self-absorbed exhibitionist's and they began to perform what by all appearances was a demented version of a Tango from across the room.

Morgan turned her attention to Felicia to avoid bursting out in hysterical laughter. The expression Felicia wore said it all. She had been in this situation before. They had a few more minutes left on their treadmills and Morgan wondered which would be more awkward, staying or going.

The woman was as enamored with her own reflection as was the man. Facing a mirror at the chin up bar, she stood with her hands on the bar, feet wide apart, gazing at her scantily clad body. She seemed not to notice as the male came up behind her placing his hands on either side of hers on the bar. Slowly and deliberately he began to grind his pelvis against her posterior as she stared into her own eyes.

Morgan's eyes widened as she flashed a startled look at Felicia. Felicia signaled with her hand to give it another minute. Although they both avoided looking at them directly, with all the mirrors it was impossible not to see what was going on.

The man's hands cupped the woman's breasts as he kneaded at them, still grinding away. Still her gaze never left her own eyes. One hand continued to squeeze her breast as the other dropped down to her crotch.

Morgan had seen enough and hit the stop button on the treadmill and made a straight path for the exit door. Felicia was right behind her.

As soon as they were outside Morgan burst into laughter. "Oh, my God. What in the hell was that?"

Felicia was trying to control her snorting. "That's Colonel Higgins daughter and her boyfriend. They're the strangest thing I've ever seen. They only do that for the shock value."

"Aren't they worried there are cameras in there?"

"Are you kidding?" Felicia shot back. "If there were they wouldn't have to try to capture unsuspecting victims working out. Besides, her dad isn't going to let his little angel get into any trouble."

"Doesn't he care that people will know she's a whore?"

"Hah! Anyone saying anything bad about her might as well look for another job. And like they say, 'the apple doesn't fall far from the tree'. The two of them are just alike."

Morgan shook her head in disbelief. Maybe Greg had been right about this job.

Three hours later, Morgan pulled out of the SOC parking lot in her old blue Toyota. She was completely unaware that anyone was watching. Felicia waved good-bye to Morgan, got in her own car, and left - noticing nothing out of the ordinary.

Neither of them had seen the gray sedan as it pulled in behind Morgan at the stop sign at Twenty-first and Eight. As Morgan turned right, so did the car behind her. It followed her to the red light at Adamo. As she continued straight ahead to the Leroy Selmon Expressway, the sedan turned left. The man driving the car smiled to himself, this was so easy.

It was an overwhelming rush, even at this early stage when the object of the hunt was unaware. The role of predator was his favorite. He especially savored the catch, but between now and then there was the enjoyment of the hunt.

He inhaled deeply, filling his lungs with the heavy, humid summer air. It was amazing how adrenaline affected the senses, heightening each one to an exquisite peak. Hearing only slightly impaired by the increased flow of blood in vessels near to the eardrum. This is what he lived for, the feeling of his own life pulsing through his veins at a frenzied rate. The reason was the power he had over another person, someone totally oblivious to the threat that loomed just outside of the grasp of their own senses.

No need to rush, there was plenty of time to enjoy every detail. There was no particular deadline to be met. As long as he finished by the first of the year, and that was months away. This would be a game to enjoy. Opportunities like this didn't come along every day.

What did it matter to him that he knew her? He had done jobs like this before, it was nothing personal. It was just the way it went. Besides, she didn't mean that much to him anyway. Sure, he could do it; maybe it would even be more fun this way. Everyone has to die sometime. He would be sure she went quickly with little or no pain. He could do that for her at least.

EIGHT

Thursday and Friday were her days off this week. Morgan slept through most of Thursday, and woke feeling hung over. She made a pot of extra strong coffee, and took a cup of it to the couch. Mercifully, the curtains were drawn. The room was thick with darkness, comforting to bloodshot, tired eyes.

As she was finishing her second cup of coffee, she heard Greg pulling up in the drive. He was early today. It was only about five-thirty. The car door closed with that new car - rubber meets rubber - solid sound. Greg's loafers made a slow, familiar crunch as he came up the walk. His key turned in the dead bolt, and he entered the room, all fresh and perky.

He seemed like he had just woken up from a nap instead of returning from work. Not a hint of his undoubtedly long and hectic day was apparent, even to a skilled observer. He was bright eyed and bushy tailed, raring to go. Greg had relentless energy.

He flashed his wide, easy grin at Morgan. "Hi! You look rough," he ventured. "How long have you been up?"

"Not long," she lied, feeling ashamed to have been sitting there so long doing nothing.

"Why don't you get showered up, and I'll take you to Ybor for dinner?"

Morgan agreed reluctantly. Ybor City, an old historical section of Tampa, was quickly becoming a hot nightspot. Almost anyone who was anyone in the city could be spotted there on any given night during the week, but especially on the weekend.

Greg was quickly becoming an important player in the local political arena. Until recently, they had enjoyed relative anonymity when they dined out. However, this last promotion to Director of Finance at County Tax Collector's Office had brought with it an increased visibility and accompanying scrutiny.

Morgan tried to keep a low profile at her job, but increasingly the law enforcement people she met were connected to Greg's political acquaintances. For her it was a little unnerving. One false step and Greg's career could be damaged. So, trying to be the perfect wife, she never discussed her personal life, opinions, or feelings with anyone. It seemed unnatural, she had always been open an honest, perhaps to a fault.

"Sounds great," she lied. "That new black dress I bought should be perfect. Where are we going, Columbia?"

"No, not tonight. I thought Ovo Cafe. Let's jump in the Jacuzzi before we go. Remember your philosophy on sex after dinner."

"Right, remember my philosophy on sex in the morning?"

"Of course, this is your morning, isn't it?" he joked, good-naturedly. "So, which do you prefer, after dinner or your morning? I know you don't like either especially, but give a fella a break."

"I think I'll pick after dinner."

"Agreed. Then after dinner, it is. We'll skip the spa for now."

"You're the sweetest man. I could never replace you."

"You only say that because I am so nice. But don't expect me to be so nice after dinner."

"Hummmmm, I'll hold you to that promise, sir!" she said as seductively as possible, considering her comatose state.

The shower proved to be invigorating, or maybe the caffeine had begun to kick in. She wondered at the falseness of her comments to

Greg. In reality she would rather have been at home alone. It wasn't his fault she had grown tired of him. It was her obligation to take care of his needs, after all he was her husband.

She slipped her new black dress over Greg's favorite black lace teddy. It was a shame not to wear stockings, but the dress was too short to hide the garters. She settled for a pair of nude panty hose, and slid into a pair of black snakeskin stilettos. She piled her rioting blond curls on top of her head, fashioning them in a loose French twist. She wore her face make-up pale, and applied her trademark lavender plum lipstick. The purple shades brought out the green in her eyes.

Greg's long low wolf whistle confirmed that the combination had the desired effect. After nearly ten years, he still thought she looked great. He could hardly believe she was his woman.

Greg was wearing a jacket and tie. He wore a size forty-four jacket and thirty-one pants. Racquetball and weight training had paid off for him. He still had the body of a much younger man, and he managed to have kept a full head of hair. He was a brunette, but was graying nicely. Morgan gave him a whistle back.

They drove Greg's Lexus, of course; Morgan's old Toyota would never do. His car still smelled brand new, still less than six months old. The white paint and gold trim was a stylish contrast with the custom dark brown interior.

The leather seats were cold against her legs, covered only by thin stockings. Greg started the car and turned on the radio, popping in a Kenny G CD.

"You look terrific. That dress is perfect for you."

"Awwww, shucks," she replied, blushing

slightly. Greg was always so complimentary.

She was never certain whether his compliments were genuine, or just a part of the facade they both worked hard to maintain. On the surface everything seemed great. The casual observer wouldn't realize the dissillusion they both had about their marriage.

He backed out of the drive and headed east to Bayshore Boulevard. Neither of them noticed the dark blue Rodeo parked on the street just across the street from the neighbor's house, nor did they notice as it pulled out behind them.

NINE

The driver straightened up in his seat, pushing his baseball cap back on his head as he started the car. He pulled out slowly, leaving his lights off, staying about a block behind. As the Rodeo approached Bayshore, the headlights switched on. The Lexus was just visible up ahead, so the Rodeo narrowed the distance between them. As he reached a comfortable distance, he slowed to forty-five, matching the speed of the Lexus.

Both vehicles wound through Hyde Park, passing Tampa General Hospital, and both turned right crossing over the Platt Street Bridge. The Rodeo came to a stop at the red light underneath the Convention Center.

The Rodeo was on the right, and stopped so that the left front fender just came up parallel to the passenger door of the Lexus. He could see her slender white neck. One little blond curl had escaped and hung loosely next to her ear. She wore small pearl post earrings. She was turned slightly to the left, semi-facing the driver, engrossed in conversation.

His heart rate quickened slightly, and he noticed his palms were moist. His fingers curled involuntarily tightening his grip on the steering wheel. These same fingers could easily be tightening around her pale stately neck, restricting her blood flow, life-giving oxygen...

The light changed and the Lexus was off. He shook himself, returning from his sub-consciousness state. Behind him an impatient driver honked, annoyed. "All right, all right," he said to himself. He rolled down the window, offering his middle finger in salute to the car behind, and sped off still pursuing the Lexus.

He reminded himself not to become too involved. Focus on the prey; get sloppy, and get caught. But something about this woman captivated him. Even from the start when he had first seen her, he knew there was something unusual about her. It was unnerving, he almost felt bad about what he was doing, but not that bad.

He had done this before, but never on this scale. He had spent literally hours re-searching her habits and desires over the past few weeks. Now she was the focus of all his desires and increasingly frequent erotic dreams. Oh, the things they had done together in his imagination. Of course, he would never harm her. He was only having fun, lots of fun.

They passed the Ice Palace and wound through the maze to the circle in front of the aquarium, then north on Channelside. He closed in on the Lexus as it turned north on Nine-teenth Street, and pulled into a parking lot between Sixth and Seventh Avenues. He tossed his baseball cap on the seat beside him.

Her husband got out of the car and walked around to open her door. One pale, slender leg slithered out of the car. One high heeled, black shoe slowly and deliberately touched the ground. Its mate followed closely behind. She shifted her weight from the car seat to her feet. Her movements were catlike. He watched her walk, her hips swaying in a slow undulating rhythm. He watched them leave the parking lot, walking up Nineteenth, and they turned right on Seventh Avenue.

He parked, following close behind them, maintaining a safe distance. She seemed to sense she was being watched, glancing behind several times, searching faces. It must have been danger she sensed because he noticed many people were watching her as she passed by. Not only men were watching her, but other women watched enviously. She walked on, seeming unaware of the appreciative stares.

There was nothing particularly beautiful about her, nothing you could put your finger on, but she had a natural sensuality. Her feline grace, combined with unusual coloring combined to create an exotic look with a hint of innocence mixed with a heavy dose of eroticism.

Looking at her he was able to imagine every fantastic dream he had ever had. He felt the heat growing in his loins as he thought of a tiny drop of perspiration dripping from that strand of gold springing down the side of her neck. How he wanted to make her sweat.

Walking behind them, he saw the two enter The Ovo Cafe. Perfect. Right across the street was Blues Ship Cafe, a perfect observation point. He pushed through the crowd, entered, and went upstairs to the second floor porch. He ordered a ginger ale and sat back enjoying the show.

Their table was close enough to the front window to give him a clear view of her every move. This was excellent. She sat facing the window at an angle. Each time she leaned forward to talk with her husband a hint of cleavage peeked over the neckline of her chemise dress.

He wore dark wrap-around sunglasses to hide his eyes from anyone who might be watching him. He certainly didn't want her to recognize him. His head was turned slightly to the left, to further disguise what was the object of his attention.

All of his senses seemed to be magnified. Each molecule of air was distinguishable from the next, with every inhalation. Vision was focused on one vortex, all periphery discounted. Stale beer mixed with the acrid scent of espresso coffee beans for a sharp, distinctive fragrance, unique to Ybor.

Loud bass that had threatened to rupture his eardrums now blended with shouts, electric guitars, and second-rate vocalists.

Out of all these senses, vision was giving him the most pleasure. He fed on the optical stimulation. His ego swelled to new proportions with the sheer power he felt. Feeling intoxicated, he was dizzy with the potent wine of his own stealth. It was like being some sort of deity, watching from afar. His prey had no tangible knowledge, but sensed something there, and yet was totally unaware of how easily life could be ended without notice.

Her back was straight as she sat conversing with her husband. A few more tendrils of hair had escaped their bonds, springing with each movement of her head. Her long graceful fingers, each tipped with long dark red nails, caressed her wine glass. She blotted her lips with her napkin and giggled as she and her husband chatted back and forth.

He imagined the two of them together, wondering what they did when they were alone. Surely she was more suited to someone more like himself. Her husband could never be worthy of her exquisite body, and yet she was his. She belonged to that small insignificant little worm of a man. If only she were his instead...

TEN

"I don't understand why they are stalling on the money, Greg," Morgan said. "If the budget was already approved, then how can they change it now?"

Greg shook his head slowly. "You know as well as I do, they can do whatever they want. The County Commissioners bend the rules to fit their needs, and I have to make it work."

"It's just not right though, everyone was expecting a raise. Some of the deputies that I know have cars that are falling apart. I even heard of one being in a pursuit the other day and his car wouldn't do over fifty. All of those old cars that need to be replaced will have to wait. Our Comm. Center is filled with archaic equipment and obsolete computer programs. There are bound to be people complaining to the county commissioners."

"There's not a thing I can do to change it, Morgan," he protested.

"I don't know how you can do their dirty work for them and still sleep at night."

"It takes money to have a house to put all your fancy clothes in. And if it I didn't do it someone else would. Don't be such a Pollyanna, Morgan, it's the nineties."

"Yes, it is the nineties, and I'm not sure I like it. Let's not talk about it anymore. I just want to have a good time tonight."

"Best idea I've heard all night," he said, reaching out his hand to grasp hers firmly. "Did I tell you, you look marvelous tonight?"

"Several times, I believe, but a few more times won't hurt."

"You look maaaavelous," he said in his

best Billy Crystal voice.

"Charmed, I'm sure," she replied in a sugary southern accent, batting her eyelashes in belle fashion.

Greg smiled pausing to admire his woman, his wife of many years. Amazing, after all this time he was still overwhelmed by her feminine wiles.

"I have something to tell you, and you aren't going to like it," he said hesitating.

"Oh, no. Then don't tell me. What is it?"

"It's not all that bad," he hedged.

"Go on," she said, relenting. "Might as well tell me. I'll find out sooner or later anyway.

"I have to go to Tallahassee for two weeks for a tax seminar."

"Two weeks!" she protested. "Why so long?"

"There are a lot of changes coming down with those new laws that are going to be effective at the first of the year. Why don't you see if you can take some time off and come with me?"

"When will you be leaving?"

"The last two weeks of October."

"I can try, but with all of the people that usually go on vacation in the fall, it may be impossible."

"Great," he said sarcastically, "let me know so I can make plans." It was no secret he resented her job, but he didn't want to ruin the evening so he changed the subject. "Now, if you don't mind, I'd like to get out of here. This place is a little too crowded for me," he said suggestively.

"Oh," she replied, "I hadn't noticed. Just what did you have in mind? Hummmm?" she asked, trying hard to change his mood.

"Don't you worry your pretty little head about a thing, ma'am. Don't I always have good

ANN BAKER

ideas?"

"Oh, yes! If my memory's correct, I
believe you do, sir."

"Then lets go."

ELEVEN

They rose to leave, and he did too, making his way hurriedly down the stairs. He reached his car before they got to theirs. As she was about to get into the car, Greg whirled her around. He placed his arms around her, and holding her close, he kissed her deeply. He watched jealously as she gave her husband a playful push away, caressing his thigh as she did.

Again he felt his pulse quicken, as did his respiration; while he watched them from the distance. They certainly didn't act like a couple married for almost ten years. And yet he was certain that they were, he had looked up their marriage license at the courthouse. If she was his woman he imagined he would do the same. And he certainly had done his share of imagining for the past few days.

It seemed she had been the object of his imagination forever. Since the first time he had seen her, he found it impossible to forget her. Even in his dreams she was there; taunting, haunting his every conscious thought. She was intoxicating and all consuming, more so that anyone he had encountered before.

For a while he tried to avoid thinking of her. It worked, but not for long. He told himself it was deranged to be thinking of her continually after only seeing her once. He had been obsessed with other women before, but only ones he had been involved with.

Thinking back to the first time he had seen her in the break room, he realized he should have known she would be trouble. He had noticed her wedding ring right away, but somehow it didn't matter.

Making up reasons to drop by Communications, he became a frequent visitor to the delight of several of the single girls. With a few inquiries to the right people he was able to get her name. Once he had her name, he looked up her home address in the computer.

It was then that he had begun his surveillance. All of his free time was spent filling in all of the details of her life. Before long he knew what foods she liked, clothes she wore, and many of her personal habits. With amazing ease he became familiar with her from a distance, and she didn't even know it.

Eventually, he became bored with just watching from a distance, and longed for personal contact with her. But all she seemed to do was go to work, the grocery store, and occasionally shopping. As weeks went by he grew more and more impatient as his craving for Morgan McGhee grew unrelentingly, demanding to be fed.

It had been in roll call one day that he had overheard a conversation. Instantly, it clicked in his mind, and he realized Austin was talking about her. He listened intently to the conversation, amazed at the dumb luck of having been there to hear it.

"Yeah, right, so this chick says to me 'How long have you been working out?' How long have I been working out?! I felt like telling her, 'Look at me stupid. How long do you think I've been working out.' Women are so stupid, always talking, just got to be saying something or they're not happy."

"What does she look like? Is she pretty?" asked Deputy Rogers, the district desk deputy.

"Hell, yeah she's pretty. But she's gotta be at least five years older than me. Anyway I have a woman, I don't need her, and I sure don't like women with blond hair, especially with curly blond hair. I've never seen one of them that isn't dumber than two rocks. I gotta admit though she don't look too bad. But I don't have nothing to do with dispatchers, they are all bad news. They all talk to each other about everything they do."

"Hey, Austin, did I hear you talking about working out?"

"Hey, yo Ian, I haven't seen you in a long time. Where have you been hiding yourself?"

"You know here and there. I try to keep busy. Where have you been working out lately?"

"I'm still going to the SOC gym. I go during the day on my days off. They've made some improvements there and added some new equipment."

"I've been thinking about checking it out again. When you going next and I'll meet you there."

"Sweet, I was just complaining about the women there talking too much. I'd be glad to have another guy to work out with. I'm going tomorrow. I'll be there about four-thirty."

"Okay, I'll see you then. Good seeing you again."

Ian left ecstatic. *What luck, what unbelievable luck.* For weeks he had searched for some way to get to know her, and now she practically falls into his lap. He could hardly wait till tomorrow.

The first day he went, she wasn't there. Wanting to bring up the subject, but not arouse suspicion, he thought long and hard before saying anything.

"So, looks like we have the gym all to ourselves. How long can you expect that to last on a weekday?"

"Just after five a few come in. There is a guy that comes in every night about six-thirty and stays awhile. If you come in late at night there are some dispatchers that come in."

"Are you going to be here tomorrow? I'd like to have a spotter to help me with that incline press. I wanted to increase the weight I've been using."

"Yeah, I'll be here, same time."

"I'm gonna head out now," Ian said. "I still have to go running."

"Where do you run?" Austin asked.

"I run on the Bayshore," he answered.

"Oh yeah, how far do you run?"

"I'm kinda out of shape right now. Only about 4 miles. When I'm in top condition I run 10 miles a day."

"Marathon man, huh?"

"Yeah, I guess you could say that, but I like it. Hey, I'm gonna have to run. I gotta work tonight. I'll see you tomorrow, about the same time."

"Okay, man, sounds good."

"See ya, bro."

Ian had a hard time sleeping that night. He kept thinking of her, over and over in his mind. His only memory of that day in the breakroom replayed itself. Imaginings merged with memory, creating new scenarios. New ways for Ian to torture himself with something he could not have. For Ian it had always been the things he could not have that he wanted the most. He always got what he wanted, though, no matter how long it took.

The next day, Ian arrived at the gym before Austin. He was already well into his workout when he arrived. He stopped for a breather and sat on a bench while he talked to Austin.

In the women's dressing room he could hear the door close and someone opening a locker. He felt the excitement building as he antici-pated the female entering the gym. Maybe this time it would be her.

Several minutes passed, and still no one came out. He heard a door open and close again. It had to be the exit door. It was the only one except the entrance to the gym. About two minutes later, he heard the door opening again, and the handle to the gym door turned. The anticipation was exquisite.

She walked through the door quickly scanning the room to see who was there, smiling a quick perfunctory greeting. She put her things on the chair, and went to the scale to weigh. Seemingly satisfied with the results, she stepped down and turned picking up a small towel, she tossed it around her neck, draping her long curls over it.

Ian could scarcely breathe. He recognized her immediately. It was her! He didn't want to seem too anxious, so he made a conscious effort to look nonchalant, but he found himself staring at her in spite of himself.

She wore black leggings and a tee shirt. As she turned, she smiled and said hello to Austin. He grunted in reply, rolling his eyes at Ian to display his obvious disdain.

She went to an open space at one side of the room. Placing her feet wide apart, she bent over at the waist, touching the ground with her hands, then stretching farther she placed her hands through her legs at the ankles. Her golden curls swept the ground as she reached for one ankle and then the other.

She didn't notice as Ian sat transfixed, watching her every move. Slowly and deliberately she stretched, sensually and elegantly. It seemed so strange to see her now after all these weeks of thinking of her. His imagination had not done her justice. She was much better looking up close that he had remembered. Of course, when he had seen her, she had been dressed in that ill-fitting uniform she was required to wear.

Quickly, he stole a glance at Austin to

check his reaction. There was no hint that he had more than a passive awareness that she was in the room. He continued his work out, ignoring her completely.
His predatory instincts were now fully aroused, and would not be denied.

When she finished stretching, she put on her leg weights and moved to the step and began doing calf raises. With one leg outstretched in front of her, she slowly raised up and down on the toes of the other foot. He watched as the muscles of her shapely calf contracted and released with the smoothness of a ballet dancer.

After completing the calf raises, she went over to the slant board and stretched out. With her hands clasped over her head, she elongated her spine, pointing her toes.

It was then that Ian found conversation with Austin became impossible to continue. Austin didn't seem to notice. He continued with his bench presses, without the grunting, now that there was a female in the room.

Ian noticed that his mouth had become dry, and he could feel his blood coursing through the vessels in his neck. Mesmerized, he watched her do stomach crunches, her long hair swaying gently beneath her head with each rhythmic movement. She avoided any eye contact with either of them, and apparently had no idea she was being so closely scrutinized. Austin remained oblivious, staring intently at his own image in the mirror.

Time seemed to stand still for a few excruciating moments. She completed what she was doing on the slant board and walked toward him, coming very close, smiling as she walked closer. Swallowing hard he tried to smile innocuously. He was certain his thumping heart must be showing through the tee shirt he wore.

"Hey, Ian, are you gonna stay in Juliet on the next shift bid?" Austin asked.

"Yeah," he grunted in reply. Even though

he hadn't done any lifting for several minutes, his reply sounded as though he were straining under the weight of a very heavy barbell.

"Well! That's a very exciting area to work," Morgan offered.

"Mmmm," Ian responded, trying to sound nonchalant.

"You are about as talkative as Austin," she said smiling.

He swallowed hard, looking into her eyes, and he said stupidly, "Ummm hummm."

She looked away quickly, not wanting to be drawn into his gaze, yet sensed something familiar. For some unexplained reason she felt uneasy about him.

Ian seemed to sense her discomfort and made a conscious effort to make conversation. "So, what schedule did you get on your bid?" he asked her.

"Oh, I'm going back to nights. This day stuff isn't for me. They made me go to days for a few weeks. I hate it."

Both men chuckled at that comment, exchanging knowing glances. All the lazy people went to days, dispatchers and deputies. They were a royal pain for the people who actually did like to work to put up with.

"By the way, I'm Ian Greer. I work in Juliet area."

"I've seen your name before," she replied.

"I hope it wasn't because of something bad."

"Oh, no, I would certainly remember if it had been something bad, but you do look familiar."

"And you would be?"

"I'm sorry. I'm Morgan," she smiled, not knowing what else to say. She began working her triceps with the dumbbells.

"And does Morgan have a last name?" he

asked, grinning

"Of course, it's McGhee."

"McGhee, Morgan McGhee... I don't seem to remember that name."

"Is there some reason you should remember my name?" she asked suspiciously.

He laughed aloud this time. "Sure, if you made me mad before - on the radio - I'd remember you. I always run the names of people who make me mad, and believe me I remember their names."

"Now, why is it that I believe that?" she countered. "It's a good thing I happen to like bossy men. Political correctness has emasculated all but the very brave."

He grinned and said, "You're a pretty sassy one, aren't you?"

"You're very perceptive Ian," she countered sharply.

"I think you're the perceptive one, ma'am!"

"Oh really, what makes you say that?"

"You've just met me and you seem to understand me pretty well already."

Morgan laughed, "Oh, it's not that I can tell so much about you. It's more of a generic thing. Seems that deputies have several things in common."

Ian stepped closer to her, looking her in the eye. "You'll find there's very little common or generic about me miss."

She blushed, taken aback by his directness. Austin just rolled his eyes and went back to his weigh lifting. Morgan took his cue and resumed her work out also. She went to the tread mill and began a brisk walk.

Ian busied himself doing some lateral pulls. The machine for laterals was coincidentally right by the treadmill. He purposely placed himself right in front of her field of vision. Now she had no choice but to see him as he slowly flexed each muscle in his bulging arms. He watched himself in the mirror, but the reflection of Morgan was right next to his. She was trying to be polite and avoid looking at him. *Great*, he could watch her walking without her knowing.

"So, Morgan, how long have you been a dispatcher," Ian asked.

"About a year now," she answered.

"Do you like it?"

"That depends on what day it is," she laughed. "Today, it's not too bad; but some days you wonder why you bothered to show up. I haven't seen you here before. Do you come here much?" she asked, changing the subject.

"Yeah, this is the gym I always use," he answered.

"That's funny, I've never seen you down here before."

"Oh, that's because I come down about three in the morning, when I get off work. I've been coming down at that time about five months now."

"Well, that would explain it," she said.

Morgan knew she had caught him in a lie. Almost every night she had been in the gym at about that time for at several months, but that ended about five weeks ago, when she had switched to day shift. Realizing that he had lied to her, she was now suspicious of everything he said.

"I guess that I'll be seeing you down here then," she ventured.

"Oh yeah, why is that?"

"Well, I'm going back to nights on the next shift bid. I'll be working out every night that I work, about that time."

"That's great!" he said, a little too enthusiastically. "So, what about day shift don't you like?"

"It's a combination of things really. There are those lazy day deputies that drive you crazy. 'Dispatch, free me from that call, I get off in two hours.'"

Both men laughed aloud at her comment. Even Austin couldn't resist. They knew what she was saying was the sad truth.

"Then there's always the dragon women that run both day squads. God forbid that anyone that has been here less than five years should bid for their squad."

"Oh, yeah," Ian agreed, "I've had my share of experience with some of those women."

"And then there's the getting up at four o'clock in the morning. And that, of course, means you have to go to sleep about eight at night. That always makes for a great family life."

"So, you have a family?" Ian asked.

"Well, no children, but I'm married. My husband doesn't really appreciate me having to go to sleep so early, or me waking him up when my alarms go off in the morning."

"Alarms? Is that plural?"

"Yeah, alarms. I have to set three to wake me up. I put them across the room or I'd never get up."

"Then I see why you are going back to nights. Send me a message when you see me logged on, we can keep in touch."

"Okay, I'd like that," she said, as she turned off the tread mill. "It's been real nice talking to you," she said as she extended her hand to shake his.

He hoped she didn't notice that his hand was trembling as he took her hand in his. She squeezed lightly as she shook his hand, the pressure sent unexpected sensations up his arm, and extended to other extremities of his body. He was unexpectedly embarrassed. Making a conscious effort he released her hand, having held it as long as possible without seeming overly long. It was the second time her hand had been in his, and he liked the feeling.

She didn't seem to notice his reaction,

and after she said good-bye, she left the gym. He heard a locker open and knew she was undressing. This thought matured in his mind as he heard the shower come on. There was nothing he would have loved more than to step through the door that lead to the ladies dressing room.

Austin was continuing his workout, still oblivious to most of what had gone on. "Hey, Austin," Ian said. "I think I'm gonna grab a shower and head out of here."

"Okay," he said straining to rise from the last squat of the set. "I'll see you around."

Ian hurried into the dressing room. He needed a shower - a really cold one. Now that he had seen her, talked with her, he had plans to make, and things to do. He knew exactly what he was going to do next.

TWELVE

The next day when Morgan went to work she checked to see if Ian was working. Sure enough, he was logged on as 2J10. She waited about an hour before sending a message, not wanting to appear too anxious.

"Hi," she sent.

"Hey, there," came the reply.

"I enjoyed meeting you yesterday," she returned.

"Thanks. Me too," he answered quickly.

"When are you switching back to nights?" he sent before she could respond.

"Two more weeks, on Monday. I can't wait." she sent back.

"That's great. I'll be glad to have someone to work out with in the gym."

"Oh, yeah. You need a gym buddy?"

"Oh, yes," he answered, smiling to him-self. She was more willing than he had hoped.

"Good then, you can be my trainer."

"I can't wait," was his response.

The messages they sent to each other were carefully crafted to have some seeming official purpose. Neither wanted the wrath of thier respective supervisors.

District One became Morgan's first choice of radio dispatch positions to work. With that assignment she had plenty of opportunity to send him messages, and the sound of his voice on the radio sent shivers down her spine.

When the schedule change did come, they were both anxious to see one another again. Both had been careful to hide any hint of the anticipation that had grown.

Morgan was sure he was coming. He had sent her a message just before she logged off.

As she finished a full twenty minutes on the treadmill, she began to wonder if something had happened to hold him up. She was just about to leave when she heard someone in the men's locker room. Thrilled, she tried to look busy as she waited.

The grin on Ian's face was almost as wide as the one she wore. "I almost didn't make it. There was a drunk in the parking lot on my way in," he explained.

"How unusual," Morgan laughed nervously.

"I know. A drunk in Ybor... Who'd believe that?"

When she explained she had to go, he hid his disappointment. There was no doubt in his mind she didn't want to go. His nonchalance would only heighten her intrest. This he knew from experience.

As far as Morgan knew, Ian had no one to answer to, and had no reason to hurry home. Her's was another story entirely. Greg would be worried if he woke up and she was late. Before she started the evening shift he had demanded that she call him just before she got home every night after work. She wondered whether he wanted to be sure she was safe, or if it was that he didn't trust her, or even worse that maybe Greg sensed what Morgan had been denying to herself; he was no longer first in her heart.

Captivated by Ian Greer, Morgan reasoned to herself that she was not cheating on Greg. At the same time she wondered where exactly adultery began. Was it the commission of a physical act or the willingness to do so?

One thing was sure - Ian had been right - he wasn't like other deputies. Everything about him was a study in contradictions. His macho bravado was tempered with a subtle tenderness, openness contrasted with mystery, and in his cynicism there was an unmistakable hint of confidence in human nature.

THIRTEEN

Greg drove the Lexus into the driveway and got out as Morgan waited for him to open the car door for her. He was always a stickler for manners. She appreciated that about him, after all this time, he stilled tried to be polite to her.

Remembering her promise she had made before dinner, she slithered out of her dress and hung it in neatly in the closet. She placed her shoes in their box on the shelf, and turned to see Greg tossing his clothing haphazardly around the room. He expected her to pick them up. After all, she was the woman. That irritated her more than anything. Always, he tossed things around the house, never putting things away. She had to admit, it was probably her fault as much as his. Effectively enabling his sloppy behavior, time after time, she picked up after him.

Once she had tried leaving everything where he put it, and after three days she had given up. The whole house had become a mass of clutter. How one man could make such a mess, she didn't know.

She turned back the sheets and got into the bed on his side. Feeling a like a not-so willing sacrifice she waited for him to come to her.

As usual, he began by kissing her. His tongue forced her lips apart and she tried her best to kiss him back. As much as was within her, she pushed back her aversion to his spit being on her. She wiped her mouth on the pillow case, hoping he didn't notice.

Knowing what he liked best she tried to hurry the whole distasteful process. But, as usual, he demanded that she achieved satisfaction first and just once wasn't good enough. Ordinarily, that might be a good quality in a man. Years ago she had mistaken it for being considerate. Now, she knew it was just another one of his needs that had to be met. Everything was always about him, even when it looked like it was for her. It had taken her years to realize how selfish he really was. At one time she found him seductive, but now she felt like she was only a tool for his masturbation.

So, she was faced with the all too familiar choice. Either she could try to urge him on, hoping he was intoxicated enough not to notice, or she could fake it. Certainly she had become practiced at that. The only problem was that if she feigned enjoyment, she was lying. Morgan hated having to do that more than anything. But, it was his arrogance that had forced her into this dilemma. She chose to lie.

After what seemed to be an interminable time of rutting, he finished. Only a few more minutes of allowing him to lie on top of her and she would be free to shove him off of her.

At her first opportunity, she rushed into the bathroom, washed up, and changed into her bathing suit. The spa would be a great way to soak away the scent of him - the smell of his copulation - that now seemed to hang thickly on her body.

Greg followed her, apparently oblivious to her disgust. She settled in next to him, relishing the steaming hot liquid that swirled around, cleansing her soul. Settling back, she placed her head on the edge, and gazed up at the stars. As she looked up at the sky, her thoughts settled to what had recently become her favorite escape, Ian Greer. She had become virtually obsessed with thinking of him, since she had met him in the gym. If only she cared for Greg like she did for Ian.

In all honesty, love probably wasn't the word for it. It was more like pure, unadulterated lust. She chuckled under her breath to think of it.

"What are you laughing at?" Greg asked, pulling her back to reality.

Annoyed, she answered curtly. "Why do you care?"

Greg gave her a look that told her he was too stunned to reply.

That really wasn't called for, she thought. *After all, Greg doesn't even have a clue how I feel. Maybe if I told him. No, that would never work. He would never tolerate his wife being attracted to another man.*

"I'm sorry," she said sincerely.

"God, you're becoming very snippy here lately. Maybe it's that job of yours. I should have never let you go to work. You're turning real bitchy."

That made her even angrier. Trying to avoid an argument, she said nothing. She knew all too well. She couldn't win, and it would go on for days. Perhaps she had gone too far already, and she knew the kind of price she would pay. Sulking was an art form for Greg. The silent treatment was his favorite form of torture.

Who gives a shit? Let him play his little game, have a pity party for himself.

"I'm ready to go in. Let's go," he commanded.

Determined not to give into him, she decided to stay. Without him next to her she would be free to indulge in her favorite daydreams, uninterrupted.

"You go in. I'm going to stay for a while," she ventured in a rare display of independence.

"You know Morgan..." he didn't finish the sentence. Instead he shook his head in disbelief.

66

Afraid he would make a big scene, she braced herself. Actually, she hoped he would make her go in. She was a little afraid to stay outside by herself at such a late hour, but her cell phone was next to her towel, and it was a good neighborhood.

Maybe he was just tired, or maybe he sensed it wasn't a good time to push his luck; but to her surprise he said nothing more, reached for his towel, and stood up to go.

FOURTEEN

Following them back home was a breeze. He was sure of where they were going. He knew where she lived. The moon was full and golden yellow as it rose over the bay. The mist from sprinklers that watered the lush landscaping that grew in the oversized median along Bayshore Boulevard, sprayed his Rodeo as he passed. Instead of turning down their street, he turned onto the street just over from theirs. Luckily their house was on a corner, and he parked behind their house and slouched down in his car. Their bedroom window was just visible above the Jacuzzi they used almost every night that she was home. The break in the hedges was just enough to allow a partial view.

As he watched the house from the back, he noticed a black Camaro driving down the road beside the house, passing in front of his car. He slid down in the car seat a little lower, even though all the side windows had very dark tint. The windows of the Camaro were also darkly tinted, and it was impossible to see how many people were in the car as it passed. It drove slowly, turning in front of Morgan and Greg's house. It passed by so slowly that it aroused his suspicion. Perhaps he had been a cop too long, but something seemed wrong. That old familiar gut feeling couldn't be mistaken. He was able to get a look at the tag, with the help of the binoculars he had been using already. Immediately he picked up his cell phone and dialed the Sheriff's Office Teletype room. After a brief moment the dispatcher answered.

"DP3."

"This is unit 6245, ID number 7534, I need a 10-28 on a tag."

"Go ahead with your tag," came the reply.

"Florida tag Lima-Charlie-Delta-one-five-Yankee, should come back to a black Camaro."

"Can you hold a for a minute?" the dispatcher asked.

"Sure," he replied. She put him on hold for what seemed a very long time. Finally she returned. "That's going to be a confidential government tag. I'm unable to disclose any information about that vehicle, sorry."

"Are you able to tell me which agency it comes back to?"

"That I can't tell you, it's a government tag, probably a cool car."

"Thank-you very much for your help."

"Your welcome."

He hung up the phone. *A government tag. That was strange.* He wondered what it was doing in this neighborhood. Maybe someone knew he had been watching her. No, that couldn't be. If they were watching her they would have been behind him, not driving in front of him. He tried to put it out of his mind, clicking on the stereo system. He put in a Phil Collins CD. He was anxious to get back to the business at hand, pleasure and fantasy.

The lights went on in the bedroom, and shadows played on the blinds that covered the French doors. In a few minutes the brightness of the lighting dimmed considerably, and it appeared as though the room was fire-lit, perhaps by candles. Imagination alive, he watched intently without blinking. Memory conjured the black stilettos and the black dress. He thought of the curls hanging around her neck and longed to touch his nose to the lobe and crest of her pale soft ear. The cleavage that had only teased him before spoke of delights he could only dream of. But dream he did, while time seemed to stand still.

The lights became brighter again, and he glanced at his watch. Forty-five minutes had elapsed. He had to give it to them. They certainly had kept things alive in their marriage. His own marriage had died after less than two years. Nothing he could have done would have kept it alive after he caught her with... *STOP*, he told himself, *you promised not to think of it again.*

The French doors swung open and they stepped out together. He could see she wore a silver lame one piece swim suit. It was his favorite of all he had seen her wear so far. She sat on the side swinging her legs over the edge and tested the water with one toe, while he sat in his car spellbound, unable to move. Finding the temperature suitable she stepped in. Her husband came in right after her, and sat on the side farthest away from the doors. Perfect he could see her clearly.

She leaned back, tilting her head back as far as it would go resting on the side of the spa. Watching the stars, she sat very still. He could see her chest rise and fall as she breathed gently.

The black Camaro re-appeared about twenty minutes after he had first seen it. It approached from the same direction, but this time it stopped just north and east of where he sat, off to his left. The lights were off when the car came up the street. When it stopped he couldn't tell if the engine was still running or not. He dared not open his window to find out. He was just out of the line of sight from the Camaro to the spa. The hairs on the back of his neck stood at full attention.

Greg and Morgan sat in the hot tub, oblivious to either of the vehicles, both of which were apparently focused on them. She sat in clear view, her head back, still gazing upward at the stars.

From his perspective - slumped down in

the seat of the car - he could see that the sky was clear, with only a cloud or two in sight. The stars were brilliant despite the city lights. Several constellations were clearly visible. For a few minutes no one moved. He was becoming anxious as the minutes went by, tension building. He kept watch on the Camaro to his left. No one moved, and neither car door opened.

The Rodeo had a great stereo system, and Phil Collins began singing one of his favorite songs, "I Can Feel it Coming in the Air Tonight". It seemed like an omen. The music was appurtenant to the moment, as if written for this very time. The percussion of the drums reverberated in his ears, even though the volume was low. Somehow, he knew these few moments would live forever, burned in his memory as with a laser. Sure enough, he could feel something in the air, but what in the hell was it?

Greg stood up to get out of the spa, reaching for his towel. At the same time the Camaro began to move forward, and very quickly, going by right in front of the Rodeo. The Camaro seemed to pause for a moment as the passenger window rolled down, a long gun barrel emerging.

A sudden flash of light was the only indication that the gun had been fired. He heard no sound inside his car except Phil Collins. As if in slow motion he looked toward the spa, where he knew the shot had been aimed. He watched as Greg's head exploded, showering Morgan with a fine red mist as she sat, her head back, still looking up at the stars. She came to an upright position, her mouth frozen open in a seeming inaudible scream.

His attention turned back to the Camaro and he watched as the shooter, masked in darkness, took new aim. He knew exactly what the sites of the gun were now lined up on, *Morgan*.

His thoughts raced for a solution and only one came to mind. He slammed the heel of his palm on the horn of his car and prayed that it would work.

For an instant he feared that he had failed. Then without warning, the Camaro sped off, tires burning rubber as it tore off. Instinct finally overcame indecision and the door of the Rodeo opened. Once committed, all caution was thrown to the wind.

He told himself he must remain calm, think clearly. What should be the next move? Each second was critical.

Think fast, think fast. His brain raced for a solution. Ideas and thoughts meshed, fantasies remembered, suddenly he knew exactly what he would do. Sure the timing was off, but there was no reason his time table could not be moved up. It had been just an idea, one he never expected to take form, but it was the only plan at the moment.

He ran to her, her mouth still open in what seemed to be a scream, but he couldn't tell for sure if he heard her or not. It seemed as though he were running in slow motion, his legs felt like they were made of rubber. Quickly he yanked her from the spa, lifting her like a rag doll, and clamping his hand tightly over her mouth. Her back was to him, and her feet dangled above the ground, as he held her there, suspended in air her ear near to his mouth.

The warm blood and water transferred from her suit and body to his clothing, quickly reaching his skin. Ian thought about the danger of exposure to the blood briefly. He told himself not to think about it. Even though it was one of his steadfast rules to avoid contamination with body fluids, he was amazed that he would be thinking of that now. *Funny how training comes to the surface at the strangest times.*

"Don't scream, don't scream," he whispered in her ear. "I'm here to help you. You know me from the Sheriff's Office. It's Ian, Ian Greer. You remember me from the gym. You're in danger. I need to get you out of here. Nod your head if you understand what I'm saying."

How could she understand? He didn't. He felt like he was rambling on and on.

She nodded her head, but he knew she was terrified. He felt her body tremble under his arm as her heart pounded wildly.

He hated for her to see her husband that way - his head fairly removed from his shoulders and blood splattered everywhere - only his tongue and teeth were distinguishable. It was important that she be certain that there was nothing she could do to help him at this point. Without that she might forever blame herself for having left him.

"Greg's dead. Look at him."

She stared at his body, crumpled in the water that was ever reddening by the moment. She struggled to free herself from his grip, but it was no use, he overpowered her with ease.

"Morgan, do you see him?"

Finally she nodded, but refused to look, as she began to wretch involuntarily.

"I saw someone watching you and followed them here. If I hadn't scared them off, you would have been next. Now, I have to get you out of here and fast. Do you understand?"

Again she nodded, but was obviously in shock. She was now staring at her husband's corpse in disbelief. Her cell phone was still clutched tightly in her hand. She must have grabbed it before he got to her, she was shaking uncontrollably. He spun her around and held her to himself tightly.

"Come on, we have to go. I can protect you, but you have to trust me."

"But, Greg, he needs me, I can't leave him."

"You don't have a choice. There's nothing you can do to help Greg now. Do you know who wanted to kill him?"

She looked stunned, making no effort to speak or move.

"Of course you don't. For all you know they may have been after you. Come with me now, they could come back at any time."

Looking back at her husband's body, then up at Ian, she hesitated. *Should I go with him, or stay and call the police?*

It was as if he could read her thoughts.

"You're thinking of calling the police aren't you?" The rhetorical question needed no answer. "Well, don't even think about it. I followed that car over here. I already had the tag run, and it's a confidential government tag. Tampa Police Department won't be of any help to you."

"I, uh I, I don't know what to do. I'm so afraid."

"Walk out here with me, and do it fast."

Still, she hesitated, so he made the decision for her. He scooped her up in his arms; towel, cell phone, and all, and carried her to the car.

Instinctively she held onto him tightly, pressing her face to his chest. *What a nightmare*, she thought. *Surely in a few minutes I will wake up and find this all a bad dream. Things like this don't just happen. This is too weird.*

As scared as she was, it felt good to have him hold her; his large body cradling her small one. Suddenly she thought, *Thank God he was here. If I had been alone, if those men had come for me... He just saved my life. How did he happen to be there? Did he explain it to me?* She just wanted to close her eyes and have it all go away.

Gently he placed her in the passenger seat of his Rodeo. She held her head in her hands, covering her eyes in denial. He longed to touch her hair, hold her again, but instead he started his car.

He reminded himself he had plenty of time to make her his. The only mistake he could make now would be moving too fast. Sure she would mourn for a while, but sooner or later she would see that she was meant for him.

"Ian, I don't know what I would do without you," she said as she leaned over and reached her arm around his neck, squeezing him closer to her. "Thank God you were there."

"Lean your seat back and close your eyes. I'll turn on the heater for you. Put that towel over you. I know just the place to take you."

He was so direct, so authoritative, she did exactly as he said. She felt safe with him driving. Funny, she never felt safe when Greg was driving. Somehow, she knew she should be terrified, but suddenly she just felt very sleepy. Perhaps it was some kind of reaction to the shock; or maybe it was just a psychological way of hiding from what she could not yet cope with, but as the heater warmed the car she relaxed, and let him take her away.

FIFTEEN

The first thing he had to do was to get her cleaned up. If she could see herself she would be horrified. In her hair and on her face, were splattered blood and brain matter, fragments of bone now hung in her glorious curls. Not a pretty sight. If he had not seen the same kind of thing so many times over the years, he might have been repulsed.

He drove straight to MacDill Avenue, and turning right, headed north to Kennedy Boulevard. He turned east and quickly found exactly what he needed, a cheap motel that catered to the prostitution trade, The Flamingo Motel. They would want little cash, ask no questions, and remember nothing.

Leaving Morgan in the Rodeo, he went inside. It hadn't been easy to extricate himself from her. She clung to him, terrified to be alone, even for a moment. But after reassuring her he would be right back, she finally agreed to wait there for him.

It was a good thing he had worn his black jeans and black dress shirt. The wetness barely showed in the hazy light of the dingy little office.

The clerk requested twenty-five dollars for two hours. Ian paid him fifty. "Do you have any shampoo, and a few extra towels?" he asked the clerk.

"Sure, hang on just a minute," he said as he turned away.

"Could you just hurry," Ian demanded. He was used to getting his way.

"Hold your horses, big guy. It'll just take a second."

Ian waited impatiently, watching the car

closely. Finally the clerk returned, cigarette hanging from his lips, ashes trailing down the front of his shirt. He handed Ian a partially used bottle of shampoo and two towels.

"Here you go, enjoy our little place," he grinned exposing his partially toothed gums.

"Have someone bring some milk and chocolate chip cookies over to the room, and there's another twenty in it for you," Ian directed.

"Now, ain't that sweet. The little lady likes cookies does she?"

"That's none of your fucking business" Ian said through clenched teeth. "Do you want to get them or not?"

"Oh, yeah, I'll get 'em for you. Just give me the twenty now, and another five to buy it with."

After giving him the money, Ian hurried back to the car. He drove over to the room that corresponded to the number on the key. Jumping out - grabbing the shampoo and towels - he opened the back of the car, and removed the flannel shirt he kept there for emergencies. He opened the car door for Morgan, put the shirt over her head, and held out his hand to help her out of the car. She hesitated just a moment, then took his hand, and got out of the car.

The key turned in the lock, and the two of them entered the room. It was just what he had expected. A large wall-sized mirror hung on the farthest wall, with smuged fingerprints visible from the front door. The room was dominated by a king-size bed, covered with a red crushed velvet bed spread, with faded tassels along the bottom. A lamp with a dirty yellowed shade stood on the wall mounted stand to the left of the bed. The carpet was a different shade of red, clashing with the bed spread. It was worn and dirty, dotted with cigarette burns. The smell of stale beer and smoke was revolting. Ian hoped that the bathroom would not be any worse that what he had seen so far, surely it couldn't be.

He looked at Morgan's eyes. "Are you all right?" he asked.

"I don't know," she answered. "I don't know if I'll ever be all right again."

He was worried that she would start to cry if he didn't move quickly. "I'm gonna get you into the shower. You can just keep your bathing suit on. Sit here in this chair, and I'll start the shower."

Disappearing to the bathroom, he found it minimally acceptable. Some of the obsolescent avocado green tiles were cracked, and the grout was stained. The shower dripped, and a trail of minerals spilled down the shower tiles. The toilet had no covering lid. Two towels and wash cloths hung on a silver rack on the wall, and a terry cloth bath mat was hanging there beside them.

Ian started the hot water running and then went to the other room and turned on the heater, even though it was about seventy-five degrees outside. He locked the bolt on the door, and took Morgan by the hand.

"Come on, you really need to get cleaned up."

She sat there in a disoriented state, but responded to his touch. Rising from the chair, she allowed herself to be led to the bathroom, catching a glimpse of herself in the mirror.

"Oh, dear God! I look like I've been in a train wreck."

"Just come in here, it'll all be gone in a minute." He turned on the cold water, and finding the right temperature, he turned the shower on.

"Here now, just step in."

The water felt great, warming her chilled extremities. As the warm water streamed down on her hair, the blood and particles of tissue flowed with it into the tub. She was startled by the sight of it, and began to cry. Ian took off all his clothes, keeping only his boxers on. He stepped into the tub and pressed her head to his chest, whispering, "Just close your eyes."

He got the shampoo from the side of the tub, and squeezed some of it into her hair. As he began to scrub her scalp roughly with the tips of his fingers, she gave into the pressure of his hands. He tilted her head backwards so that the water rinsed her hair as he scrubbed. The bubbles from the shampoo were pink, tinged with the blood of her dead husband.

Ian struggled to remain in control of his responses. Somehow, she seemed even more vulnerable than before with her head back like that, her neck exposed. He could see her blood pulsing just below the surface in the large vessels that fed her head. It would be so easy to harm her. No one knew where she was, no one had seen her enter the room with him.

Ian's thoughts were interrupted by a knock at the door. "Stay right here," he instructed. "I'll be right back."

He wrapped a towel around his waist, and went to unlock the door. Before he opened it he looked through the peep hole to make sure who it was. Mr. Fewteeth grinned at the door, knowing he was being watched. Ian opened the door, but only partially.

"Here's your cookies and milk."

Ian just grabbed them and slammed the door in the man's face. He really didn't want to play games with this guy today, or ever. Then he remembered he needed some ice. Partially opening the door he yelled to the disappearing clerk.

"Hey!"

"Yeah," came the reply.

"How about some ice in this bucket," he

said as he reached around to the table and grabbed the small plastic tub.

"You sure want a lot of service."

"Yeah, and I've paid for everything I asked for. Just get the ice."

"Okay, okay, don't be so pushy."

Ian stood there by the door dripping while he waited for the clerk to return. The ice machine must have been close by, because it only took him a minute.

"This one's on me," he said as he handed the ice in.

"Thank you so much," Ian replied with more than a little sarcasm.

He set the ice next to the sink, and put the quart of milk on the ice to keep it chilled. Locking the door behind him, he hurried back to the bathroom.

Morgan had cleaned herself up fairly well in the time he was gone. Almost all the blood and other matter seemed to be gone. But Ian wanted to make sure. He helped her get out of the shower, and rinsed the shower curtain thoroughly, checking the sides of the tub for anything that may have splattered. He flushed the pieces of bone that had collected in the drain of the bath tub. When he was satisfied that it was all clean, he went into the other room.

She was sitting in the chair next to the heater, drying her hair. He threw another towel in her direction, and walked over to where she was.

"We'll get out of here as soon as you are dried off. I apologize for bringing you here, but it was the closest place I could think of."

"Apologize?! Are you kidding? Thank you for taking care of me. I don't know what I would have done if you hadn't happened to show up when you did."

She began to cry again, and he got some tissue from the bathroom for her. "Thank God you were there. I don't know what I'm going to do."

"Don't worry about anything now, there will be time to figure it all out," he promised. He hated it when women cried.

After they had both dried sufficiently, he dressed himself first, and then put his extra shirt on her. It was a good thing she was so small. The shirt covered her for the most part, looking something like a short dress on her. He rolled up each sleeve for her, and seated her on the edge of the bed.

"That chair is too dirty sit in. I don't want you to have to touch that bed, but it's only for a minute."

He went over to the sink and removed the wrapper from each of two plastic cups that were sitting there. He poured each of them a glass of milk. Then he opened his wallet, and removed the two Benedryl he kept there for his allergy emergencies. He had an extreme reaction to a bee sting a few years ago and kept them with him always. After opening the package he gave her the capsules, instructing her to take them both. She took it reluctantly, but by now she was thirsty, and the events of the past few hours had begun to take their toll. Thinking something with sugar in it would do her some good, she nibbled on one of the cookies.

"These are my favorite kind of cookies. I have cookies and milk every night before I go to bed. Isn't that funny?" she asked, laughing. She was still in shock, confused from the events that had just occurred, nothing seemed real.

Ian just smiled as he watched her drink her milk. He was satisfied when the whole cup had been emptied. Now, it seemed was as good a time to leave as any. It was surreal to be talking about cookies at such a time.

"Come on, let's get out of here. We will be safe in no time."

They left the room, Ian again opening

the car door for her. He hurried around to the driver's side, and got in. Starting the engine in a hurry, he sped out of the parking area, and headed west on Kennedy to Dale Mabry, the quickest way to get to the Interstate.

Once in the car, Morgan began to feel very drowsy. She tried to get comfortable in the seat. She was warmed with the car heater, and was finding it hard to stay awake.

"Here let me help you," Ian said. He reached over her to the lever on the side of the seat that enabled it to lie back.

"Thanks," she said sleepily.

"You just rest," he said. "We'll be there in no time."

He smiled to himself. This had been smooth, too easy actually. He could not have wished for a better scenario if he had planned for weeks. Other than the fact that he had just been an eye witness to a murder, tampered with evidence, and fled the scene, things were perfect.

SIXTEEN

When she woke, Morgan was in a four poster bed covered with a beautiful wedding ring quilt. She was wearing a white cotton, ankle-length night gown, and wondered how she happened to have it on. The windows were covered with heavy curtains that blocked any light that may have tried to enter the room. On the table next to the bed a Big Ben wind up clock ticked a steady reminder that life was passing by. Morgan looked at the clock's faintly glowing face. Three-thirty was the time it displayed. *Three-thirty in the morning or in the after-noon*, she wondered.

She looked around for a bathroom, and suddenly remembered what had brought her there. Immediately her hands flew to her face to cover her eyes. It was like a bizarre dream, only an imagining. But Morgan knew what had happened had been real. She had seen Greg floating in the spa with herself. There were so many things to think about. She wondered how she would ever sort it all out.

A light knock at the door startled her. "Come in," she said.

Ian opened the door, holding a tray of food. On the tray were scrambled eggs, orange juice, coffee, toast, and peach jam. All of her favorites, and it was garnished with a lavender rose in a short bud vase. On the side of the plate was a small dish of ketchup. Morgan was amazed that every item on the tray was exactly what she would have chosen for her self. Even the rose. It appeared to be an Angle Face. She had several of the same bushes in her yard.

"Wow, you've gone to a lot of trouble,"

she remarked.

"Oh, it's the least I could do, considering." He lowered his head, avoiding her eyes, seemingly out of respect for her grief.

"Just one silly question. Where is the bathroom?"

"Oh! It's that door right there. Let me get you a robe." He walked to the closet and retrieved a long white terry cloth robe. It was just like the one she had at home hanging on the back of her bathroom door. What a coincidence, she thought to herself.

He walked her over to the bathroom, and left her to have some privacy. A new brush lay on the counter, and next to it was a new toothbrush and toothpaste. It was medium firmness and the toothpaste baking soda gel, the kind she had at home. She finished using the rest room, washed her hands, and used the brush to tidy her hair.

Returning to the bedroom, she noticed the walls were filled with Norman Rockwell prints and Ansel Adams photographs. How unusual, she thought. *Ian likes the same artists as I do.* He was sitting at the desk, in the corner of the room, with the tray of food he had brought for her.

"Just sit over here next to the lamp," he instructed. "It's all ready for you. You really need to eat something."

"Thanks, Ian. You're so thoughtful." She tried to be enthusiastic about eating, but as soon as she picked up the fork she started to cry.

Ian pulled some tissues from the box on the desk, and handed them to her. He reached over and pulled her to his chest, cradling her head in her arms, pressing her closer to him. "It's okay," he assured her. "I'm here for you."

"Oh, Ian, what would I do without you? I'm so scared. This is the worst nightmare. I never thought anything like this would ever happen to me."

"Don't worry," he said. "I'm here for you. We'll figure everything out. I promise. I'll be right here for you. I'm not going anywhere.

"I called in a welfare check at your home to Tampa Police. I said I was Greg's brother and hadn't been able to get ahold of either of you by phone for a few days. That way they'll be sure to have found him and start an investigation."

"Don't you think they'll wonder where I am?, she asked.

"Of course, let them wonder. It's more important to keep you safe right now. I'm not sure they can do that. I can."

"They'll think I had something to do with it," she protested.

"I'm sure they will. There's a friend of mine I can ask to check into it. While he does, it's better for you to sit back and wait."

"I sure hope you're right," she said.

"Me too."

SEVENTEEN

Ian was reluctant to call Lieutenant Moreno, but there was no other choice. He had to ask someone to help him, and the lieutenant was one of the few people he knew he could trust with something as sensitive as this. It was just that he really hated bothering him at home on his day off. The last thing cops want to do on their days off is police work.

"Hello," Patrick Moreno said.

"Hey, Lieutenant. This is Ian Greer. I hate to bother you at home, but I really need your help with something," Ian apologized.

"No problem. What's going on?"

"Well, I have a tag I need some information on."

"Why don't you just call communications and have them run it through FCIC for you?" he asked.

"The problem is, it's a government tag. Seems that it is a little too sensitive for me to be checking into without a lot of explanations. So, I had hoped that you would be willing to check it out for me. I wouldn't think that anyone would question a supervisor about it."

"I guess I could do that for you. Why do I feel that I'm getting into something here?"

"Could be that you know me too well," Ian joked.

Lieutenant Moreno had been his supervisor for three years, off and on. As a boss he had been a great guy to work for. Get the job done, and have all the fun you want. But if you didn't do your job, God save you from the wrath of the lieutenant. Ian gave him all the information, along with his pager and cell phone numbers. Patrick promised to get right on it and get back with him quickly.

With nothing more to be done but wait, Ian turned his attention to taking care of Morgan.

ANN BAKER

EIGHTEEN

Several days went by before Morgan ventured outside. She had slept almost all of the time for the past few days, wasn't sure what day it was, and even less sure what day of the month it was. So far, she had not even worried where she was. Ian kept feeding her Benedryl to make her sleep. Eventually she would have to snap out of it and deal with the reality of the situation.

Ian would bring her meals to her, and leave her to sleep. He had been so sweet and supportive. She felt herself bonding to him, becoming dependent on him for every thing. It was not a good connection to be developing at this point. With Greg's death so recent, she surely didn't need to start clinging to someone she barely knew. However, there was no one else to cling to, and for some reason she trusted him.

Morgan had found clothing in the bedroom that was her size. There was a complete wardrobe of everything she needed, jeans, tops, dresses, shoes, and under things. When she asked Ian where they came from, he told her they belonged to his ex-wife. Not being one to pry, she didn't ask him about her.

She jumped out of bed this morning, tired of sleeping, tired of doing nothing. A quick shower cleared some of the cobwebs from her mind and partially returned her to reality. Still, after having slept for so many days, she felt as though she was in a fog.

The blow-dryer she held in her hand was familiar and comforting. It was the same type she had at home, but a different brand. The warm air flowed over her skin, giving it a

88

tingling sensation. Her hair tickled her cheeks as it was blown forward. Hanging her head up side down, she allowed the air to finish drying the underside of her thick mane. Then with a flip of her head the hair was flinging backwards and hung down her back in a thick cascade of curls.

Morgan noticed she had started her period. Too many days without her birth control pills no doubt. Luckily all the things she needed were there in the bathroom. At least she didn't have to ask Ian to pick something up for her. She had noticed three packages of birth control pills, the same kind she used in the medicine cabinet. Not wanting to use something that belonged to someone else, she had left them there. The date on the packages had been current, however, but then those kinds of things stayed good for years. Oddly there was no name or label on the packages. Perhaps the woman who owned them had ordered by mail like Morgan did. She thought she remembered the label being attached to each of hers but she couldn't be certain. *Oh well*, she thought, and put the matter behind her without dwelling on it further.

She arranged her hair around her face with her fingers, and began to apply some of the make-up she found there. The sun-screen in the drawer was SPF 50, hypoallergenic, the kind she used. She applied a thin film, and then used some brown eyeliner. It was the first time in days she had even thought about putting on make-up. After brushing her lashes with some brown mascara, she picked up a lavender lip stick, and got a tissue to wipe off the end. To her surprise it was new, showing no sign of being used before.

Without another thought, she turned and left the bathroom. It felt a little strange to be leaving the bedroom, the room that had served as a haven, a womb for her for so many days.

She was surprised at what she found at the end of the hall. The living room was a charming country room. There was an oval braided rug in mauve and blue that was placed directly in front of the river rock fireplace. The mantle held a kerosene lamp and several beautiful candles that had obviously been used.

The furniture consisted of a blue and beige checkered couch and love seat. There was a large chest positioned between the couch and fire place, just perfect for putting your feet up on. To the right of the fireplace was a large rocker with beige eyelet cushions on the seat and back. On each arm of the rocker there was a crocheted oval doily, they matched the curtains. Each curtain was intricately crocheted, and obviously had been done by hand. Behind each curtain was a thick room-darkening shade to block out any sun that tried to break into the room when unwanted.

A large rustic dining table heralded the transition from living room to kitchen. Blue gingham checked curtains hung around the window over the sink. A country hutch augmented the cabinets, and held the dishes. They were a beautiful combination of antique plates, bowls and cups that were all in shades of blue, none matching the others. The glasses were a beautiful dark blue. She recognized them as the dishes Ian had been serving her meals on. The tray he had been serving her on sat at the back of the hutch. Someone had taken great care to decorate this home, and it was lovely.

Morgan sank into the cushions on the couch and thought about starting a fire even though it was probably hot outside. All the shades were closed, and she had no idea what time of day it was, or even if it was day or night. It felt like early evening, but she really didn't care. She had no ambition to even go to the window and look out. It was enough to just sit there enveloped in the quiet.

It was frightening for her to think. She had no idea what she was going to do next. She didn't even know when it would be safe to go home. The people at work must be wondering where she had disappeared to. If only she had the newspaper. She scanned the room for a television set, but saw none.

Surely the news would have something on Greg's murder. Channel Two News had a twenty-four hour local program. There must be a television in the house some where. She got up and went to look for it.

First, she went down the hall to the room she had been staying in. A cursory glance around the room confirmed what she already knew. There was no television in the room. There was a large hutch in the corner of the room, but it was locked, she had tried to open it before. A quick search of the closet was unproductive.

Morgan decided to try the room at the end of the hall, to the left of the bedroom she had been using. She assumed it was Ian's room.

Walking down the short hall, she felt a little uneasy. It felt as though she were spying on him, doing something she shouldn't. The door handle was one of those lever types, silver and black. The design was an intricate floral pattern. She gripped it in her right hand, and found the metal was cold against her palm. As she pressed downward on the handle, she realized the door was locked.

At the same moment she felt warmth on the top of her head, as if someone were breathing behind her. She felt a chill through her whole body, knowing someone was behind her.

"Good morning my lady," Ian said in a low liquid voice.

"Oh, Ian, you terrified me. Why didn't you tell me you were in the house?"

"I just got here," he defended. "I didn't know you'd be awake. You've been sleeping for days now."

"I know. I finally woke up." She felt a little too close to him, standing there in the hall. His large body seemed even larger here in this close space. How could she have forgotten his imposing size? Her breathing quickened and she felt a little warm. He stood behind her, blocking her exit. One hand touched each wall, arms outstretched in front of her. She looked up her eyes meeting his. The tension was unnerving. She could feel his eyes penetrating her very soul.

"Let's get out of this hall," she suggested. "I'm getting hot standing here."

Barely managing to prevent a chuckle at the obvious ambiguity of the statement, he smiled. "Sure," he said, but then paused a few seconds before turning.

He loved being in control, catching her off guard. He reminded himself to play fairly, after all, she had been through a lot, and he had plenty of time, not to mention a great advantage.

Morgan followed Ian to the couch in front of the fireplace. "You really should be, ashamed , scaring me like that. Considering all I have been through, it's a wonder I didn't start screaming like a hysterical fool."

"You're right. I'm really sorry. Do you forgive me?"

"Of course I forgive you. Ian, you're the best. You've been so good to me. I really don't know how I'll ever thank you."

Could she really be this naïve? He knew exactly how she could thank him, and intended to be compensated. It was only a matter of time.

"It's no problem. I'm glad I can help you," he stated.

"That's a beautiful fireplace," she offered, feeling uncomfortable with the lull in conversation.

"You want me to light the fire?" he asked.

"Oh, would you? I love a fireplace. I have one at home, but not nearly as charming as yours."

"Sure thing. I'm a bit of a pyro myself," he mused.

She watched quietly as he removed the fire screen. He reached to top of the mantle and removed one of the long matches from its tube. The logs were already set up, and Ian wadded some old newspapers he kept in a basket next to the hearth.

"Ian," she ventured, "What has the news been saying about Greg?"

There was a long pause. He didn't answer, but kept working at the fireplace. She watched as he methodically returned the screen to the front of the newly beginning fire, and put the tube of matches back on the mantle. She was beginning to wonder if he had heard her, when he came and sat on the couch next to her.

He wore a green button-down shirt with blue stripes creating a checked pattern. It was her favorite kind of shirt. It set off the unusual color of his eyes. They were a kind light olive-drab, very unusual. His jeans fit snugly, showing off his muscular body.

"I don't know if you are ready for all of this yet," he stalled.

"Of course, I've been through a lot, but I still want to know what's going on. That's what I was doing in the hall. I was looking for a television. I want to see the news."

Ian sat there thinking for a few minutes. It was so awkward trying to talk to him today. He seemed strange and different, unlike other times she had been with him.

"I don't know how to say this without scaring you."

"I have always admired your directness and honesty more than anything else about you, and I wouldn't expect any less of you now. You don't have to protect me you know."

She was so trusting, so gullible. Protection was what she needed most right now, and he was the only one who could give it to her.

"It seems there has been a twist added to the story, one we could not have foreseen at the time."

"If you don't tell me I'm going to go crazy. Just tell the story, *PLEASE*."

"Okay, here goes. I know for a fact, the person in that Camaro was working for the government. That much you must have guessed already."

"Right, that much you've told me."

"I haven't been able to find out which agency they worked for so far. But the media is reporting that Tampa Police Department is considering you as the number one suspect."

"ME!!! Oh, great. I knew it."

"Apparently, they are treating your disappearance as an indicator of guilt."

"Perfect, that's just perfect!" she shouted. "I guess I should go and turn myself in somewhere."

"Oh, no! You can do anything like that. Who would you go to? We still have no idea which agency that tag came back to. It could have been TPD for all you know, or it could be some federal agency."

"Yes, of course, you're right. What am I going to do Ian?"

"Well, right now I have a friend looking into the tag. It may take a little bit of time, if we want to avoid arousing suspicion. No doubt there are a few people looking for you. You'll be safe here. No one would guess that you're with me."

"I can't believe how good you are to me. But, I've got to start doing something. I can't just sleep all the time. I don't even know what day it is, or what time it is."

"That's understandable. Let me catch

you up then. Today is Saturday, September twenty-seventh in the year of our Lord, nineteen hundred and ninety seven, and the time is approximately twenty-two hundred hours," he said with mock formality.

"Oh," she sighed with relief. "You don't know how confused I was."

"I think I might be able to imagine," he mused. "After all you are a female."

"Great, that's all I need now, some lame attempt at male humor."

"Sorry, it's hard for me to deny my true nature for any length of time, and I love to hear you laugh."

She hung her head as she began to cry. "I don't know if I will ever laugh again Ian."

Feeling genuine sympathy, he moved close putting his arm around her. "It's all right, Morgan, it'll get better." It felt good to hold her in his arms, to protect her. She needed him, and that was right where he wanted her.

Ian held her there for the better part of a half hour. He was an expert on how to comfort a woman, instinctively knowing when to talk and when to listen, and when to do nothing at all. Armed with a box of tissues, he was a man with a mission, one he was well qualified to carry out. He could have stayed like this for hours.

Finally he ventured a word. "You must be starving. Let me fix you something. What would you like?"

"What are my choices?" she asked, attempting to hide her reddened eyes. A lot of good putting on make-up had done. It was probably smeared all under her eyes, raccoon style.

"Well, I have the ever popular chicken noodle soup, with accompanying sandwich of your choice. Then there is the frozen lasagna or sweet and sour chicken, also frozen. For dessert I can offer you chocolate cake, or vanilla ice cream, or both."

"Sounds like bachelor heaven. Do you happen to have any Frosted Flakes?"

"Oui, Madame, we do have the Frosted Flakes. And how would Madame prefer her Frosted Flakes served, with milk in the bowl or milk on the side?" he said using his best French accent.

"Ummmm...," she paused for dramatic effect. "I think the milk in the bowl would be preferable, sir. Thank-you very much. You really are considerate."

He set a place at the table for her and made some coffee, decaf because of the late hour. "Maybe you would like to go outside for awhile when you finish eating. I have some lounge chairs out there and the sky is clear, the stars are beautiful."

"That sounds great. Just let me wolf down some of this cereal. This tastes great. I didn't realize how hungry I was."

He laughed to himself as he watched her slurping down the cereal. It was wonderful to have her here. Even in her grief it was a joy for him to watch her. Something about having her with him made him feel complete and at peace.

When she finished her cereal, he took the bowl and spoon, and put them in the dishwasher after rinsing them. He got a jacket for her and offered her some insect repellent.

"Believe me you'll be glad you used this. The mosquitoes are the size of sparrows out here."

"Ian," she paused. "Where is out here? I don't even know where I am."

"You are in a safe place. We are in Hillsborough County, and you are right in the very middle of no where."

"But where?"

"You probably wouldn't know if I told

you. The Alafia River is just to the west of us, though. When you are stronger we will walk over there."

"That's right, I wanted to ask you. I really need to start exercising again. Is there anywhere I can get some leg weights and a few free weights."

"I think I could accommodate you, if you were to ask me just right."

"Would a 'pretty please' help?"

"Ahhhhh, you have found my weakness. Pretty pleases are my weakness. And coming from you, pretty please will get you anything you want... anything."

"I'll have to remember that one and use it in the future."

"I sure hope you do."

"You are quite the charmer. I don't believe I remember seeing this side of you before."

"Super Deputy has many sides. It depends on the color of the cape he is wearing, and the color of hair the person in need of rescue has."

"Oh! I see. Well, then, what color would elicit undying devotion?" she mused, playing along with his game.

Ian stopped dead in his tracks, as they were on the way out the door, she following right behind him. He turned, grabbing her by both arms and pulling her close. Looking into her eyes and becoming gravely serious he said, "That would be the color you have. And then if her eyes were green like yours, then undying devotion would only be the beginning."

She pulled back, frightened, breathless. "Ian, you scare me. I'm not used to anyone being so direct."

"So sorry to have disturbed you my lady," he said, lifting her hand to his mouth and kissing it lightly. "I'm telling the truth. If you don't want to hear it I'll try to keep quiet in the future."

"I'm sorry, Ian. I guess I sound silly. I've been out of the loop for a very long time."

"I can see that. It only adds to the appeal, I'm afraid."

"Oh, no, I'm the one who's afraid."

"Do I really scare you?" he asked obviously concerned.

"Honestly? Yes, you do. You scare the hell out of me."

"Why?"

"You're just so, so," she hesitated, "your size has something to do with it. But it is probably more the fact that you're so direct, so honest. I don't believe I've ever had anyone be quite that way with me."

"Oh, I see."

She felt the pressure growing, and wanting to escape, changed the subject. "Let's go outside now. I can't wait to see the stars out here away from the lights. And I haven't been outside for a long time."

"Okay, let's go." He led the way. "It may take a few minutes for your eyes to adjust. There isn't any light out here this time of night. Here, take my hand."

She did take his hand, it was big and warm, comforting. Just like him, he was all those things, and more. Touching him sent a delicious tingle through her. Her hand was completely lost in his. She knew that, like her hand she could become completely lost in Ian Greer, and forget who Morgan had been. In fact, she was already beginning to have difficulty remembering who she had been just a few short days before.

He was right about the darkness, as soon as she left the house and the door closed behind them total darkness enveloped them. How ironic she thought, she was totally at his mercy. If not for his care she would be without direction and totally lost. But did she trust this man she hardly knew? Did she have a choice?

"Here we are, and here's your front row seat to the best show in town."

Morgan sat in the lounge chair that was already lying back. "Oh, Ian!" she exclaimed. "How beautiful! I forgot how beautiful the sky is at night away from the city. I always loved looking at the stars in town, but this is beyond comparison."

"I know," was his only response. He wasn't looking at the stars. He was watching her. It brought him pleasure to know that he had pleased her in some way.

They sat there for the better part of an hour, not speaking. She entranced with the beauty of the stars, and he entranced with her. He was the first to break the silence.

"Morgan, there's something I have been wanting to ask you?"

"Sure, go ahead," she replied.

"Do you remember about a year ago, in the break room below Communications, the downstairs break room?" he paused as he spoke. "Do you remember a guy helping you with your candy bar?"

She searched her memory for a few seconds. "Yes! I remember that. I was so embarrassed. Were you there?"

"Yes," he admitted. "I was there. I was the one that helped you with the candy machine."

"You're kidding!" She was very surprised. "That's too much. I can't believe I didn't put that together. I've always thought there was something familiar about your eyes, but I just couldn't put my finger on what it was."

"I thought I noticed you trying to figure it out more than once."

"You should have said something a long

time ago. That's unbelievable. What a small world."

The reality of what he had said began to sink in, as her memory of that day unfolded. She had been so taken by him, and yet not recognized him as the same person. Of course, a long time had passed between seeing him the first time and actually meeting him.

Ian just watched her. He enjoyed doing that. But this time it was particularly interesting. She struggled with the details of this new information, and was visibly trying to reconcile other details to make them fit.

"Why didn't you mention it before?" she finally asked.

"I don't know," he answered truthfully. "It didn't seem all that important before."

"I've got to tell you, quite honestly, I was really taken by you that day."

"Yeah, me too," he admitted. "Morgan, I don't know if it's the right time to say this or not, but I'm fascinated by you."

Morgan felt her face reddening, and wondered if he could see it in the darkness. "Well, I'm flattered, of course," she stammered.

"I just wanted you to know that. I want you to feel safe with me. Say the word and I'll leave you alone. Do you want me to leave you alone?"

"Alone? Of course not. But you realize that I can't trust my feelings at this point. No matter what I might or might not feel for you now is greatly affected by Greg's murder. It has only been a few days. I don't even know if he is buried yet or not."

She began to cry again, and he pulled her out of her chair, and picking her up, carried her into the house. He deposited her in her room, in the four poster bed she had occupied for the past few days.

"Here, you rest. Don't think about anything. I'll see you in the morning." He turned and left the room, closing the door behind him.

Morgan couldn't rest with insect repellent all over her. She rose and went to the bathroom and undressed to shower. Reaching over to turn the shower on she caught a glimpse of herself in the mirror. Looking more closely, she hardly recognized the person gazing back at her. It wasn't that she looked any different on the outside, but something had changed, something you couldn't see, but it showed just the same. What was happening, and where would it end?

She stepped into the warm water, allowing it to flow over her. The liquid river of warmth poured over her, melting away her fears. For a moment she gave up thinking about the past, Greg and her fears.

Through the mist in her mind thoughts of Ian permeated her awareness. Just like the warm water that enclosed her in fluid comfort, Ian's presence surrounded her consciousness. The feeling was much more than just pleasant, and Morgan found herself surrendering to the sensation willingly, wantonly. She wanted to forget all of her problems, and he was the perfect escape. Just how long had she wanted him? Was it something that had been there all along and she had just ignored it?

An involuntary gasp of pleasure escaped from low in her throat. Surprised and shocked with herself, she instantly turned off the water and shook her head scolding herself for such a breach of proper morals. What was she becoming? His, was the more than obvious answer.

NINETEEN

She tried to sleep, but it was impossible. The truth of what he had told her added a new dimension to the puzzle that she was already overwhelmed with.

Who had shot Greg? Were they still after her? Could she trust Ian? And could she trust herself with Ian?

Morgan remembered her reaction to him that first time she had seen him very vividly. No wonder she felt the way she did about him. No wonder he intimidated her. It was nothing else but lust, pure and unadulterated. Perhaps some people called it love, but she knew what it really was.

Her relationship with Greg had never been based on that. They had something far different from that, love based on friendship first. It had been a wonderful few years. Especially the last few when they were able to afford to go places and do thing. But now Greg was gone forever. Surely the reality of this would begin to sink in sooner or later.

Right now Morgan felt as if she were still married to Greg. She wondered if his mother had planned the funeral yet. More than likely they had already held the funeral. Almost a full week had gone by since that fateful night.

Morgan stayed awake most of the night. Maybe she dozed off for a few minutes, but certainly not much more than that. So many questions raced through her head. When would her life return to normal? What would normal be like now? And exactly how was it that Ian happened to be there just at the right time?

She seemed to remember him giving her

some kind of explanation, but couldn't remember what it had been. None of the pieces seemed to fit. Searching her every conscious memory, she tried to remember any hint of a reason that someone would want to kill Greg. But there was no mistaking what had happened. Even she could easily see that this was no accident or coincidence. Someone had meant to kill him. There was no doubt about that. Just who that had been was yet to be seen. And until she knew who it was her life was in danger too.

Before she knew it morning had arrived. Ian was busy in the kitchen frying bacon. This man was really a dream. If he only did windows he would be perfect. No, that would be too much to ask. Surely a man with all his talents must have some flaws somewhere.

Morgan dressed and freshened up before coming out to the kitchen. Ian greeted her with a big broad smile, two rows of perfect white teeth gleaming. "How do you take your coffee?" he asked.

"Sweet and light," she responded.

"I should have guessed. And I would bet you take your eggs scrambled dry."

"That's right!" she exclaimed. "You really are too much. What's a nice guy like you doing single any way?"

"I guess the right one just hasn't come along. Not since my divorce anyway. And so it seems, not before the divorce either, although I thought differently at one time."

"I'd love to hear what happened, if it's not prying to ask."

"No, it's not prying, but I'd rather talk about something more pleasant to start the day."

"Sounds fine to me, you name the topic."

"You mentioned you wanted to start working out. I've got some weights for you and some running shoes. I hope they're the right size. I thought we'd go running a little later this morning."

"Well, that sounds like fun. I really need to get back into doing something. I'm going crazy sitting still. When do you have to go back to work?"

"Not for a while I took a couple of days off, to spend time with you."

"How thoughtful. I'm growing very accustomed to having you around. I'd hate it if I became dependent on you."

"And I'd like nothing more than that."

She stopped and looked at him quizzically, "Do you really mean that?"

"Except for the horrible circumstances that brought you into my life, nothing better has happened to me in a very long time. I really look forward to coming home, knowing that you're here."

The meaning of his words made her feel unexpectedly safe and scared at the same time. Her reactions to him were never singular and always seemed to be conflicting. It felt good to be needed and wanted by him. At the same time she realized she was becoming someone else; a person completely encompassed in someone she didn't know at all.

They finished breakfast and Morgan cleaned up the dishes. Ian disappeared outside for a few minutes, and reappeared with weights and running shoes. Morgan found socks and leggings in the bedroom she was using, and an appropriate T-shirt. The shoes fit perfectly, and after waiting for their food to digest properly, they went out for a short run.

Ian proved to be quite the runner, running circles around Morgan with ease. After not having any physical activity for almost a week, she became tired quickly, and returned to the house, waiting outside for Ian to return.

The area was very remote. There were

plenty of live oaks, and some maples; Spanish moss hung thickly from the branches of the oaks. The crickets hummed loudly in the midmorning heat, and the call of the mocking-birds pierced the air. Morgan tried to get her bearings, based on the rising sun, but it was hard to tell where she was.

Ian came walking up, cooling down from his run. He had been running for the better part of an hour. His physical condition was superior in every way. Standing on the edge of the porch with his back to the trees, he stretched his calves, alternating one then the other. She watched entranced and wondered how she could be so lucky to have someone like him to help her through this hard time.

Morgan was the first to break the silence. "Ian, I can't stay here forever. They must be wondering where I am at work. I can't imagine what the news is saying about my being missing, and TPD considering me a suspect. I can't just sit here and do nothing."

"You're right," he agreed. "And as soon as we get cleaned up, I plan on the two of us going to work on it." He opened the door to the house and motioned her through.

On her way in, Morgan noticed for the first time, the burglar bars that covered all the windows. There were matching wrought iron doors for each entrance. She thought it odd to have them this far out in the country. Perhaps that was the very reason, the remoteness of the location. She shrugged it off without further thought.

TWENTY

Felicia arrived at work early. She was really troubled with Morgan's disappearance. It wasn't at all like her not to have been in contact. They had been very close to each other. She knew Morgan would call if she could. And she knew Morgan well enough to know that she would never have shot Greg, no matter what Tampa Police Department was trying to say.

Randy happened to show up early too. "Hey, Randy!" Felicia called out. "Hold up, I want to talk to you."

"Hey Felicia, you are here awful early. You don't usually show up till half way through roll call."

"Yeah, I know, but I wanted to talk to you so I got here early," she said, ignoring his tease. "I'm really worried about Morgan. She wouldn't have taken off like that. If there was any way possible, she would call me."

"Maybe she's afraid your phone is tapped," Randy countered.

"Right, but she has my pager number and my cell phone number. She would have tried to contact me somehow."

"That was before she offed her husband."

"I don't believe that crap for a minute. Do you?"

"You know her better than I do. I think people are capable of just about anything, given the right circumstances."

"Maybe, but not Morgan. She never even owned a gun. Do you know anyone over at TPD that could get us some information on the gun that killed Greg?"

"No, not at TPD, but a friend of mine has

a friend that works at the Medical Examiner's Office. I'm sure we could get some information from there."

"Great, I want you to get to work on it today."

"Sure thing Felicia, but it's gonna cost ya."

"Wouldn't I know it if it were you. What's your price Randy?"

"I'm not sure yet. How about just an open ticket?"

"Not with you. No telling what you will demand down the road. How about just doing it out of friendship for Morgan?"

"Hey, I'm not her friend if she's a murderer."

"That sounds just about like what I'd expect of you."

"Whatever," Randy ended the conversation with one of his favorite expressions.

Later that afternoon, Randy paged his friend with the Medical Examiner connections. It was a lieutenant friend of his, one that was just cynical enough about law enforcement to be discreet. Within a few minutes Lieutenant Moreno returned Randy's page.

"Hey there LT, what's up?" Randy greeted.

"Not much here. What's up with you?

"I really need to talk to you. Name a place and I'll meet you after work, somewhere around sevenish."

"You live in Town and Country now don't you?"

"Yeah, but Ybor might be a good place. You like Frankie's Patio."

"Fine with me. See you there."

With that out of the way, Randy began thinking just how to approach the subject with him. He thought it best to be open. Lieutenant Moreno could spot a lie a mile away, probably because he had told so many of his own over the years. He had spent several years in homicide. You don't get through that without a good sense of character.

Everyone in the county must have heard every detail about the case that had been released to the press. Greg and Morgan were having marital problems, and she had simply gone nuts and shot him, and now there was a nation-wide search on to find her. Pretty clear cut and self explanatory. The only person that wasn't buying it was Felicia.

TWENTY-ONE

Finally, the shift ended. Randy went down to the gym for a quick work out and shower. He always kept a change of clothes in his trunk. You never know when an emergency party session will occur.

After a light upper body workout, he hit the shower. He kept a blow dryer in his locker for just such an occasion as this. After he was satisfied with his hair, he had just enough time for a quick shave.

Now he was ready for Ybor, and he was still the man. Even if he was in his early thirties, he was irresistible. He thought of himself a little like a younger version of John Travolta, and he hummed to himself, thinking he was a ladies' man, knowing how to use his walk. Yep, he hadn't lost it yet, and probably never would.

Lieutenant Moreno was waiting at a table in the corner at Frankie's just as agreed. He was a tall good looking man, with a full head of silver gray hair. Silver Fox was what they called him. Fox was an accurate description literally and figuratively. He was sharp, even now in his mid-fifties his mind was quick, with an eye for detail. His blue eyes were brilliant and clear, seeing things others missed. His frame was an athletic one with barely an ounce of fluff, nearly all rock hard with defined muscle tone.

"Hey Randy," he offered. "Good to see you. I thought you had disappeared entirely after you got married."

"Whole new lifestyle LT. Gotta keep a low profile. But every now and then, you just got to get out. You know what I mean."

"Yeah, Randy, I sure do. But I'm sure you didn't ask me down here to discuss the social life of a former bachelor."

"You're right LT. I'll get right to the point. You know about the Greg McGhee murder right?"

"Who doesn't? It's the talk of the town. Wasn't his wife a friend of yours?"

"Coworker," he corrected. "I don't know if I would go so far as to say she was a friend."

"What's up with that anyway? You think she really did it?" Patrick asked.

"That's exactly why I came to you. A friend of mine really doesn't buy this domestic violence thing. Seems she knew Morgan real well, and there wasn't a hint of it before this."

"Really?" The Lieutenant perked up now, sitting a little taller in his chair, his innate reaction was automatic. The nose of the bloodhound, trained for years to smell the slightest scent of malevolence, now tweaked. "Tell me more."

"There's not much more to tell. I promised I would ask you to check with your sources and see if you can find out what kind of gun killed Greg McGhee."

"That shouldn't be too hard," he offered, reluctantly, still thinking. "Why would that be of any significance?"

"It seems that Ms. Morgan never owned a gun. Didn't know how to shoot at all according to her friends."

"You know, I have been following all of the news reports, and I haven't heard mention of the murder weapon being located."

"Exactly, see, there are too many questions. There may be perfectly logical explanations, but my friend just can't seem to put the pieces together," Randy explained.

"I'm sure I can look into it. What else

does your friend know about this?"

"She only says that she was very close to Morgan and that if there were any way possible, she surely would have tried to contact her some way."

"Maybe she is just afraid of being traced," said Lieutenant Moreno.

"That's the first thing I said, but she insisted she knew her pager number. She could have called that without fear of a trace."

"True, true... Well, Randy, I promise I'll look into it for you. By the way, have you heard I plan to retire at the first of the year."

"No way! Congrats man! You deserve it. You gonna just hang around Cheval and golf every day?"

"As tempting as that sounds, no. I bought a fishing camp in the Carolinas. Think I'll go up there and run the place and kick back for a few years and see what turns up."

"Sounds great. Be sure to give me all the particulars. I'd love to have a place to escape the home scene from time to time."

"Say, how can I contact you? I really don't want to call up to the Comm. Center. All those recorded lines make me nervous."

"You and me both. Call my cell, anytime day or night. I'll be waiting to hear from you. I'll take care of the check on the way out."

"Don't even think about it buddy, it's my treat. I make the big bucks, remember?"

At that they both laughed. Randy left, but the Patrick sat there for long time thinking. Something didn't seem right to him about this case from the beginning. It wasn't any of his business, but this was real close to home. He had plenty of contacts over at TPD. After all, that's where he came from. He had a contact at the Medical Examiner's Office, although he would rather avoid calling that particular old flame for information.

Moreno didn't wait till in the morning to start making a few phone calls. Right after he got home he started calling in some favors he was owed. Before long, he was sure this story was missing more than just a few details. Too many people were being way too tight lipped about the whole thing. Something was up, and he was going to find out what it was.

He would have to bite the bullet and call Rhonda. Knowing she wouldn't be at the morgue, he dialed her cell. She answered right away, and after a few minutes of raking him over the coals she agreed to talk.

"I did some work on the McGhee case," Rhonda said reluctantly."

"You know me, I can't wait for the report to be made public. It's not like I'm gonna tell anyone. Hell, you know how bad I hate the press."

Patrick listened intently as Rhonda explained what she knew about the case. Particularly interesting was the type of bullet that killed Greg McGhee.

"Whoa, .223 caliber, hollow point boat tail match grade Federal ammunition, huh? Shit! Not your typical women's firearm. That's the same ammo we all use in our carbines. I can see why you guys are keeping it quiet."

"Yeah, two police detectives came in for the autopsy. That's unheard of. I've been wondering who McGhee was. It seems like he was pretty high profile."

"Rhonda, you're the best. I'm really sorry about how things worked out. I'd like to take you to dinner sometime. Could we do that?"

Rhonda told him she really didn't think so, but would keep it in mind. She had moved on. he was glad to hear it. No one deserved his brand of romance.

Patrick switched into high gear. The tag Ian had asked him to check out and now this. He would get to the bottom of this, and quick. This was right up his alley.

TWENTY-TWO

Morgan was glad to be getting back into the swing of regular exercise. It was the one thing she could actually say had been constant in her life as long as she could remember. It felt good to run again, and Ian was a wonderful companion. Although, his abilities exceeded her own, he never gloated or tried to make her feel inferior. He seemed to naturally assume that she would not be able to keep up with him, and made concessions when appropriate.

Usually when she came to the end of her endurance, he would continue on with his run and meet her back at the house. Today was different however; he stopped to rest when she did.

"Hey, remember I promised to show you the Alafia," Ian offered.

"Oh, I forgot all about that."

"Come on then, we'll walk over there. Unless you're too tired?"

"Not at all. Sounds like a great idea."

He took her hand, leading the way. It felt awkward to be touching someone, even in such an impersonal way. Somehow the simple act of holding his hand seemed to take on an intimate meaning. Perhaps it was the circumstances, but something inside Morgan was telling her she should be afraid - afraid to become involved with this man. He seemed to be way out of her league, much to smooth and polished to have not had considerable experience.

Her feelings were not to be trusted at this point. Before she had met Greg, she had been a poor judge of character, always picking the wrong kind of guy. Greg had been the only one that had seemed worthy of spending a life-

NO COINCIDENCE

time with. Even Greg had turned out to be vastly different from what she had hoped for.

"Smell the jasmine," Ian said breaking the uneasy silence. "It blooms every year about this time. You should be here when the citrus trees bloom."

"The jasmine smells wonderful. Roses have always been my passion though. I wonder if mine are doing okay with no one to take care of them."

"They'll be fine for a while. They grow in the wild with no attention at all."

"You're right, it's only been a little over a week anyway, but I would be fertilizing them this week, and I need to spray for mildew."

"Don't worry about your roses. You can take care of them when this mess is cleared up."

"Right, but I have no way of knowing how long it'll be. Do you think the police are investigating any other leads, or are they just looking for me?"

"I am sure they'll investigate every possible avenue. That is, of course, unless they are the ones that were behind all of this to begin with."

"That's a scary thought. When do you expect to hear back from your friend about that tag?" she asked anxiously.

"As a matter of fact, I'm hoping he'll call this evening."

"How will he call you? You have no phone at the house."

"I keep my cell phone in the car, or he'll page me if he can't get me on the phone," Ian explained.

Morgan didn't reply. There was no need for words. Their communication did not need to be verbal. What he wanted to say could be best expressed through touch. He continued to hold her hand loosely, his thumb stroking the inside of her palm occasionally. It seemed strange to her that such a simple motion could be so sensually stimulating, causing far reaching reactions that were quite unexpected. More than once she started to withdraw her hand, but against better judgment, she did not.

"Look, just through those trees, that is the Alafia," Ian pointed out.

"Greg and I went canoeing on the Alafia once," she offered.

"Really? I love canoeing. I'd love to take you sometime."

"Sounds great. You almost convince me that there is a future," she mused.

"Of course, there's a future. You will go on breathing, just like the sun comes up every day in the east. It may take some time, but eventually, the truth will come out."

"Later rather than sooner is my fear though. By then I could be breathing the air from inside a prison cell."

"Never fear, Super Ian is here."

"You are that Ian. I mean it. You've been great... You're so sweet."

"Sweet? Did you say sweet? Don't repeat that. If any of the guys I work with ever heard that I'd have to quit. You'll damage my reputation madam," he said laughingly.

"Of course, it'll be our secret. I'll never say it in public, you have my promise."

Even this whimsical promise to keep something secret between the two of them seemed to magnify the bond that was growing. Growing slowly, but growing nonetheless.

As they reached the banks of the river, Ian offered Morgan a seat on a log. He sat down beside her.

"I'm surprised how wide and fast the river is here," she remarked. "I have always seen the Alafia as a small creek-like thing."

"We're a little farther south than you may be familiar with," he explained. "The closer you get to the bay, the deeper and wider the Alafia becomes, and there are a couple of branches of the river."

"The water's darker here than I remember too."

"Right, but it is perfectly clean. It's the tannin from the trees along the banks. The same thing colors iced tea."

"Well, all we need is a little sugar and some ice then."

"Mmmm," he responded suggestively. "Sugar."

There was another awkward pause. He watched her like a spider watching a fly trapped in its web, scrutinizing her every move. When he first brought here he did not realize how deep his feelings would become for her. At first it was just a game, like so many other games he had played. But now it was turning into something different, something more enduring. He didn't dare admit to himself that he was falling in love with her. Love was something Ian avoided. He avoided it because of the potential pain associated with the emotion, but here he was, helpless to stop himself.

A yellow butterfly made its way up the opposite side of the river and Morgan followed it with her eyes, her head automatically turning to follow. She noticed Ian watching her, and against her better judgment allowed herself to be drawn into his gaze. At that moment, she knew all resolve to resist him was lost.

Ian leaned forward and downward, brushing his cheek against hers. The subtlety of the touch, the brevity of contact startled her. She caught his scent, warm and masculine, musky and moist. Her arms almost reached out to keep him from moving away again, but she forced herself to keep them at her side. A deep sigh escaped her lungs, exiting her in an audible, "Mmmm."

Before she had any more time to react, he was tearing off his running shoes and socks. Once he was barefoot, he helped her out of hers. Morgan squealed in protest, but he did not stop. When he had completed his task, he scooped her up in his arms and waded into the water. Without hesitation, he dunked under the water, taking Morgan under with him. The chill of the water took her breath.

"Ian, you are crazy," she said in protest. "But I have to admit, this feels great."

"You feel great," he said, looking deeply into her eyes as he held her. He released her legs allowing them to float vertically, but still held her body next to his. "You are so, so enticing."

He stopped talking and covered her lips with his own. She expected him to kiss her, but instead he just brushed his lips lightly across her own. Combined with the cold water the effect was totally exhilarating. She could feel his body as it tensed next to hers, his leg muscles flexed as he withstood the considerable current. His powerful arms encompassed her, pressing her against his chest. The hardness of his arms and chest were a stark contrast to the tenderness of his embrace, and more comforting than she could ever have imagined.

She longed to stay there forever, protected from harm, but she reminded herself that her feelings could not be trusted. It took a significant effort, but she pushed herself away from him. Had he not willingly released her the push she gave would have been purely ineffective.

He was able to overpower her with ease. But overpowering her is not what he wanted. What he really wanted was for her to give herself to him willingly, then and only then would she really be his. He wanted to own her as his own; body, mind and soul. Little did he know that he was much closer to his goal than he dreamed.

Morgan allowed herself to enjoy the water. She dove time and again, turning flips and standing on her hands like a little girl playing in the ocean. She almost forgot all the trouble of the past few days, lost in the feeling of the moment. It was almost like being another person, having no resemblance to the one she had known only a few short days ago.

Ian enjoyed watching her, pleased to have made her happy. It was like watching a child at play, unrestrained with no immediate worries. He wanted to frolic too, but it seemed so undignified for a man. Eventually he gave up his dignity and joined in with abandon.

Nearing exhaustion, Morgan dragged herself up the bank and stretched out on the grass nearby. Ian followed her, lying right next to her, their sides touching. They stayed that way for a long time, panting together, watching the clouds as a gentle breeze blew over them. It was unusual that it was so warm so late in the year.

Morgan was reminded of when she and her brother had spent so many hours lying on the grass looking at the clouds when they were kids. Never had she shared this experience with anyone else, and the intimacy of it seemed very personal.

Ian was the first to speak. "Look at that cloud just over that oak tree. Doesn't that look like Goofy?"

Morgan laughed aloud. "Yes, it does, and that one over there looks like an angel. See the halo."

"Yes, but the angel appears to have horns growing."

"You're too funny," she laughed.

"Funny! So you think of me as funny do

you."

He turned to her and loomed above her, staring into her eyes. Morgan found her self helpless to the captivating power of his gaze.

"You know I'm crazy about you, don't you?"

Her only response was an uttered, "Mmmm." It was an increasingly common response she had to him.

"I wish we could stay like this forever."

"I love being here with you," she responded.

The words she spoke visibly stirred him. He looked away for a moment, and then returned his gaze to hers. "You don't know how much it means to me to hear you say that. There's nothing I want more than to have you here with me. I really mean that."

"What I can't understand is why you're single. I'm sure hoards of women chase after you."

"You flatter me. I guess there are plenty of women out there, but none that appeal to me. I told you before, the minute I first saw you, I knew I wanted you."

"Now you flatter me."

"No," he protested. "It's true. There's something different about you."

"Yeah, I've been told I'm different before, but usually it's not a compliment."

"I can't imagine that," he said sincerely. "How many other women do you know that would like cloud watching in the grass?"

"You may have me there. I am rather childlike in some of my activities."

"Mmmm," was his response this time.

He placed his mouth on hers and this time it was no mere brushing of lips across hers. This time he made demands of her, pressuring her to give of herself. At first she responded, finding it hard to resist him. This was something new to Morgan - raw and powerful - unlike anything she had ever experienced before. But within seconds her conscience stopped her, reminding her that her husband was only just newly planted in the ground, or at least was soon to be. A proper widow would not be cavorting with a man so soon after his death. She pulled herself away from him. Morgan ran in the direction of the house, wanting to outrun her feelings for Ian, but she knew it was impossible.

She didn't look behind her, but she knew he wasn't far behind. She could feel him more than hear him. Somehow she realized it would be this way forever, always feeling his presence, whether near or far.

When she reached the house, she waited by the door for him to return, panting. It wasn't long before he rounded the corner, and she felt her pulse quicken as he came toward her.

"Now why did you want to do a thing like that?" he asked as he pinned her against the wall with his body.

"I can't breathe when you're so close to me."

"What do you mean? What am I doing to affect your breathing?"

"Oh, God," she answered breathlessly. "It's just that... The air seems to be sucked out of the room when you walk in. When you are close to me I think I may just disappear and become part of you. Look at my hands shaking. It's not right for you to do that to me."

"You're wrong Morgan, it is right. It's just this feeling that people live and die for. It's right, and not only that but it's what you really want, if you will admit it to yourself."

"It's too soon, Ian. I just can't."

"No, maybe not now, but you will. You're mine now. You can feel it, can't you?"

Morgan turned her head to avoid his gaze.

To her surprise he took her face in his hand and turned her face to his. "Can't you?" he demanded.

"Yes, yes, you know it's true. Why do you have to force me to say it?"

"Because I like to hear you say it. It's that simple."

"No matter how uncomfortable it makes me feel. Right?"

"I wasn't looking at it that way."

"Of course you weren't. You were only thinking of how you feel."

"You're right. I apologize," but his grin belied any sincerity.

"Do you really think I wouldn't like to throw you down on the ground and attack you?"

Now he laughed at the thought of this. "Oh, sure, that's just what I thought you wanted to do to me."

"Don't make fun of me," she protested.

"I'm sorry," he offered. "But the thought of you trying to throw me on the ground, it's just too funny."

"I can't imagine you'd resist."

"Not at all. In fact, let me stretch myself out here on this porch, and you can attack away."

"Now you are making me laugh. Don't you even think of it."

"You're the one that made the suggestion my lady."

"Why do you call me that?" she asked.

"What?" he countered.

"Your lady."

"It's just an expression, but it sure sounds like a good idea."

"Doesn't it seem a little possessive to you?"

"Maybe, but I can't imagine being happy without you being mine."

"Wow! That certainly is a mouthful. I don't think I've ever belonged to anyone. I have always thought I was free, even after almost a decade of being married."

"Morgan, I won't ever lie to you about how I feel about you. I'm sorry if it makes you feel uncomfortable, but I want you to know how I feel."

"I do appreciate your honesty. You know I'm terrified of you."

The truth of her statement empowered him, his ego feeding off the realization that she really did fear him. It was the kind of power that satisfied him the most.

"Exactly what about me scares you so much?" he continued.

"If I'm not mistaken, I believe we have been through this one before."

"Well, explain it one more time for me," he urged.

"Why do you always want me to say everything? To spell it out verbally?"

"Because that's the way I am. I know what I want, and I always get what I want."

"Fair enough," she paused, breathing deeply. She hoped she had lost him in the diversion.

"Well..."

"Well what...," she countered.

"*What are you so afraid of*?", he said loudly.

"Please Ian, don't shout," she stalled.

"My lady, you do drive me to it."

"I am scared of just that, Ian. I am afraid that I will become part of you, without my own identity. I've only been here with you a few days, and already I don't know who I am anymore. I have no job, no things of my own, my thoughts are completely fragmented. I don't even know if my husband has been buried yet or not."

"Okay, I can see your point. How about if I bring you some newspapers? And I'll bring out the television."

"I'm wondering why you didn't sooner."

"Do you think I'm hiding something from you?"

"Actually the thought had occurred to me."

"I'm sorry you think that way, truly. My only intention was to protect you. I thought the news might upset you."

"And I appreciate that. It just scares me that's all; having someone else make decisions for me."

"I see. You've always been the one in control."

"Not true," she admitted. "Greg always told me exactly what to do. I guess I always got my way anyway though."

"Then it comes down to a power thing, doesn't it? You don't want anyone bossing you around anymore."

"I guess so. Yes, you're right."

He spoke no more, but responded by covering her mouth with his own. Morgan knew she was lost, lost in something far more powerful than herself. The most frightening thing was - she loved it - finding it more intoxicating than any thing she had ever known.

TWENTY-THREE

Lieutenant Moreno couldn't rest peacefully that night when he went to bed. It was his night off, and usually he turned in early. But something in the back of his mind kept nagging at him. After hours of tossing and turning, he pushed the button on the clock next to the bed to light the display. It read three-twelve. He decided to get up and head down to District One Office. Surely the information he had requested on that tag would be in by now.

He slid one long leg in his jeans and then the other. Even at his age he still wore Levi's thirty-four - thirty-sixes. His legs were quite long, but not out of proportion to the rest of his body. From the hanger in the closet he pulled a long sleeved blue chambray shirt. It was his favorite one, soft and worn. The color of the shirt brought out the blue in his eyes. After slipping on a pair of deck shoes he was ready to head out.

On his way to the door he picked up his keys, pager and cell phone; then slipping his gun into his shoulder holster, he felt ready to leave. He marveled at all the contraptions he continually had strapped to him. If he ever fell in the water he would likely drown to death because of the weight of all the gadgets he carried.

He just needed one more thing - a cup of ice water for the car. He always had ice water with him. It kept him from drinking endless carbonated drinks saturated with sugar. That, more than anything, was what he attributed his ability to maintain a normal physique. A glance at the mirror over the table in the hall confirmed what he knew already. He still looked really good.

As he placed his hand on the knob of the front door to exit, the phone rang. He headed back to the kitchen to answer it. "Hello."

"Lieutenant Moreno?"

"Yes, who's calling?"

"This is dispatcher 203 from the Sheriff's Office," she replied.

"What can I do for you 203?" he responded.

"Sir, I was calling you about the tag you requested information on."

"Great, what do you have?"

"The Florida Department of Law Enforcement just called about the tag and they want you to contact them by phone. Can you copy the number?"

"Sure," he said as he automatically picked up a pencil to write. "Go ahead with that number."

"Okay, it's going to be 222-3333, ask for extension 452."

"Thanks, I'll call right now."

"You're welcome," and 203 hung up.

Wow, that's certainly unusual, he thought. In all of his years in law enforcement he could only remember one time before when FDLE had asked to be contacted directly about tag information. That had been when President Bush had been in town at the same time as Queen Elizabeth. He had inadvertently run a tag from one of the Secret Service vehicles behind the motorcade.

He was not one to put things off, so he dialed the number immediately. The voice mail recording answered instructing him to enter the extension number. How he hated voice mail. It was one of the worst things he could think of in the new electronic age.

"Agent Larkin," answered the voice at the other end.

"This is Lieutenant Moreno with the Sheriff's Office. I received a message to call you."

"Yes, I asked that you call about that tag information you were requesting. Uh," he hesitated. "Is this information you requested pertinent to an essential investigation you are conducting?"

"Well, yes… you could say that," he replied.

"It's just that this type of request usually comes through other channels.

"Just what is the problem with releasing this information Agent Larkin?"

"There's no real problem, it's just highly sensitive information. If you want, you can come down here and I'll hand deliver the information to you. Under current regulations, I can't discuss it over the phone or send it through ordinary mail channels. The fastest way would be for you to just pick it up."

"That's not a problem. Can I come by now?"

"Sure, I'll be here till 1500 this afternoon."

"Great, I'm on my way now. I should be there within the hour."

"Okay, I'll be waiting."

"Thank you, Larkin."

What's up with this? he thought. *This is really too weird.* Apparently Ian had stumbled on to something very sensitive. No wonder Ian had asked him to run the tag for him. An ordinary street deputy would have aroused quite a bit of suspicion if he had requested the detailed information on this confidential government tag.

True to his word, he arrived before the hour was up. He parked his Jeep in the parking lot and walked to the front door at a brisk pace, curiosity urging him forward. Buzzing the front door he looked into the camera so the security person could see who he was. Satisfied, someone buzzed the door and it unlocked to allow him entrance.

He stopped at the front desk and introduced himself to the clerk and explained Larkin was expecting him.

"Have a seat and I'll page him."

After a few protracted moments of waiting, Larkin finally appeared. He clasped Patrick's outstretched hand with a firm grip.

"Hi, I'm Pete Larkin. Step into my office and I'll give you the information you requested."

Moreno followed becoming more irritated by the moment. But he played the game, no use becoming impatient; they would only become suspicious of him.

They wound through the halls of the building, either Larkin was very important and needed a very secure work place or he was at the bottom of the totem pole. It was obvious that the former was more accurate as they made their way through two locks with numerical combinations required to gain entry.

Agent Larkin motioned to the empty chair in front of his desk and Moreno took the cue and sat down. Larkin then offered a manila envelope, passing it across the desk.

"Oh, hey, just a minute. I need you to sign for this." He handed the clip board over with a form to be signed.

Not wanting to appear overly anxious, Moreno resisted the urge to tear into the envelope and see what the contents held right there. He signed the form and took the enveloped, and thanking Larkin left the building as he had entered.

He got back in his dark green Jeep, drove back north on Lois, and pulled into the parking lot of the Driver's License Bureau at the corner of Dr. King Boulevard. Opening the envelope carefully, he extracted the papers inside, and turning on the inside dome light; he read the information.

It wasn't what he had expected at all. Actually he was quite surprised. The vehicle the tag had been displayed on indeed had been a black, 1997 Chevrolet Camaro. The kicker was that the vehicle was owned by the Sheriff's Office, used by the deep cover operatives within the agency, in cooperation with the feds. Only a handful of people within the agency even knew who they were. Once, several years ago, he had inadvertently arrested one of them along with a group of others. He was told about it, but still didn't know which one of the group had been the one.

Now the obvious question was, why Ian Greer had wanted information on this tag? It was time to contact Ian and find out exactly what was going on. Lieutenant Moreno dialed the Comm. Center on his cell phone.

"Sheriff's Office, how may I help you?"

"This is Lieutenant Moreno, PID 13077. I want you to page Deputy Ian Greer to my cell phone number."

"Yes, sir, I'll do that right now."

"Thanks," he said automatically as he hung up.

He wanted to wait right there for Ian to call him, but he knew from experience it might be a few hours before he returned the page. He headed east on Dr. King Boulevard and turned left heading north on Dale Mabry. He hadn't even reached the overpass at Hillsborough Avenue before his cell phone rang. Thinking it best to stop while he talked he pulled over in front of Bill Curry Ford so he could devote his full attention to what Ian was going to say.

"Lieutenant Moreno," he answered.

"Lieutenant, this is Ian Greer returning your page."

"Yeah, Ian, I need to meet with you. It's about the tag information you wanted me to check for you."

"Name a 20 for 56."

"Right now?" he hesitated.

"Yeah, right now," Moreno responded a little forcefully. He knew Ian wasn't working tonight, because they were both on the same schedule.

"How bout Village Inn's on Dale Mabry, south of 275."

"Perfect. Thirty minutes?"

"It'll take me a little longer than that to get there, how about an hour."

"That'll have to do. I'll be waiting so make it as fast as you can."

"Sure thing Lieutenant, see you in a few."

TWENTY-FOUR

Morgan woke up from a deep sleep, having finally drifted off after hours of tossing and turning. She heard Ian's Rodeo as it started up. Quickly, she jumped up and ran to the window just in time to see his tail lights as they faded from view. Suddenly she felt afraid and lonely without him. It was an unusual thing for her, normally she preferred being alone.

She went back to her room, threw on the white terry robe, and went to the living room, switching on the television Ian had moved out there just yesterday. Immediately she turned on Channel Two, knowing they would have the most information on local news at this time of morning. The wait wasn't overly long. Within the first hour the story came on.

"And now for the latest on a perplexing murder that occurred in Tampa, in an upscale neighborhood within Hyde Park. Police are reporting no new leads in their search for Morgan McGhee, the prime suspect and wife of slain Director of Finance of the County Tax Collector's Office, Gregory McGhee. The couple are said to have been having marital difficulties and it is believed that Mrs. McGhee may have shot her husband to death at their home early last week. Funeral services were held yesterday, with police vigilant, just in case Mrs. McGhee tried to attend the funeral. At this time police have no information on where Mrs. McGhee may have fled, but are confident that they will find her in the near future. If you have any information regarding this case you are urged to contact either the Tampa Police Department of if you prefer to remain anonymous you can call Crime Stoppers. You may be eligible for a reward."

The footage they showed was of Morgan's house and a bad photograph that was taken for her work identification card. She hoped the reports were not complete and accurate. Surely she wasn't the only lead in the case. From her own experience during the past few years, she knew the police would not be revealing any information they had to the media. Not unless the media already knew and they could not deny it.

If only she could talk to Felicia, she would know what was going on. Morgan decided to go outside to see if there was a phone line coming into the house. She tried to open the back door, but there was a dead bolt, the kind that only opens with a key from either side. She tried the front door, it had a different type of lock. When she opened the front door she was confronted with the wrought iron door on the other side. She tried the lever handle, but it was locked.

Suddenly she became frightened and infuriated. Why would Ian lock her in? What if there was a fire? How would she get out?

Now that she was angry, she knew just what to do. Heading straight for her bathroom, she opened the drawer on the vanity and extracted a bobby pin. She peeled the plastic tips off with her teeth and spit the tips on the floor. Marching down the hall to Ian's bedroom door, she stuck the bobby pin into the lock and within a few seconds, she had gained entry.

The door swung open with an eerie creaking of the hinges. The bed was neatly made with a quilt. A rustic wood frame surrounded the bed made of rough timbers. Pillows were propped at the head and a fluffy down comforter at the bottom of the bed. The room smelled like Ian.

To the left of the bed there was a large

drafting table with a light suspended overhead attached to an arm at the back of the table. Morgan hesitated to enter the room, but taking a chance, she decided to go ahead.

The switch on the lamp clicked, and the fluorescent bulb flickered before it came on fully. The light illuminated the room, darkened by thick shades that covered both windows. She was amazed at what the table lamp revealed. The entire table was filled with snapshots of her. Some of them when she was going into work; some of them were of her running on Bayshore Boulevard. There were others at various locations in the city, apparently when she had been running errands. One or two had Greg in the picture.

Rage and fear overcame her at the same time. Ian had obviously been watching her for some time. Now details began to make sense to her. She looked over the items on the table more closely. On the on side of the table there was a stack of papers. She picked them up and a chill ran through her entire being. Here were papers that had belonged to her. Prescription labels, letters, grocery lists and a list of product names; products she used all the time.

It was no wonder all the items she found in the room she was staying in were her favorites. That explains why he had Frosted Flakes. She remembered the chocolate chip cookies at that sleazy motel on Kennedy Boulevard.

Ian had obviously spent many hours and risked being caught to find out these intimate details of her life. How long, she wondered, had he been following her? Why had he followed her? Had he killed Greg? But the real question that scared her was, what did he intend to do with her?

So far Morgan was a willing guest. What would happen when she tried to leave?

Quickly her mind began to think over the

possibilities. First, she didn't know for sure where she was. Second, there appeared to be no telephone anywhere in the house. Searching her memory of the past few days she realized she had not heard the sound of a phone ringing the entire time. Ian did wear a pager, but that would be of no use to her. She must remain calm and think everything through. If he had put so much planning into this, he must also have planned for her attempted escape.

Not knowing when Ian would be returning, she closed the door and turned out the light, being careful to lock the door behind her. Morgan hid the bobby pin she had used to open the door over the door jam on the inside of her bedroom door.

This was going to take a lot of thinking on her part. Obviously, Ian was much smarter than she in many areas, areas that would be critical to her escape. But she knew if she could deceive him, if he didn't know she was on to his game, she could trick him. The element of surprise was her number one weapon, her only weapon.

Morgan debated with herself whether or not to mention to him that she had discovered herself locked inside the house. She wondered if this would cause him to leave her in the house with the doors unlocked, or make him suspicious. She had wanted to trust him, love him, and stay with him, but he was a liar. The contemptible thing about it was that it had been so easy. How could she have been so stupid, so naive? Her education had been amended. She would never allow him to deceive her again.

TWENTY-FIVE

Lieutenant Moreno was waiting inside when Ian arrived, and on his third cup of coffee. He waved to him when he came through the front door.

"Hi, Lieutenant," Ian said. "This must be important to have you out so early on your day off."

"Pretty important Ian. I just got back the information from FDLE on that tag you asked me to run for you."

"What's up?" Ian said trying not to appear too eager.

"Before I give you any information, I want you to come clean with me. I don't like being used, and I think you have attempted to do just that. Now you can trust me or not, the choice is entirely yours. But if I sense any untruth or if I catch you in a lie, I will personally see to it that you get burned. Is that perfectly clear?"

"Yes, sir, it's clear, perfectly."

"Where did you get the tag number you asked me to run?"

"I saw it displayed on the back of a black Camaro," Ian thought it best not to divulge any additional information unless asked.

"Where did the Camaro happen to be when you saw it?" the lieutenant asked, closing in quickly. He certainly didn't want to play games.

"On a street in Tampa."

"Which particular street, Ian?" he demanded, becoming increasingly impatient.

"It was on Fountain, just west of Mac Dill," he answered reluctantly.

"And just what day would this have been

on?" the lieutenant asked, quickly locking in on the real heart of the matter.

"It was shortly after midnight last Friday, week before last. It sounds to me like you already know all the answers." Ian was becoming defensive.

"Not quite all the answers young man. Bear with me." Years of experience had produced a flawless technique.

Ian hated not being the one in control. It was clear who was in charge here, and he knew enough from his military and law enforcement experience that he had better submit. And it wasn't hard to trust Lieutenant Moreno; he had been a close friend for many years. Still, this was no ordinary situation, and Ian clearly was breaking some laws here.

"Would that happen to be in the neighborhood of the McGhee home?"

"Yes, sir it certainly would."

"Do you happen to know where Mrs. McGhee is hiding at this time?"

Ian thought long and hard before he answered this question, carefully calculating which words he wanted to respond with. He bit his lower lip. The muscles in his jaw twitched as he struggled within himself. Direct honesty seemed the best policy at this point.

"Yes, sir, I do know where she is."

"Is she in a safe place, I mean a really safe place?"

"It's as safe as I could manage. What have you found out on the tag?"

"Apparently it's caused quite a stir that anyone was inquiring in the first place. FDLE was not very willing to divulge this information. The tag belongs to a Sheriff's Office covert vehicle. It belongs to one of our deep cover agents."

Ian was visibly shaken at this information. "I would never have expected that, not in a million years. Now I'm really confused," he said, rubbing his chin.

"Why is that?" the lieutenant pressed.

Ian looked around him before answering. He wanted to be sure no one was close enough to hear what he was saying. He also placed his hand on the side of his mouth to hide his lips, just in case someone was watching. Even so, he spoke in a whisper.

"It wasn't Morgan McGhee who shot her husband," he stated emphatically.

"Really? Then who did?"

"I saw the whole thing, Lieutenant. Who ever shot Greg McGhee was in that Camaro. I couldn't get a good look at their face, so your guess is as good as mine as to who in the hell the actual shooter was."

The lieutenant was quiet for a few minutes, thinking over the information he had just received. He was limited in what he could do. The Tampa Police Department was handling the investigation, and although he might be able to get some of the details, they would be very reluctant to share information, even though it did involve an employee of the Sheriff's Office. Also ,the lieutenant was no longer involved directly in homicide investigations, and suspicion would be aroused if he were to ask too many questions.

"Ian," he finally responded. "I hope you know what a big chance you've taken getting involved in this at the level you have."

"Yes, sir," he answered. "I do realize. It could cost me my career, but I had no choice. I had to protect her."

"How long have you two had something going on?" the lieutenant asked.

"I'm not sure I know what you mean," Ian hedged.

"I mean, you're obviously crazy about this woman. Why else would you risk your career? How long has it been going on? How deeply were you involved with her before her husband was murdered?" the questions were coming rapid fire now.

"You'll probably have a hard time believing this one, but I wasn't involved with her at all. We were simply casual friends. I met her at the gym, and have seen her around a few times, nothing more."

"And you want me to believe you just happened to be in the neighborhood when someone blew her husband away in the middle of the night? You're right, that is a hard one to believe."

"I don't blame you for being suspicious about that one."

"Ian, there's just got to be more to it than that. Surely you don't think an old blood hound like me is that gullible, do you?"

Ian weighed just how much he should trust him, but at this point he didn't have much of a choice. He wouldn't have believed that story either. "Truth is, sir, I have been watching her for some time," Ian admitted reluctantly.

"You've been watching her? Just what in the hell does that mean?" the lieutenant said, almost shouting. Looking around he repeated it more quietly. "What do you mean, 'watching her'?"

"Just that. I've been nuts about her since the first time I saw her. I have been, well uhh, keeping an eye on her."

"Don't you think that's a little fool hardy in this politically correct day and age, son? Stalkers aren't tolerated in the 90's."

"When you put it that way... Well, of course, it seems a lot different from how I have been seeing it. You're right though, a hundred percent. There's absolutely no justifiable reason for what I've been doing. I'm just glad, for what ever reason, I happened to be there when I was. The next target for the shooter was Morgan. I watched as he took aim on her. I had to stop him, and I had to protect her. I just took her. She came with me willingly. She was terrified; she had no choice. "I had already called about the tag on the Camaro, and I knew it was a confidential tag. I didn't know it was deep cover cool car. Now you're confirming that my fears were well founded."

"Does anyone know about your association or friendship with this woman?"

Ian searched his memory before answering. "Not a soul. A couple of people may have seen us talking to one another, but no one would ever guess there was anything more than a casual friendship between us. I had to stop them. They were about to shoot her next."

"And just exactly how did you stop them from shooting Mrs. McGhee?"

"The only way I could at the moment. I hit the horn long and hard, and thank God it worked. They were scared off by the sound and tore out of there in a big hurry. I don't think they saw me at all."

The lieutenant assimilated what Ian had told him, his chest rising sharply as he inhaled slowly. As he exhaled he grinned at Ian shaking his head, he didn't know why, but he decided to believe him. He watched his eyes when he talked. The eyes told him everything, and Ian's eyes said that he was telling the truth.

"Okay, son, I'm gonna help you. I don't know how I could allow myself to get sucked into something like this, but what the hell. I'm retiring soon anyway. They don't hang anyone in the United States anymore. But you'll have to be totally honest with me. I want to know everything, no details overlooked. Can you do that?"

"Sure thing… What do you want to know?"

Ian told him everything, how he met Morgan, how he followed her, collecting details about her life. He told him how he found out what kind of foods she liked, her clothing sizes, even what kinds of cosmetics she used. It had taken lots of time, but it had been very easy. Watching her in the grocery store had been very productive, especially the time she had dropped her shopping receipt in the parking lot.

Find her clothing sizes had been a breeze. Morgan had left bags of clothing marked for pick up by the Sunshine Thrift store at her curb one morning. He simply picked them up and went through them. They still smelled like her perfume. He made sure they all got to their intended destination. He dropped them in the collection bin himself at the store on South Dale Mabry Highway.

Actually, his ex-wife matched her in size very closely. He bought foods he knew she liked for himself. It made him feel closer to her to be eating the same things she was. He had collected some of her items that she used and placed them in the extra bathroom. Secretly, he hoped someday she would live there with him.

Ian was disgusted with himself as his story unfolded to the lieutenant. Patrick just shook his head from time to time as the tale continued. Somehow, it seemed so much more immoral to Ian as he spoke aloud of his actions of the past few months. But he had promised honesty, and he was going to deliver just that.

After Ian had exhausted all the details he could think of the lieutenant spoke. "Son, does she know you've done all this?"

"No, sir! It would scare her to death if she knew."

"Oh, I'd say you're right about that."

"I just told her all of the things I had at my cabin belonged to my ex-wife. It was partially true."

"And she believed that?" the lieutenant

asked, incredulous.

"She seems to, so far anyway. She's been pretty scared, so she probably hasn't been thinking too clearly. I kept the television from her for a long time, and there is no telephone. So, all she knows of what is going on is what I tell her."

"She must trust you quite a bit to accept that."

"To tell you the truth, she's been far more cooperative than I'd hoped. But, realistically, I can't hope to keep her hidden much longer. The only reason no one has thought to look for her with me is that were only very casually acquainted. No one knows how crazy I am about her, or that I was watching her."

"It worked out well for her, all things considered. You know you're going to have to come clean with her. She'll hate you if she finds all this out on her own. She'll likely hate you anyway when you tell her."

"You're right again. All she needs is another shock in her life. I'm just afraid she'll think it was me that killed Greg. She couldn't have seen everything from where she was. I just appeared right after he was shot. It could have been me from her point of view."

"That may be the least of your worries. Anyone else who knows you will think the same thing. If you're not careful, you won't just have to worry about tampering with evidence and obstruction of justice charges, you may be facing murder charges. I seem to remember you're a master on the gun range. Are you not?"

"Yes, unfortunately I am. I realize all this. That's why I came to you. I knew you would help me if there was any way you could."

The lieutenant sighed deeply before replying. "I'll do all that I can. I can't promise anything though. This thing may be too big for me to be of any help. But, you're right, if I can help you, I will."

"You'll never know how much I appreciate that," Ian said sincerely.

As they rose to leave, Ian was relieved to have shared his long held secret with someone. The lieutenant was invigorated to have something interesting to devote his time to for a change. And this was something he could believe in. For some reason, even he didn't fully understand, he wanted to help Ian. He felt an urgent compulsion to assist him in this mess he had involved himself in.

Lieutenant Moreno wasted no time beginning his search for the reason Greg McGhee was murdered. He went directly home and made a few phone calls to some friends he had in the homicide department at the Tampa Police Department. It was early, so he had to leave messages on voice mail, but he knew his phone would start ringing as soon as people started arriving at work.

Patrick stretched out on his bed without bothering to turn back the covers. He got out his notebook, and began to review notes he had already made. The only real lead he had was the tag, and he wasn't going to get very far with that alone. It would take a lot more than that to find out who was responsible, but more than that the lieutenant needed a motive. No one just drove up and shot Greg McGhee from a Sheriff's Office vehicle without a very good reason. And if what Ian had told him was accurate, Morgan had been the next target. Someone had to have had a good reason to eliminate the both of them.

There was always the possibility that Morgan had been the target to begin with and that Greg had been the accident. Lieutenant Moreno made a note to page Ian later in the day and arrange to meet with Morgan to interview her. There was no doubt in his mind, she would hold valuable information that would unravel the puzzle which lay before him.

It was not beyond the realm of possibility that it had been a crime of passion. Perhaps Morgan had gotten involved with the wrong person, gotten herself in too deeply with a dangerous man. The fact that the shooter was in the passenger seat of the car didn't make sense though. If it were a jealous lover, it proably would have happened much differently. Passion as a motive could probably be discounted altogether, based on that fact alone.

Then there was the possibility of a random act of violence. Obviously, that was not the case, given the vehicle information. That was of course assuming that Ian had told him the truth. For some reason he believed Ian. He seemed too sincere to be lying, but cops were good liars. Many of them practiced their skills on a daily basis, conning people into incriminating themselves when silence would have prevented them from being caught. Ian could be one of these people, able to lie with such mastery that he convinced himself of is own lies.

Lieutenant Moreno still trusted his gut instincts. He had always been able to spot even the most convincing of liars from a mile off. Ian didn't give even a hint of any falseness. On the contrary, he seemed genuinely concerned. So, why would anyone want to harm the McGhees?

Patrick Moreno looked at the clock, it was almost six. There was still plenty of time to burn before anyone at TPD would begin to arrive at work. He was not the least bit sleepy, and had precious little to work with at this point. Walking across the living room, he flipped on the television with the remote control and selected the local twenty-four hour news station, Channel Two.

Tossing the remote on the table with his

notebook, he sauntered into the kitchen and took a glass from the cabinet. He opened the refrigerator and took out the carton of orange juice. He liked the kind that was full of pulp, and not that reconstituted stuff either, and ice cold. Quickly, he drained the glass and rinsed it, and put the glass in the dishwasher.

Patrick had never needed a woman to take care of his home for him. Maybe that is why he was never able to stay married for very long. Women like to feel needed, taking care of their man. He enjoyed doing all his own shopping, cooking, and preferred his clothing to be pro-fessionally laundered. Twice a week a cleaning service came in and took care of the mundane chores that he preferred not to do. It wasn't that he didn't like the company of women, he just never liked being at their mercy. They were too changeable. One day everything was fine, and the next some hormonal change would occur and everything was wrong. It was too much for a man to have to try to understand.

In his younger days, Patrick had been quite the womanizer. Variety had been key to him. Sometimes he prefered a mindless, firm-bodied young woman. Other times he enjoyed the company of a mature person he could converse with, one who understood the world from his perspective. After his last disasterous marraige, he had given up on the idea of having anyone live with him. He was too comfortable doing things his way to make any consessions to another person.

Ambling back to the dining room table, the lieutenant's ear picked up on the news story being broadcast. It was the Greg McGhee story. Quickly he grabbed the remote and turned up the sound. He raced to the VCR and slipped in a blank tape. Pushing the record button he stood and watched as the brief biography of the McGhees unfolded.

Greg McGhee was a Tampa native and was

going to college at Florida State University when he met Morgan. They had been married for nearly ten years and had no children. Greg was employed by the County Tax Collector as the Director of Finance. Morgan was of course a dispatcher for the County Sheriff's Office. None of their friends reported any knowledge of previous marital problems. Patrick noted that this was a contradiction to the official "domestic violence" story. There were several pictures of them taken over the years that the media had been able to gather, but not much more substantial information was given.

The first thing he wanted to know was which of them had been the primary target. Had it been Greg, or Morgan? Realistically, it could have been either one of them. It appeared to have been a paid hit. The overtones were reminiscent of the mob hits so prevalent in Tampa as late as the 70s In all likelihood, it had been Greg they were after.

What were the possible motives? He began the usual list. The primary three were love, money, power, or combination thereof. Love and lust were both interchangeable as motives.

Quickly, he eliminated love. Someone with Greg's job description couldn't have kept a secret like that in Tampa; it would have surfaced quickly after the shooting. As for Morgan, Ian had been following her for some time, and almost certainly would have discovered any affair she may have been having. The thought that more than one person had been stalking her - while possible - seemed ludicrous.

So, it had to be either money or power. Surely that narrowed the primary target to Greg, because Morgan didn't seem to have much of either. Greg, on the other hand, working at the Tax Collector's Office in the capacity that he did, meant he had access to a great deal of influence over both. The fact that he was shot first, and then Morgan was targeted, spoke very loudly. Patrick decided he would concentrate his efforts on Greg McGhee, which would prove a little more difficult considering the limitations of his investigative resources.

As Patrick Moreno pondered the situation, his phone rang. *Great*, he thought, *that will be someone from TPD.* He wasn't disappointed.

"Hello," he said with enthusiasm.

"Morning old man," Detective Lockwood said, good-naturedly.

"How the hell have you been, Danny?"

"Great, and you? I hear you're getting ready to retire on us."

"Yeah, can't wait to get up to the mountains and start living. How are Cynthia and the kids?"

"Didn't you hear? Cynthia and I got divorced last month," Danny told him sadly.

"No way! I thought you two would be together forever."

"Me too," Danny said. "Guess it just wasn't working for her. It just about killed me. I was crazy about that woman."

"I'm sure sorry to hear about that, Danny. I know what you're going through. Nobody should ever have to go through that."

"Yeah, but we do don't we."

"I'm living proof of that one," Patrick said honestly.

"So, I know you didn't' call me to sort out my personal life for me. What's up?" Danny asked.

"It's that McGhee murder."

"Oh yeah, what a weird case. Do you know the wife?"

"No, I sure don't. I can't remember ever having seen her before. Her pictures look like she'd be someone you would remember."

"So I've heard," Danny laughed.

"I was wondering what you could tell me about it. I have a couple of friends that know her, and they've shared some concerns with me."

"Sure thing, but I'd rather not discuss anything over the phone, you know."

"I understand completely. Can we meet for coffee this morning, or would lunch be better?"

"I think lunch would be best. I'm pretty busy around here this morning. What have you got in mind as far as a place?"

"How about the Seabreeze on the Causeway? I'll buy."

"Sounds good, I'll take a free lunch anywhere these days. Child support is killing me. You did say you'd buy didn't you?" Danny joked.

"I bet. How many was it the last time you counted? Nine?" Lieutenant Moreno asked.

"Come on now LT, you know I only have three. You're right though, three is a lot."

"I'll see you about eleven. Is that convenient for you?"

"Sure thing Pattie boy. See you then."

"Okay, Danny baby. Bye."

Patrick was happy now, things were moving. He loved investigation, and he was good at it. Leaving the homicide division had been a hard decision. It was the most satisfying work he had ever done. Several things caused him to leave, the most significant being Major Crawford.

Major Douglas Crawford, butt-head extraordinaire. He was the number one suck-up to Colonel Thompson, his superior in rank, superior in butt-headedness. The two of them had nearly forced Patrick to leave the Sheriff's Office before he could retire. He was just biding his time as a street lieutenant for a few more months. Then they could do what ever they wanted with the whole state for all he

cared. But nothing prevented him from having a
little fun in the interim.

TWENTY-SIX

Ian made the long drive down Interstate 75 to Big Bend Road, then south on 301 Highway, then across 672 to 39 Highway, finally arriving on Thatcher Road.

He drove a little farther east on Thatcher and stopped at the end of the bridge. The cabin was a long way from anything, and had appealed to Ian for that very reason. He preferred an isolated spot, with no nosy neighbors to intrude on his privacy. It was a place to escape his congested Northdale residence.

Getting out of the Rodeo, Ian walked over to the gate and removed the key to the padlock from his pocket. He swung the gate open and drove through, and then he returned to lock the chain securely back in place. It began to rain lightly. He noticed the wind had shifted and picked up quite a bit. He hadn't had time to watch the weather; it seemed the least of his worries. Usually this time of year it was an early cold front if there was any rain. It would be a good excuse to light the fireplace.

Only a few more minutes of driving now and he would be back at the cabin. Ian was tired - bone tired - he couldn't wait to drop into bed and sleep. Rain would be the perfect thing for a nice long nap. When he entered the house he was surprised to find Morgan in his kitchen cooking. She had a big smile on her face, and seemed genuinely pleased to see him.

"Good morning!" she greeted.

"Hi. You look all bright eyed and bushy tailed."

"Sorry to say, you don't. What kind of truck was it that ran over you?"

"I was too tired to look," Ian laughed.

"I didn't sleep at all last night."

"Well, if you'll just tell me how you like your eggs, I'll fix you up with breakfast and you can sleep for a while."

"Are you sure you don't mind?" he asked. "I'd think you would be anxious for some company."

"Okay then, you can sleep here on the couch. Then I can be close to you."

"Wow!" he responded. "I like the sound of that. What gives you this sudden affinity for closeness, my lady?"

"I missed you when you were gone," she said, pouring it on a little thick. "I woke up and found you gone, and I was a little scared, that's all."

"No need to be afraid. I can't stay away from where you are."

Considering her recent discovery his words took on new meaning.

"I like that," she said. "It's nice being here with you." She looked into his eyes. The intensity of what she saw there scared the hell out of her, but she had to play the game.

"By the way, do you have any decaffeinated coffee? If you're going to sleep, you sure don't need the real thing."

"Don't worry about making coffee, I'll get it," he offered.

"No way!" she protested. "You've been taking care of me for a long time, now it's my turn." She poured him a glass of milk and placed it in front of him on the table.

"Now, how did you say you liked your eggs?" she asked.

"I didn't say, but over easy would be nice."

"Coming right up. How many do you want?"

"Two will be fine."

"Your wish is my command. Do you want any toast?"

"Two slices white, if you please ma'am. I'll be right back. I need to wash up before I eat."

"Sure thing, but hurry back. Your eggs will be ready in a couple of minutes."

Morgan breathed a sigh of relief after he left the room. How could she have been so foolish as to have trusted him? The answer was obvious. It was because he was a big powerful, gorgeous man who was in charge of everything around him. He was easy to trust, easy to love. As much as she hated to admit it, she did love him. She was crazy about him, but he was not what she thought. He had deceived her, followed her, and quite possibly had been involved in Greg's murder somehow. She had to remember all of these things if she was going to escape him.

If she did escape where would she go? Morgan had been thinking about it for hours. She knew exactly where she would go. There was only one person she could trust right now. Felicia would take her in; help her find the answers to the problems that now faced her. If the police believed that Morgan murdered Greg, the best thing she could do would be to turn herself in, explain what had happened. Surely, they would believe her.

"Ahhh, that's much better," Ian said, stretching as he reentered the room.

Morgan was taken aback at the sight of him. He had changed into a plain white T-shirt, her favorite kind. She could imagine the scent of it even from the distance, clean and fresh like the sunshine. His pale blue jeans hung low on his trim waist. With his hands extended above his head in a stretch, the shirt was hiked up, revealing his tight, tanned abdominals. The dim sunlight meandering through the kitchen window played in the golden hairs that surrounded his navel. There was a line of them that descended southward from there, bringing to mind things Morgan would rather not have been thinking about. On the other hand, it was exactly what she wanted to think about. Suddenly it seemed as though the room was in a vacuum, and Morgan found herself in a battle with instinctual reactions she had thought she had under control. They were animal reactions and irresistible, brought on by this superb male specimen.

She finally found her voice and attempted to speak, "Maybe you'd better sit down here and have your breakfast."

"Yes ma'am," he purred. He was well aware of the power he had over her. Ian pulled out the chair and swung one leg over the back of it, sitting down cowboy style.

"You are something else," Morgan admitted breathlessly, and placed his breakfast before him.

"Oh, yeah, what am I?" he asked, watching closely for her reaction.

She just looked at him, unable to speak. Just the spectacle of him sitting there took her breath away. He just sat there, watching her intently, looking like a centerfold from some women's magazine.

Tilting his head to the side he spoke first. "What are you going to do, stand there all day? Come on and sit down here next to me and keep me company while I eat."

She just smiled, "I don't think that's such a good idea."

"And why not," he said coyly, knowing exactly why she didn't want to sit next to him.

"You know," she stated simply.

"Do I? Now how would I know that?"

Morgan chided herself for not being able to resist his charms any more than a moth could resist the light of a candle. He was able to cut right through the chase and make her say just exactly what he wanted her to say. He was so good, so smooth. How would she ever be able to deceive him, even for a few minutes? It was painfully obvious that he could read her every thought, sense what she was feeling even before she knew herself.

"Let's stop playing this game, Ian. We both know what's going on here."

"And what is that, my lady?"

"Oh! Your eggs are getting cold. You'd better eat them," she said in an attempt to avoid the obvious.

"I'm not going to eat until you talk about it."

After a few seconds of pregnant silence she acquiesced and spoke, "Okay, where were you all night?"

"You have this annoying habit of always changing the subject of the conversation when you feel uncomfortable"

She grinned in spite of herself, "Really? And just when did you notice this?"

Now he smiled, "The first time I talked to you."

"Well, if you didn't make a habit of making people feel uncomfortable, maybe they wouldn't have to use defensive tactics in conversation."

"Oh, is that what it is, a power thing?"

"Isn't everything a power thing with you?" she joked.

"Oh, yes, ma'am it is. Everything is about power. And the power you have over me is not just unfair, it should be illegal."

Morgan blushed. "Ian, you're so... I'm just not used to people talking so plainly about..."

"Go ahead. Plainly about what?" he urged.

"You know. Don't make me say it. You must not like my cooking very much; those eggs are just sitting there petrifying. Why don't you eat them?"

"Is that what you want?" he asked.

"Uhhhh, yeah, that's exactly what I want!"

she said in exasperation.

"Okay, I'll eat them, but you have to sit down here and stop changing the subject. Agreed?"

"Agreed, but it doesn't sound like a very fair trade."

She reluctantly took the chair next to him. Morgan clasped her hands in front of her, on the table, twining her fingers together nervously. She felt like a child about to be lectured by an overbearing parent, only worse. She looked around the room futility for something to focus on to avoid his direct gaze.

"Now, what is that I talk so plainly about that bothers you?" he asked as he ate the food she had prepared for him.

Several minutes passed, and the hush between them expanded like a storm cloud on a hot summer afternoon. He used the silence like a weapon against her - knowingly - with calculation. She saw that he would not let the matter rest, and so she finally spoke.

"It's the attraction between us. I hardly know you well enough to be..."

"Be what?" he was relentless.

"To be... Well, to be… becoming so involved with you."

Ian took a deep breath and took her hands in his, prying them apart. "You really need to relax. I'd never hurt you. You really are afraid of me, aren't you?"

"Should I be afraid of you? I hardly know you." Morgan began to cry, even though she had promised herself she would not. "Please let me go get some tissue."

"You sit right here, I'll get it for you," he said, rising to fulfill his promise. "Tell me something. Do you cry every time you cook for a man, or am I just special?"

Morgan had to laugh at this. "You're bad, that's what you are."

"Bad? Bad you say? Now, what have I

done that would make you say that?" he asked honestly.

"Nothing, nothing at all Ian. You've been very good to me, and that's the truth."

He handed her a tissue, looking down at her as he did. "What have I done that makes you so afraid of me then?"

"It's not anything you have done that I am afraid of," she paused searching for the right words.

"So, what is it then?"

"It's me that I'm afraid of."

"You?! I agree. You're very scary," he chuckled.

"Don't try to make me laugh. I'm afraid of becoming too involved with you. I don't need to be depending on you. My husband was just murdered. Don't you think that I should be mourning for him instead of... of... well, for lack of a better word, lusting after a perfect stranger."

"So, I'm perfect you say. That's the best thing I have heard all day, other than the word lust; which by the way, I find to be a wonderful word," he mused.

"You're absolutely impossible to talk to!"

"I don't know. I was enjoying the conversation," he was being honest. He was enjoying seeing her squirm. "Let me change the subject for you this time.

"You are a superb cook, ma'am. I don't know when I have ever enjoyed eggs and toast as much."

"What am I ever going to do with you?"

"Well, I have a few suggestions you might like to try. Oh, now there I go again, being, what was that you called it, direct. That's it, direct, isn't it?"

Ian took Morgan by both of her hands, pulling her to her feet effortlessly. She was like a rag doll in his hands, a marionette under the power of a skilled master. "I can't help it," he confessed. "When you're close to me, I want you."

He placed her arms around his neck, pulling her body close to his own. "I wish you'd let me thank you properly for the breakfast you made for me."

Ian looked down at her, into her eyes, just like that first time she had seen him. Her reaction to him had not diminished in any way, on the contrary they had increased alarmingly.

Outside the rain beat on the tin roof, and thunder was announcing the storm that followed. She would be stuck inside the house with him. Ian liked that idea.

"Would you like that, ma'am?"

"Why do you always insist that I say it, Ian?" she said, angered at his perseverance.

"Because it means a lot to hear you say it. And because I'd never do anything that you didn't want me to. I want you to feel safe with me."

"Hah! Safe with you? How about safe from myself?"

"What are you so afraid of Morgan? I'm not going anywhere. I'll always be right here for you."

Tears rolled down Morgan's face. This time her tears were for Ian. She knew without a doubt that he was telling her the truth. He would be there for her. It was almost enough to make her forget what she knew. Forget that in the room at the end of the hall was all the evidence that she needed to prove that her fears of him were well founded.

Ian began to kiss her where the tears were falling down her cheeks. Tilting her head up slightly, he pressed her to his chest, and held her close.

Dear God, he is so good, so smooth. I could stay right here forever, Morgan thought.

Her defenses were nearing their end. She was disgusted with herself, all the resolve she had earlier was fading away.

They stood together for what seemed to Morgan to be an eternity, his heart beating in her ear, the warmth of his body permeating hers. She could have died at that very moment happy, content to be with him alone.

It was no surprise to her when he lifted her from the floor, carrying her to the bedroom where she had stayed since she had come to stay with him. He placed her gently on the quilt, and placing one hand on each side of her head, he knelt over her. As was fast becoming his usual practice, he looked into her eyes, searching for an answer.

"I want to know if this is what you want. You'll have to tell me, because I would never force myself on you. I'll leave you alone if that's what you want. Just say the word either way."

"Ian, please," she begged. "Don't force me to say it."

"No, Morgan, you can't change the subject this time. You can't run from me. Just tell me what you want, but you have to make the decision."

"You know what I feel without asking. We both know what the other feels, thinks. I can almost feel every breath you take in my own lungs. It has been that way for a long time. I just never admitted it to myself."

"It's a yes or no answer Morgan," he demanded. "I won't take any other kind of answer. You won't be squirming out of the conversations with me by changing the subject anymore either. Not this time, not ever," he was angry and exacting, near the end of his ability to control his own responses.

"My lady, you need to answer me now. I've been very patient with you, and I can only be put off for so long."

Morgan knew what her answer would be. She could leave him tomorrow, run away later. Ian was what she had wanted for a long time, or at least it seemed like a long time. What ever the price might be - and there would be one to pay - she would pay it when the bill came due. Right now, her entire being ached for him, not just her body, but her soul cried out for union with his. Ashamed of herself before she answered, Morgan threw all caution to the wind.

"Yes, yes! Of course I want you. I want you more than I want to breathe."

An audible sigh escaped from Ian. It mingled with a deep throaty groan, as if from one long tortured by something. Tortured he had been, mostly of his own doing. He knew that all the waiting, all of his dreaming, would be worth it. This woman had enchanted him and eluded him for way too long. Now she was his. Not just his in flesh, but he knew he had claimed her spirit for his own. She would never be free of him.

It took a great deal of restraint on his part not to devour her at once. This was a moment to be savored, tasted delicately, and that's exactly what he intended to do. He wanted to experience all five senses at the same time with this woman, and remember every detail forever. Any fatigue he had felt when he had come in was now gone, adrenal potency sustained him.

Morgan did not make any effort to move for some time, afraid to allow herself that liberty. She nuzzled against his chest, savoring the smell of his T-shirt. It was exactly as she had expected, like it had been hung out in the sun. She inhaled deeply, catching the scent of his cologne. "What is that scent you're wearing, it's heavenly."

"Obsession," he replied with a grin.

Now Morgan could not restrain herself. She broke into a fit of hysterical laughter.

"That's rich. I don't believe I've heard anything so funny for a long time."

Ian laughed with her, for if any one word would sum up the essence of what the two of them shared; that would be the word. He loved the way she was able to change tempo without skipping a beat, going from one emotion to the next like changing directions without notice. Being with her was like going downhill in a car with no brakes. Constantly he battled to remain the one in control, the one with the strength, but constantly, he found that she had turned the tables on him. It was exhilarating.

As she began to unbutton her shirt, he watched her intently, enjoying every second. He slipped his shirt over his head and pushed her onto her back and moved to sit atop her hips. His body rested lightly on her thighs as he straddled her, careful not to allow his full weight to rest on her.

Opening the front clasp that had held her bra together, an involuntary gasp escaped his lips. Taking one creamy white pink tipped breast in each of her hands she pressed them together, beckoning him to come closer. Trying to restrain himself he moved slowly. The bait taken, he suckled first one and then the other, biting each tip gently.

"Wait, wait, wait," she said, slithering out from under him. "Let's lose the pants."

He laughed, "And you were the one that called me direct? You want it bad don't you baby?"

It was her turn to laugh. "If you can't tell, you shouldn't be asking."

He just grinned and tossed his pants on the floor. Watching as she removed all but her tiny red lace thong panties, he shook his head as she started to take them off. They were much too seductive to discard now. Glad that she seemed to understand, he had to remind himself to go slow; as she snapped the elastic waistband on her hip.

Ian was even more impressive undressed than he had been with clothes on. Morgan tried hard not to stare. It was apparent he was a real blond and she thought how much his coloring resembled her own. They could have been fraternal twins.

Her heart was beating so wildly she could hear the rush of blood in her ears as he came closer. With one hand on each side of her head he ran his fingers through her hair, pulling her head back. He gazed into her eyes as he searched for any hint of hesitation. Finding none he covered her mouth with his own, and as she parted her lips to receive him, he filled her with himself. Her eyes closed in surrender, and she knew in moments she would be his in every way.

Morgan had never enjoyed kissing, but this was so much more. It was hot and wild and ever so much more than lips and tongues touching. He was making love to her mouth with his.

Pushing him away she laughed, "Oh my God."

Confused, he asked, " What?"

"I never did that before."

"You never kissed before?"

"Not like that," she whispered as she stretched out on the bed.

He had expected her to be inhibited and a bit shy. To his surprise, she was not in the least. He was amazed as she touched herself in places he had only imagined for so very long, welcoming him.

Torn between enjoying the exhibition and participating, he found he could wait no longer.

"God, you are so hot," he said.

She only smiled as she began to touch him in all the ways he had hoped she would. Reality was ever so much better than imagination.

Wrapping her slender legs around his waist

she beckoned him to enter her, raising her hips to meet him. He had wanted to be tender and gentle, but the pain was too sweet to linger. Like a wild animal out of control he thrust deep and hard within her, steady with deliberate purpose.

Just as he thought he could wait no longer, she took her hands and pushed his hips away. He paused and waited for her lead. Nudging him over on his back she began to gently kiss his chest as she climbed atop him. Her hair surrounded his face as she rocked gently bringing him to ecstasy.

There were no words to be spoken as they lay entwined. She listened as his heart beat slowed and his breathing changed signaling sleep before slipping away to the shower. He would sleep well now. She could not remember ever having to do anything as difficult as what she had to do now.

TWENTY-SEVEN

Patrick grabbed the keys to his Jeep and was off to do a little research downtown. The morning traffic was thick on Interstate 275 heading south into town, and with the rain coming in, there were sure to be several accidents. Switching on the radio, he tuned in to 990 WTTN the AM news channel for the area. He hoped to catch the latest report on the McGhee case.

The morning show was a call-in hosted by an outrageous woman named Cindy Simmons. She could argue for hours on just about any topic, regardless of how frivolous or inconsequential the subject matter. As luck would have it, this morning's topic was the McGhee murder. He had happened to tune in right in the middle of an obvious "expert" caller.

"So, in my opinion, it had to be her. Why else would she have disappeared? It don't make no sense otherwise. Hell, if I plugged my old man, I'd run too," the caller whined with a nasal, southern twang.

"You know, Mavis. That was your name, wasn't it, Mavis?" Cindy said setting her up.

"Yeah, Mavis. That's right."

"Mavis, if I were married to you, and you shot me, killing me instantly, I would count myself one of the most fortunate people in the world. You are not only totally ignorant, but that contrived southern accent of yours just doesn't come close to being as utterly obnoxious as that irritating voice of yours. Consider for a moment that Mrs. McGhee could be missing because she was abducted by her husband's murderer."

Obviously, Mavis had either been disconnected altogether, or she was being muted out, but any response she might have had would never be shared with the rest of the listeners.

"Morgan McGhee was an exemplary wife and citizen, never in any trouble in her whole life. No history of violence in the home existed. To think that she suddenly killed her husband, and disappeared without a trace seems extremely foolhardy."

Answering the next call, Cindy switched tones. "990 WTTN, you're live with Cindy. Go George from Lakeland."

"Hi. It's obvious," George said trying to talk fast. "You won't listen to any opinion other than your own."

"Not true," Cindy defended. "Let's hear the first intelligent presentation of Morgan McGhee's guilt as articulated by George of Lakeland, Esquire, no doubt."

"Okay, you think she didn't do it. Then who did? I knew this guy in high school, Greg that is. Some things never change. Greg was a run-around then, and he probably ran around on her too. My guess is that she came home and found him with another woman in the hot tub. Then she killed him because she couldn't stand seeing him with another woman."

"Time out George," Cindy said, allowing a pregnant pause. "I have only one simple problem with that theory. Morgan McGhee's purse, containing her driver's license, credit cards, check book and ATM card was found inside the house. What woman would leave those behind?"

"Uh, well," George stammered.

"As I thought," Cindy finished him off. "Next caller, Bob from Thonotosassa. Welcome Bob."

"Hi! Cindy, first let me say that I think you are the greatest. I love your show!"

"Thank you, Bob, but I won't go easy on you just because you are right."

"Fair enough. I think she did it for the insurance money. I think it was planned way in advance. She probably was the one with a lover and he is hiding her."

"So, you, like, think she took off with some guy, hoping to make it look like she was kidnapped. I'm more inclined to combine your theory with George's. Probably they had a little three-way going and she decided she liked the third person more than Greg and so she got rid of him. Now that makes sense. The obvious sex of the third person is female. That's why Morgan didn't need her purse, the other woman had one."

Patrick had been so entertained he almost passed the Ashley exit. It was a quick trip from there to Madison and Twiggs where he parallel parked at a meter. It was a ridiculous amount they charged, a quarter for twelve minutes. The city had wanted to buy new meters that sensed when a car left and dropped any remaining time on the meter. What a bunch of money hungry people the city council was.

Crossing the street, he entered the blocklong building through the center, west entrance. He flashed his badge at the security guard and sidestepped the metal detector.

"Hey there, Lieutenant," the guard said.

"How's it going Bill?" Patrick said and smiled as he hurried on.

He turned right down the long hall to the Clerk of Circuit Court's Office. Upon entering he went right to the carousels of microfilm. Selecting the ones corresponding to McGhee, he found a seat at one of the obsolete viewing machines. Snapping in the cassette he began scanning to the right entries.

There were one or two entries under Morgan's name, but the listings under Greg's name were of more interest to Patrick. He wrote down the number of each cassette where the document could be viewed as well as the page number. He selected the corresponding cassettes, five in all, and stacked them next to the viewer, and began searching.

He located the most recent document. It was the mortgage on the McGhee's home, held by the Tropical Bank of Central Florida. The mortgage was for $125,000. The house had sold for just under $250,000. Quite a down payment. The mortgage was recorded in March, 1990. The builder was Lakeside Development Corporation.

The next document was the sale of a tract of property, twenty-five acres. The sale price was $10,000, recorded in June, 1987. Patrick sat bolt upright in his chair as he read the name of the person purchasing the property from McGhee. It was Douglas T. Crawford, his old buddy, the major.

The property was part of what was now being developed as the Aviary Trails Subdivision. That tract would have increased in value astronomically right after the sale.

The next entry explained where Greg got the property. In January, 1984 a Raymond McGhee had given the property to Greg through his will. Patrick guessed it was his father.

On a hunch, Patrick copied down the folio numbers, before filing away all the cassettes and went to a computer with access to the Property Appraiser's files. With the folio number of the property it was easy to research the ownership history. Also, the value and purchase prices of the properties were listed.

After a brief wait, the history of the property appeared on the screen. Patrick could hardly believe his eyes. The whole parcel that had been given to Greg McGhee had been purchased in 1977 for $150,000, with a $100,000 mortgage to the Tropical Bank of Central Florida. The mortgage had been satisfied in 1982. Unbelievable! Why would Greg have sold it at such a low price. The value assessed by the Property Appraiser for the twenty-five acres was $232,000 at the time of sale in 1987. Ordinarily the Property Appraiser's assessment was lower than market value.

The records showed that Crawford sold the five acres to Lakeside Development also. His sale price had been much more reasonable, but still modest at $287,000.

There had to be an explanation, but what it was he could not imagine. He could just walk up to the major and ask him what was going on. *Yeah, right!* Greg McGhee sure wasn't available for questioning. Maybe Morgan would have some information that would shed some light. He made a mental note to page Ian and make arrangements to interview her, something he should have done long ago.

Searching some other files he found the record of their marriage license. That was dated June 18, 1988. Nothing very interesting there.

Still having an hour to burn before he was to meet Danny Lockwood for lunch, Patrick went to check the McGhees' driving records. Before he walked over to the Courthouse Annex, he stopped in the lobby for some Cuban coffee and cheese toast with bacon. The Blind Services Division made them both superbly. He stood in the line waiting to pay for his breakfast.

"Hey, Pattie boy! How's it going?" came a voice from behind.

Patrick turned to see who had spoken. "Good morning Judge Franklin. I haven't seen you in ages."

" Well, if you came downtown more often you might run into some of your old friends. How have you been anyway?"

"I'm doing pretty well, getting ready to retire. In fact I have an appointment later this afternoon with the retirement clerk. Thanks for reminding me."

"Good for you! I won't be far behind you. What are you planning to do with all that free time?" the judge asked.

"I'm moving to North Carolina. I think I"ll fish for a couple of years, then hunt for a few, and then I plan on just thinking about what I'm gonna do next," Lieutenant Moreno joked.

"Sounds like a winner to me. I've got to run to court, but be sure to stop by and see me before you leave town."

"I'll be sure to do that," Patrick promised. "It was good seeing you. Be sure to give my best to Mrs. Franklin."

Judge Franklin waved over his shoulder as he exited the door, sipping his coffee as he went. He was one of the few totally honest people Patrick knew in the entire court system. How he had escaped the moral compromises that just seemed unavoidable in the scheme of things, was unclear. He admired him immensely for his long standing ability to be functional in his job and yet remain politically aloof and detached. It was a real talent, a God given gift and a mystery how he managed to rise to his present position without playing ball with the city's big boys.

Patrick ate his breakfast without further interruption and walked over to the annex, again displaying his badge to the building security guards. The traffic division was just behind the metal detectors, and fortunately there were no lines.

"Next," the clerk said.

"Good morning. I'm Lieutenant Patrick Moreno, with the Sheriff's Office," he said as he showed his badge to the clerk. "I happened to be downtown this morning and wondered if you would be kind enough to run a driving history for me?"

"Sure thing,' the attractive young girl offered. "Do you have the license number or the name and date of birth?"

"Name and birth date," Patrick smiled. "And if it's not too much of a problem, I'd like to have the complete history, not just the last five years." He was the king of charm. It didn't matter that he was old enough to be her father. She was smitten with him and he could get whatever information he wanted, and he didn't need a badge to get it.

He wrote down the information on a piece of paper she offered him. He had memorized Greg McGhee's information already. When he finished writing, he slid the piece of paper towards the clerk, flashing her a grin as he did and turning his baby blues down to meet her gaze.

He could have sworn he heard her sigh as she said, "I'll have that information for you in just a minute." She walked away giving quite a performance as she went, knowing he would be watching.

True to her word, she returned just a moment later, bearing Greg McGhee's driving record on two pieces of paper. "Here you go," she said smiling. She leaned over the counter just enough to display as much of her generous bosom as possible, all the while attempting to appear as if she didn't realize what she was doing.

Patrick chuckled to himself. This girl was not near as innocent as she was trying to appear. There were the usual obvious signs of her experience, the hardness in her eyes, the way she didn't look away when he gazed down her low cut blouse, and then the exaggerated sway in her walk.

If he left his card on the counter, she would be calling him by dinner time. It was like that when you were a cop. Some women just fall all over any guy with a badge and a gun. Patrick had long since ceased to be flattered by such women, no matter what their age or looks.

"Thank you. You've been very helpful," he smiled.

"You're very welcome," she said, a little too warmly. "Hope to see you again sometime." She leaned forward to reveal what her low-cut blouse was designed to show.

Patrick left the building eager to see the results of the search. He stopped on the sidewalk just outside to have a look. There was an interesting DUI entry, in January 1987, adjudication withheld. That meant McGhee would have been twenty years old at the time. That was something to look into. Other than that, there were only the usual moving violations you would expect for a young man.

Checking his watch, Patrick realized it was almost time to meet with Detective Lockwood for lunch. He hurried to his car and drove through the port area over to Twenty-Second Street Causeway and over to the Seabreeze.

Danny Lockwood was already seated when Patrick arrived. He waved to him, and stood as he approached the table, right hand extended. Grabbing Patrick's hand, he squeezed it tightly, as he pulled the big man close slapping him on the back with his left hand.

"Hey, old man. You are looking good. I sure hope I look as good as you do when I get to 70," he joked.

"I bet you would like to look like this at seventy. I'd love that too."

As they seated themselves in their chairs a waitress approached with a menu and a glass of water. "Hi. I'm Sandy and I'll be your server today. I'll be right back for your order."

"Hang on there," Patrick said. "I don't need any time to know what I want. I'll have the grouper sandwich, extra onion and mayonnaise, and a glass of sweet tea with lemon."

"Hey, I like a man that knows what he

wants," she said smiling. "I'll have your tea for you in a minute." She removed the menus and left.

"So, what's going on, man?" Danny offered.

"Nada, buddy, just waiting to retire."

"I hear that. I wish it was me," Danny said.

"It'll be your turn soon enough. Don't wish your life away."

"So, what's this lunch all about anyway? It's sure good to see you, but I'm sure there's more than a friendly chat about the McGhee case going on here."

"Now I see why you made detective. You're sharp!" Lieutenant Moreno joked. "You're right. I need to pick your brain. A friend of mine works with Morgan McGhee. He's very concerned about what is going on in the investigation of the murder of her husband."

"He's in good company then. A lot of people want to know," Danny admitted. "Not the least of which is me."

"Right, I knew you were working on the case. What is up with the .223 ammo? That's pretty telling isn't it?"

"Not necessarily. We have good reason to believe that Mrs. McGhee killed her husband," Danny stated.

"Based on what, Danny?" Patrick asked.

"Well, the fact that she fled. That's a pretty good indicator of guilt. Wouldn't you say?"

"Ordinarily, yes, but this is different."

"How so?" Danny asked as he sipped his water.

"Was there any history of domestic violence in this case?" Patrick pushed.

"No, not that I know of. That doesn't mean anything. Just because it hasn't been reported in the past doesn't mean that it didn't happen."

"Okay. I'll buy that one, but how about the neighbors. Did you interview them?"

"They all said they were the perfect couple. Never a sound, but still..."

"How about the gun? Did either of the McGhee's own a gun, especially one of they type likely used?"

"Not that we have been able to tell... But again..." Danny stalled.

"You know I'm with you a hundred percent. I see where you are coming from, but there are too many holes in that theory."

"Such as?"

The waitress returned with the lieutenant's tea, and the men paused their conversation. She placed her hip as close to Patrick's shoulder as she could without arousing suspicion.

"There you are," she said seductively. "Just let me know if there is anything else you need," she said, with emphasis on anything.

Patrick just smiled. "Thanks," he responded in an awwww shucks-like manner.

"Man you are still the chick magnet. Aren't you?" Danny teased.

"Well, when you got it, you got it. I can't help it. They just swarm like moths to a bright light," Patrick answered, perplexed. He had never understood why women always threw themselves at him.

"Okay, now what exactly are the holes in the wife done it theory?"

"First, there was no history of domestic violence. Second, she didn't own a gun, or have any shooting experience," Patrick argued.

"That may be true, but then where is she?" Danny countered. "And why did she run?"

"There may very well be an explanation for that, detective," Patrick said, adding a little light sarcasm.

"Such as?"

"Such as, maybe she is afraid. Maybe she thinks someone is after her. Maybe, she is right." Patrick leaned forward and spoke softly for effect, "Boat tail, 69 grain, hollow point ammunition."

"Come on, Pattie boy. We both know any-one can buy that type of ammunition. It's not just law enforcement that uses it."

"Of course, but a woman who has very little experience with guns? What would she be doing with that type of ammo? Look, all I want is a little information. I promised a friend that I would look into it. You know me, I've got to give it my best shot."

Detective Lockwood breathed deeply, sit-ting taller, stretching backward in his chair as he weighed whether or not to help his friend. Technically, he should not discuss any details of the case with him. But on the other hand, this was a trusted friend of many years. And what was his purpose anyway, to solve the mur-der or convict a handy suspect?

"Okay," Danny acquiesced. "But, what-ever we discuss stays between the two of us. If I hear any of this on the news, my butt is dead meat."

"Danny, Danny, this is me you're talking to."

"Yeah, yeah, yeah. I've heard that one before. I'm sure you have too, more than once. But I would trust you with my life, man. You have always been straight with me. What do you want to know?"

"What ever you know will do nicely. And thanks for the vote of confidence. I appreci-ate that more than you know," the lieutenant said sincerely.

"Okay, here's what I have, but I warn you, it isn't much. It appears the shot came from the street. It was a clean head shot. Splattered the poor guy's brain everywhere. From the clothing we found inside the house, we think his wife was in the spa with him before it happened. At least we know she changed after dinner. And there were still wet footprints on the patio when we first came on scene."

"Is there any reason to believe anyone wanted him dead?" Patrick asked.

"Well, I've talked to some of the neighbors and got nothing. I did get some rather interesting information from the guy who is filling in for him until they name a replacement."

"Oh, yeah. Go on," Patrick encouraged.

"I interviewed him two days after the murder. Seems that Mr. McGhee had an important conference coming up in Tallahassee. Something to do with the Florida Retirement System, and the money that is being expended when county employees retire."

"Now you're talking. Keep going."

"Seems there is this county commissioner that is a little concerned because of some recent legislation about non-funded costs associated with county government. Some people are retiring with tens of thousands of dollars in pay outs, and a few hundreds of thousands. Problem is that the money isn't in the budget for these kinds of pay offs. When the cost of employees is considered, the expectation is that they will use up their sick and vacation allowances. A few too many people across the county are playing the system to their own advantage. And who could blame them?

"So, this guy says to me that Mr. McGhee had some sort of moral dilemma that he was dealing with. Apparently something was bothering the guy, and it was related to this whole issue in some way, but he wasn't sure what. Maybe he had planned his retirement in expectation of being able to exploit the whole thing."

"Okay, but how does that add up to murder?" Patrick asked.

Just as he was voicing his question the waitress arrived with two superb grouper sandwiches. "Here you are fellas," she said.

"Ummmm, ummmm," Danny said. "Nobody, but nobody makes grouper sandwiches like the Seabreeze."

"You can say that again," Patrick agreed. "This may be one of the things I'll miss most about Tampa. You will have to mail them to me in North Carolina. They sure don't have these up there."

"Don't you know it. So, back to the point," Danny continued. "How do these thing figure, if at all?"

"I don't know, but if I did, I think we would have the answer to this whole puzzle. But give me the time, I always get my man. So far, anyway," Patrick said.

"So, does that mean you're involved?"

"Not so fast, just checking into a few things."

They finished their lunch and after both men made false promises to keep the other apprised and went their respective ways. It seemed the more answers Patrick found, the more unanswered questions arose to take their place.

TWENTY-EIGHT

Morgan was drying her hair when Ian stretched out on her bed. His towel was still wrapped around his waist, the edge tucked tightly in at the waist. As he lay there she watched the rise and fall of his chest as he inhaled and exhaled. The golden hairs on his chest covered him like a light blanket. Arms outstretched as though he awaited her embrace, he slept soundly, not suspecting her plan. She noticed that even his underarm hairs were pretty. It was almost sinful for one human being to be so perfect, almost.

She regretted having to leave, but then she remembered the photographs at the end of the hall. This beautiful male creature was a dangerous predator - wild and malefic - and he was not what she had thought in the beginning. She had to keep reminding herself of this. His allure was overwhelming. His feet were uncovered and she laughed to herself thinking how much he looked like a little boy. Yes, he resembled a little boy in many ways, but indeed he was not.

Morgan dressed in sneakers and blue jeans, and chose a long-sleeved T-shirt. She applied sun screen, and grabbed a pair of sun glasses, now that the early morning rain had ended. In the kitchen she found the insect repellent and applied a generous amount. She filled a zipper seal type plastic bag with packages of peanuts and some packaged cookies. She went over the list of things she would need in her mind. If only she knew where exactly she was, she could find help more quickly. But she didn't know. She hoped for some sort of a break that would help her.

Before she left the house she took a quick look around, wanting to remember just how everything looked. Unable to leave without seeing Ian one more time, she made her way down the hall to the bedroom. Ian was still there in the same position. He hadn't moved at all. He had to be very tired, having been up all night the night before. Timing could not have been better. It was a perfect opportunity for her to leave.

Leaving proved harder for her to do than she had imagined it would be, and yet she knew she must go. She walked over and placed a light kiss on Ian's forehead. He didn't move a bit. In the back of her mind she hoped he would wake up and stop her. Having made her farewells, she turned her back and left. This time she didn't look back.

Once she was out the door she felt free, and intensely alone, more so than she had ever been. The glare of the sun hurt here eyes, and she put on her sunglasses. The Rodeo sat parked in the front of the cabin. She was glad it was not near the bedroom where Ian slept.

Trying the passenger door first, she found it locked, and she prayed by some fortunate circumstance that the driver side door would be unlocked. Sure enough, Ian had left it unlocked. Quietly, she opened the door and slid into the driver's seat. She looked in the console for his cell-phone, but there was nothing there except a couple of maps. Stepping out of the car she folded herself into the floorboard and checked under the seat, still nothing. Next she checked the glove box, finding only a tire gauge and some tissues. She tried to look under the passenger seat, but couldn't reach across well enough to get a good view under the seat. Morgan unlocked the passenger door and walked around to open it. As she opened the door she spotted her cell-phone just underneath the seat, wedged between the seat and door. She must have dropped it there that night not so very long ago; and yet so very distant. The memory had already faded to a dim recollection.

Immediately she felt an odd combination of relief and nostalgia as she dialed Felicia's number. She was relieved that she would be able to contact someone. There was no time to stand around thinking. Ian could wake up at any time, and she was more than certain he would not be happy to find her snooping around in his personal things. She put the cell-phone in the plastic bag with her food, and tucked the edge of the bag into the waistband of her pants, wedging the phone securely into her front pants pocket. Closing the door as quietly as possible, she looked around, surveying the area. She decided it would be best to head west. That was the direction of the Alafia, and beyond that there should be a more populated area. She started off jogging, it was best to put some distance between herself and the house.

It was only a few minutes before she reached the river. The river was high today, dark and swift. She thought it looked a little like a giant snake ready to swallow her up. There was no time to stop and think things over, she had to move fast.

Morgan said another quick prayer that her cell-phone battery had retained at least some of its charge as she waited for someone to pick up.

"Hello," Felicia answered.

Morgan was elated to hear her voice. Felicia, Felicia, it's me, Morgan."

Felicia was at the gym and gave a quick glance around the room to see who might be near enough to hear her speaking. She was glad that she was isolated on the women's side of the room, and no one else was around.

"Where are you?!" she whispered.

"I don't know exactly."

"What do you mean you don't know?" Felicia asked.

"I mean I'm not sure. I'm somewhere on the Alafia, out in the middle of nowhere."

"What are you doing there? Do you know the police are looking for you?"

"Yes! I know. Write this down. Ian Greer, do you know him?"

"I've heard the name from you."

"He brought me out here. There's been no phone. I just escaped from his cabin. He's sleeping right now. He'll be looking for me, and I've good reasons to be afraid of him. I think my battery is getting low, so I have to talk fast.

"All I know is that we are somewhere in Hillsborough County, and I am on the Alafia. I'm going to try to get to a road. If I can find a pay phone I'll call you collect. Be sure to keep your phone on and accept the charge."

"I will. What do you..."

Felicia never finished what she was saying because Morgan's cell-phone went dead. Morgan tossed the phone near a tree on the bank; it would be of no use to her now. She felt like sitting down and crying for a good long while, but knew she had better keep moving. Already it was well into the afternoon, and it wouldn't be any fun to be out here in the dark.

Morgan stepped into the water, walking toward the middle of the river. She gave herself over to its swift flow, allowing her body to be carried downstream by the current. If it had not been for the circumstances that had brought her there she would have been enjoying the float down-river. Eventually, Ian would wake up, and he would be right behind her. Without a doubt Ian would be moving much faster than she was and increasing the distance between them was essential, if she were to get to help.

The buzzing of crickets and chirping of birds in the trees surrounding the river lent an air of normality, a sense that all was right with the world. But Morgan was more than aware that all was not right. A man she had trusted, yes, even loved, lay sleeping not far away. She was certain that he was some sort of psychotic control freak at the very least, and quite possibly her husband's killer.

Just a few minutes down-river of where she began, Morgan found herself nearing a small bridge. At first she was elated, the bridge would mean there was a road, a road leading to safety. But she was also worried that there would be snakes under the bridge. She was terrified of snakes, and for some inexplicable reason felt certain she would encounter at least one there. She told herself there was no time now for foolish fears. She made up her mind to get out of the river at the bridge.

At first it seemed a simple thing to pull herself from the river just before the bridge. To her surprise there were many broken beer bottles littering both sides of the immediate shore. There was also broken glass visible beneath the water in the shallow area near the shore.

She decided to float down past the bridge and walk back. Even though she had gotten around the majority of the broken glass, it still proved tricky getting out of the swiftly moving water. The rocks were covered with a slimy algae type growth, but Morgan managed to haul herself onto the bank with some difficulty. Surely anyone looking for her would notice that someone had exited the river at this exact location. All she could do at this point was to hope for the best. The bank was muddy, and there was no way she could camouflage her unavoidable footprints.

Morgan headed toward the stand of cypress trees that grew along the road, but quickly found the going too rough. Her sneakers were soaked and already squishing each time she took a step, but the ground was so soft that each time she took a step her foot sunk deeply enough in the mud that a suction trapped her foot. Legs already tiring from trudging through the mire, she decided to go back to the river, go farther downstream. She had simply gotten out too far from the road, and it would be too difficult to make it.

Sitting on the bank, she rested and ate some of the nuts from her snack bag before plunging back into the frigid water of the Alafia. She drifted with the water part of the time, swimming along to speed her progress from time to time. It seemed like a very long time before she reached a dirt road that ended at the river bank. This would be a perfect spot to exit as the bank sloped gently into the river in a sandy beach area.

She felt safer now that there was considerable distance between Ian and wherever this was; this remote location she happened to find herself in. The sun was shining brightly through a thinning of the trees at the sandy portion of the bank, and Morgan decided to rest there for a few minutes while she allowed the afternoon sun to partially dry her. Evening was fast approaching, and if she did not find someone soon, she would become very cold in these damp clothes. Fatigue was becoming a factor already. She opened her plastic bag and ate some cookies hoping the sugar would give her energy.

The cookies reminded her of Ian. How he had taken care of her that night at that cheap hotel on Kennedy Boulevard. He had been so sweet, so considerate. If she had only known it was no coincidence that he got chocolate chip cookies and milk for her. All along, he knew everything she liked because he had been investigating her life for a long time. She shuddered to think of it. Even though the sun was warming her body, a chill that came from deep inside negated its warmth.

If only Ian had been what she had thought, everything would have been so different. She was stupid to have trusted him, and even more stupid to love him. Morgan thought about how frightening it was not to be able to trust her own impulses and instincts. She had not realized her own vulnerability. Now that Greg was gone, she would have to be a lot smarter than she was before, guard against emotions that can carry one to places of delusional sanctuary. There was no one to protect her now - she was all alone - literally and figuratively.

TWENTY-NINE

Patrick Moreno hated taking time out of the day, today of all days - to keep his appointment with the retirement clerk - but he wouldn't miss it for the world either. He was punctual as usual. The appointment had been made two months prior.

He entered the office by the front door, and walked up to the receptionist. "Hi, I'm Patrick Moreno. I have an appointment," he offered.

The woman at the desk looked at her appointment book, without as much as a glance in Patrick's direction. "Oh, yes. I see your name here. Have a seat over there and I'll call you."

Patrick was amazed. *She never once even looked up. Government workers! No one but the government would employ some of these people.*

He took a seat and picked up a magazine - staring at it blindly - not seeing anything on the page. Instead he mulled over the information that Danny Lockwood had given him. There was nothing to put his finger on yet, but he knew he was closing in on something. He could smell it, just like a cake baking in the oven, the scent just kept getting stronger as each moment passed.

"Patrick Moreno," the receptionist called, startling him out of his deep concentration.

"Yes," he replied.

"Step this way please."

He followed the clerk to an office down the hall. A pleasant older woman sat at the desk smiling.

"Lieutenant Moreno, have a seat. I'm Mrs. Thompson," she offered an outstretched hand.

Patrick shook her hand and had a seat next to her desk.

"I see here you work for the Sheriff's Office," Mrs. Thompson said.

"Yes, for more years than I care to mention," he countered.

She smiled at him, a kind and warm smile. It was refreshing to talk to a woman that wasn't interested in him sexually. He felt at ease with her, even though he had never met her before.

"No need to mention how many to me, Lieutenant, I have the information right here," she said gazing into her computer screen like it was a crystal ball.

"May I ask you a couple of questions, just out of curiosity?" she ventured.

"Ordinarily, ma'am, the answer would be unequivocally no; but you're such a lovely lady, I have to say yes," he answered her, pouring on the charm for some reason.

"Well, nothing personal, mind you," she blushed.

He thought she was cute the way she was flustered by talking to him. She had to be very near 65 if she wasn't already. Somehow her amiable nature appealed to him in a way he could not explain.

"You can ask me what ever you like, and I'll try to give you as honest an answer as I can."

"That sounds fair," she countered. "I was just going to ask what type of work you have done with the Sheriff's Office."

"Little lady," he said. "Is that all you wanted to know? I'll be happy to share my rather uninspired career in as much detail as you can stay awake for. I was a street deputy for a few years, and then I became a supervisor. I was a narcotics detective for a few years, but that was never my cup of tea."

"And what exactly was your cup of tea, Lieutenant Moreno?" she asked sweetly.

"Homicide, ma'am, homicide. There is nothing like it for stirring the blood. It was an absolute passion for me," Patrick said candidly.

"I can tell by the way you speak of it," Mrs. Thompson said. "I love a good mystery myself."

"Really? Then we share the same passion," he smiled.

"Yes, sir, we do. And now, let me explain your benefits to you."

Mrs. Thompson answered all of his questions patiently and with painstaking detail. She knew her job well, and Patrick was confident she was giving him the best information he could have gotten from anyone.

"Now, sir, is there anything else I can help you with?" Mrs. Thompson asked.

"I don't think so. Not right now anyway. Is it all right if I call you later if I think of any other questions?"

"Lieutenant Moreno, I'd be deeply hurt if you didn't. If you'll wait right here I'll put together some paperwork for you to take with you. That'll give you a better recollection of what we have discussed when you have time to look over it at home." She rose from her desk slowly.

At first Patrick was surprised when Mrs. Thompson came around the desk. She had some difficulty getting out of the chair, but when she tried to walk she had obvious trouble. Her dress was mid-calf length, and she had braces on both of her legs. Now he felt bad for her, she had such a positive attitude, and so many obstacles to overcome. Patrick reflected on the irony of how many times it is the people that have the most adversity in life are the most happy and pleasant to be around.

When she returned to the room she was smiling. "Now, here you are Lieutenant. All the things we discussed are right here in this folder. I hope you'll take it home and go over it carefully, paying close attention to all of the details."

"I'll do it," he promised, taking the folder from her. "I have really enjoyed talking to you and I appreciate all your help."

She smiled extending her hand to him once again. "Feel free to call me about any questions you have. And remember the sooner you look over the papers I gave you, the better you'll remember what we talked about."

Patrick squeezed her hand warmly and left without any further conversation. He jumped into his car and tossed the folder on the seat next to him. For the first time he felt really excited about his retirement. He had waited for this for a long time, and now it was finally within his reach. There was a sense of freedom that had not been there before.

Turning his thoughts back to the McGhee case, Patrick thought over the things that Detective Lockwood had shared with him. Odd that he'd mentioned the Florida Retirement System, today of all days. Patrick had learned that there were no real accidents in life. Everything happened for a reason, and somehow always seemed to fit together in a pattern.

When he got home he disabled the alarm system and tossed his folder Mrs. Thompson had given him on the dining room table. He went to the kitchen and removed a glass from the freezer, then removing a bottle of beer from the refrigerator he twisted off the top and poured. Placing the glass on the table, he went to the bathroom to wash up before he began working in earnest on the McGhee case.

Patrick took out his notebook and began to go over the list of facts he already knew.

They were beginning to add up. One thing he was certain of at this point was that Morgan McGhee did not murder her husband. She would have faced the same fate if Ian Greer had not hidden her very carefully for the last few days.

He thought about the case for the remainder of the time he ate, making notes occasionally on his pad. There was nothing new on Channel Two News about the case, and he mulled over what he should do next and came up with nothing. A tactic he had long employed was to think of something else entirely. Sometimes when you disengage your conscious thinking from a topic the sub-conscious will click and things will fit.

With this in mind he opened the folder Mrs. Thompson had given him and began to page through the thin stack of documents. The first page was an accounting of the number of years he had been employed with the county. Turning the page, he glanced over the information concerning the total contributions by the Sheriff's Office.

When he turned the next page, he was so startled that he came to full attention sitting there in his chair. A name from the past jumped off the page at him. Harlan Boswell! *What in the hell was a page on Harlan Boswell doing in his retirement file?*

He remembered the name well. Harlan was a murder victim from five years ago. Patrick had successfully investigated the murder and the suspect had been sentenced to life. His brother-in-law had murdered him. He killed him with a machete, because he was beating up on his sister, Harlan's wife.

Patrick picked up his portable phone from the table and dialed the district office. "Lieutenant Moreno here, I want you to look up something on the computer for me. What is the date of birth for Harlan A. Boswell? The entry will be from about five years ago, he was a signal five victim," he barked. "Murdered by his brother-in-law."

He could hardly wait for the answer. When the response finally came, he was completely dumbfounded. The date of birth matched the one on the print out that had been in his file. From the looks of the paper, someone was collecting retirement benefits under the name of Harlan Boswell, now dead for some five years.

There was a lump sum payment of $27,500. The monthly payments were $894.

Patrick didn't wait to start making phone calls. In a matter of a few minutes he had managed to raise more than just a couple of eye brows, and was certain that the matter was being researched, and he would have an answer in a very short time. Unless his memory was failing him big time that Harlan Boswell had never been an employee of any state or local government agency, and had earned no retirement benefits from the state. Harlan had owned a bar in Wimauma for over ten years, at the north end of Railroad Street. He had only been thirty-three at the time of his death. Hardly old enough to retire from the county, in light of the length of time he had owned the bar.

Patrick found Mrs. Thompson's card and called her without wasting a second. He was irritated by having voice mail message he got on the phone. It took several minutes on hold to break through the circular maze of numbers and actually get a person on the line.

Mrs. Thompson had left for the day. He thanked the clerk, but declined to leave a message. Not really wanting to wait till the next morning to talk to her, he dialed communications to see if she had a phone number on file in the computer. Sure enough, her number was published. If her first name had not been Verna, he probably would not have located her, Thompson being such a common name.

As he dialed her number his pager went off. He didn't recognize the phone number, but the numbpoerator number that was entered after it, he certainly did. It was Randy's.

"Hello," Mrs. Thompson answered.

"Mrs. Thompson, this is Lieutenant Moreno. I met you today at your office."

"Oh, yes, I was expecting your call."

"I imagine you were. You're a very crafty woman. Is there any additional information you have for me," he asked hopeful.

"Why, yes, I do. How about copies of the canceled checks that were issued to Mr. Boswell?"

"Mrs. Thompson, you are a dream. When can I get them?"

"How about you stopping by the Court House Coffee Shop at lunch time. I'll meet you there at 12:00."

"Great, and I'll even buy," Patrick promised.

"Twelve o'clock it is then. See you then," she said as she hung up.

Patrick had more information coming at him at one time than he had time to assimilate. He had a hunch that Randy would have some more for him. Dialing Randy's number, he grabbed his ever handy note pad.

THIRTY

Felicia was thrilled to finally hear from Morgan. Thank goodness she had remembered to take her cell phone with her when she left the house this morning to work out at her neighborhood gym. She almost didn't hear the phone ringing in her gym bag, sitting off to the side of the free weight rack.

Without hesitating after the connection was lost she called communications on the supervisor's line because she knew it was unrecorded. "Hi. Who is this?"

"Operator 203, Joe. Who is this?"

"Joe, this is Felicia. Can you please give me Randy's home phone number." Felicia tried not to sound overly anxious.

"Sure. Hang on a second. By the way, have you heard anything new yet on Morgan?"

"Nothing new yet. I sure hope she turns up soon though. I'm so worried about her."

"You and a lot of other people," Joe said.

After she got Randy's number, she dialed immediately. There was no answer. She knew Randy liked to sleep late, and more than likely had the phone turned off. Felicia decided to go straight home to change, just in case she would have to drive over to Randy's house and wake him up. As she drove home she continued to dial his number, but still no answer.

When she got home, she showered quickly, and threw on a T-shirt knit jumpsuit, and a pair of comfortable sandals. She was ready to go in less than fifteen minutes. Hoping Randy would answer, she dialed the phone once more.

"Hello," Randy answered cheerily.

"Randy, it's Felicia. I need to talk to

you right away."

"Shoot," he replied.

"Cute choice of words," Felicia said dryly.

"As always," was Randy's retort.

"I just got a call from Morgan," she blurted out.

"No kidding!" Randy almost shouted. She didn't say much, her phone went dead. Apparently she's in some danger. She mentioned a name. Do you know Ian Greer?"

"Deputy Ian Greer? I've heard the name, but I don't know him personally. Why do you ask?"

"She said she has been with him and has reason to be afraid of him. Apparently he's chasing her or something. Oh, Randy, you have to help me find her right away. I could tell by her voice she was very afraid."

"Okay, give me a few. I have to think," Randy stalled.

"That might take too long. You better let me help you with that," Felicia joked.

"Let me call Lieutenant Moreno and let him know right away."

"Can he be trusted?" Felicia asked.

"I can't see that we have any choice at this point."

"You're right. Call me back on my cell phone and let me know everything that is going on. I'm going down to the SOC and look up Ian Greer's personnel information in the computer. I don't want to ask anything on the phone, just in case anyone becomes suspicious. I'll meet you somewhere as soon as you find out what the lieutenant wants to do."

"Sounds good," said Randy. "I'll get back with you as soon as I hear from him. If I don't hear from him right away, I'll call you back and let you know."

"Okay, bye."

It didn't take Lieutenant Moreno more

than five minutes to return Randy's page, but it seemed more like an hour. Randy used the time throwing on a pair of jeans and some deck shoes, and was fully dressed by the time the phone rang. He ran from the bedroom to the kitchen to answer the phone.

"Hello," Randy said, out of breath.

"Lieutenant Moreno here."

"Hey, Lieutenant. You won't believe who just called me."

"Who was that?" he asked.

"Felicia Langston. She's that dispatcher, best friend of Morgan McGhee. Seems that she just got a call from Morgan."

"Oh, yeah? Did she say where she was?"

"Well, apparently she doesn't know exactly where she is. She said she is somewhere along the Alafia, and is apparently in danger. Is there somewhere we can all meet right away?"

"I'm home now, at Cheval. Where are you?"

"I'm in the Sunset Park area. Felicia is on her way to the Comm Center. Where do you think would be a good place to meet?"

"You said Mrs. McGhee is somewhere on the Alafia, right?"

"Right, but that covers quite a large area."

"Okay, then let's meet at Denny's on 60 Highway. It'll take me about thirty minutes to get there. How about you?"

"About the same," said Randy. "Felicia mentioned something about Deputy Ian Greer. Do you know him?"

"Yes, I do. What did she say about him?"

"Not much. Apparently Morgan is in some kind of danger involving him. Felicia is on her way to the SOC to get information from his personnel record in the computer. She didn't want to call and arouse suspicion. So she is in her super stealth mode."

"That was a good move," the lieutenant

agreed. "I'll meet you there in just a few."

THIRTY-ONE

Chuck James felt the vibration from one of the two pagers he carried on his side. He always laughingly equated it to kidney dialysis. Checking the number, he recognized it as one that would be related to his "extra-circular" employment - his off-off-duty job - the Greg McGhee job, to be specific.

He knew the number that appeared on his pager very well. It was the number for the Special Operations Deep Cover Wire Division. These were the guys that listened in on people's phone conversations. Ordinarily that required a court order, authorized by a warrant signed by a judge, but not in this case. This request was strictly off the record. No documentation would be made. Chuck knew his request for the phones of the friends and relatives of Morgan McGhee to be monitored would be approved without being encumbered by any court document.

A few inquiries were all that were needed to get a list of people that Morgan was known to associate with. It was a short list. She knew a lot of people, but didn't spend time with more than three. The job was made easier by her tendency to be a loner.

Chuck pulled the Firebird into the gas station at the corner of Twenty Second Avenue and 60 Highway. Digging a quarter out of the pocket of his tight fitting blue jeans, he deposited it into the pay phone. He almost forgot he needed a dime to go with that quarter. Finally finding one, he deposited the extra coin and dialed from memory.

When the phone picked up, no one spoke. Chuck knew the drill, he was expected to identify himself first, and so he did.

"Detective 251, Sterling Hope," he said, giving the password for the McGhee case.

"We have just had a positive contact in regard to your request for information. The call that was monitored was made at 1438 hours from the residence of Randy Spencer, and originated at the residence of Felicia Langston.

Chuck listened as the voice on the other end of the telephone read the conversation verbatim. He then asked if Chuck needed any part of the conversation repeated, and was he ready to hear the details of the second conversation. Intrigued, he told the man to go ahead.

"Right after he hung up, Randy Spencer paged someone. A short time after he made the page, a man identifying himself as Lieutenant Moreno called, advising he was returning a page."

Again, the conversation between Randy and the lieutenant was read exactly as it occurred. The man asked Chuck if anything need be repeated, or if there were any further instructions.

"No, thank you," Chuck replied hanging up the pay phone.

So, she had surfaced. He knew it was only a matter of time until she did. Originally, Morgan McGhee had not been part of the job. Perhaps he would have declined if he had known. He had been able to handle the job based on the parameters of the husband only. Things were getting deep, even for an ass with no conscience, such as himself.

Greg McGhee had meant absolutely nothing to him - just a hit - but Morgan was another story altogether. Chuck had first come in contact with her when he was doing surveillance for another job. He had gotten a little closer out of curiosity, and had found her a naive and unusual person to say the least. She was an exotic beauty, one that made you believe just by looking at her that she was wildly sensual, having an inherent knowledge of the needs of men. Yet there was a quality of innocence that made one doubt what you knew to be true. He found the mixture almost maddening, and had distanced himself from her to protect his own mental detachment. Chuck never allowed any woman to get under his skin. His motto was, "Treat them like the whores that they are." It was a crude and heartless way to think, but it fit him like a glove.

He had known when he accepted the assignment that the job could possibly expand to include Morgan, but he told himself it would not. Even now, he had his doubts whether he should, or even could continue on. Nevertheless, he knew it was way too late to turn back. The major would never agree to allow him to abandon the job at this point.

Chuck thought it best to start heading towards Denny's. He checked the battery on his radio that monitored the Sheriff's Office channels. This new 800 MHZ system was worse than the one they had replaced it with. The batteries were notorious for going dead after a very short time of use. For this reason he kept a couple of spares charged, just in case he needed them. The Firebird started up with a rumble and Chuck headed east on 60 Highway to Denny's, more than just a little heavy of heart. This was something he would have preferred not to do. He had no choice. An order is an order, and he was in too deep to go back now.

THIRTY-TWO

Lieutenant Moreno scanned his notebook for the pager number of one of his most trusted friends, Jake Reynolds. Jake had been a canine deputy for about five years. He was one of the most experienced of handlers with the department. Not only due to the length of time he had been on the job, but he really loved his work.

Often Jake would listen to the radio waiting for an opportunity to take his dog out to track a criminal. It wasn't unusual for him to just show up on a scene and go to work. Everyone was used to it, and no one even raised an eyebrow.

Within minutes Jake returned Patrick's page. "Yo, Jake here."

"Jake, this is Patrick Moreno. I need your help if you aren't busy."

"Sure thing Lieutenant. What you got?" Jake asked. He knew if Patrick needed him it was something unusual.

"Why don't you meet me at Denny's on 60 Highway in about twenty-five minutes and I'll fill you in."

"Great, I didn't have anything going on this afternoon anyway. I'll be 51 that way."

"Hey! Don't forget to bring Thor with you. I might have some work for him too."

"Sure thing LT, see you in a few," Jake said as he hung up the phone.

Patrick's mind was reeling, assimilating all the recently acquired information he had received. What had made Morgan run from Ian? Had Ian been as truthful with him as he had thought? Where exactly had Ian been hiding her all this time?

A big gaping hole in Patrick's investigation so far suddenly occurred to him. He hadn't checked for property owned by Ian when he had been at the courthouse. Patrick dialed information and got the number for the Property Appraiser's Office. He asked for the Customer Service Department, identified himself, and asked for the address of any properties owned entirely or in part by Ian Greer. The list was short, there were only two. There was a home in Northdale, and an unimproved property on Thatcher road in southeastern Hillsborough County.

Absolutely perfect. This narrowed the area to be searched considerably. Still, it might not be a piece of cake, but this was a real break.

Patrick Moreno parked his Jeep in the front of Denny's. He hardly remembered the drive there, he had been so preoccupied with his thoughts. Recognizing Randy's car in the parking lot, he went right in, glad he would not have to wait for him to arrive. To his surprise, Randy was seated at the table with a dispatcher he vaguely remembered seeing before. She wasn't in uniform, but her distinctive look was unmistakable.

"Lieutenant Moreno, I'd like for you to meet Felicia Langston. She's Morgan McGhee's best friend," Randy explained.

"Pleased to meet you," said Patrick, extending his hand to her. "I'm certain I've seen you before, but don't remember being formally introduced."

"I'm sure you're right, but I've talked to you many times on the phone in teletype," said Felicia.

"I understand, Morgan McGhee called you this afternoon," Patrick said, changing the subject and getting straight to the matter at hand.

"Right, she called me on my cell. It was

a very brief conversation. Her phone went dead."

"What exactly did she say to you?" Lieutenant Moreno asked as the waitress arrived. "Just coffee for me," he said waving her off impatiently.

"Sure thing. I'll tell you exactly what I remember. First she said that she was somewhere on the Alafia, and wasn't sure where. She also said that she was afraid that her cell phone was going to go dead. She was right about that, the phone went dead just a couple of minutes later. Also she asked if I knew Deputy Ian Greer. I told her I knew his name, but only because she had mentioned him to me previously. She mentioned that she was afraid of him for some reason, and that she had escaped from a cabin he owned. Then she said she was going to try to find a road and get to a telephone.

"I don't mind telling you Lieutenant, I'm really afraid for her. She's a real wimp. If she's lost in some remote area, no telling what she'll do. She's terrified of bugs and snakes."

"We're going to do what we can, Ms. Langston. Randy, I 've called a friend of mine, Jake Reynolds. He is a canine deputy," said Patrick.

"Right," answered Randy. "I know who he is. He's a real gung ho kinda guy. Isn't he?"

"Yes, he is. He's just the kind of help we're going to need if we're going to find Mrs. McGhee this afternoon."

Jake Reynolds went to his back yard and called Thor, who was sleeping in his dog house, under the shade tree. "Thor, come here boy, we have work."

Thor jumped up immediately, and ran to Jake. He placed his neck next to Jake's leg, in a position that allowed him to clip the leash to his collar easily.

Jake stood a little over six feet tall and weighed two-hundred, thirty-five pounds. There wasn't an ounce of fat on his body, unlike some other deputies in the department. He took pride in his appearance, even now at near thirty-five years of age.

Thor was a good dog, not a lazy bone in his body. He enjoyed his work as much as Jake, and was in his prime. They had won several awards over the last couple of years; for the number of apprehensions, and for handling and obedience at state competitions. Jake wondered if he would ever find another dog like Thor. Probably not.

Most police dogs barked incessantly. Sometimes the handlers went deaf in one ear from the dog barking in the car right next to them year after year. Not Thor, he was liked to sneak up on his victim, having never been noticed in his approach. They had been together for three years.

Jake smiled to himself as he put Thor into the back of his Sheriff's Office Blazer. The truck was already hot inside from sitting in the sun, so he hurried to turn on the air so Thor wouldn't get too hot. Even with the unusually cool weather, the car would heat up fast.

The drive would only take minutes, and Jake was anxious to find out what the Lieutenant wanted. He had been off for two days now and was excited to have something to do.

Unlike many other men his age, he wasn't interested in all the usual hobbies. It had always been a problem for him, because he was somewhat hyper-active. He had never been diagnosed by a doctor, but he knew in his heart he was. Nowadays they called it Attention Deficit Disorder. Jake just called it plain wound tight, and wound tight he was.

Married for nearly three years now, Jake

and his wife still had no children. He really didn't want any, but his wife did. She had placed a family on hold for her career in marketing for the present, and Jake hoped it would stay that way.

Still, there was little in his life that held his attention for any length of time, other than his work. Jake's father was a cop, and his grandfather had been a cop. It was more or less a family tradition. There had never been any question about what he would be when he grew up. He would be a cop too. He never felt pressured to make the decision, knowing it was what he was meant to be.

Traffic was slow on the way to Denny's and Jake parked his Blazer next to Lieutenant Moreno's Jeep. He left the car running and the air conditioner on to keep Thor cool. He always double checked to be sure he had his spare key on him before locking the door. He felt an air of anticipation as he walked inside. It was always this way with him. The excitement of a chase, the thrill of the hunt excited him in a way almost comparable to being with a woman. Jake had often wondered if any of the other canine deputies felt the same way.

It took a minute for his eyes to adjust to the light of the restaurant and he scanned the room for Patrick, finding him in the corner, facing the door. It was the habit of cops to face the door so they could see who was coming in, and it was even better if they could locate a spot with their back to the wall. Most people wouldn't ever notice, but any cop would.

After the brief introductions Jake took a seat. Patrick quickly filled him in, surprising Felicia and Randy with some of the details he knew. He told him that he thought they needed to search the area of Thatcher Road along the Alafia for Morgan McGhee. Purposely he left out the reasoning for why he thought this was a good area. Jake didn't need a reason why, he trusted the lieutenant's judgment. Years of seeing him in action had earned Jake's respect.

The discussion ended. They all got into their respective vehicles, and began the drive southward with Patrick in the lead in his Jeep. The traffic was light on the way there, unusual for this time of day. The whole Brandon area had exploded in the past few years and traffic was one of the major drawbacks to living in the area.

The convoy drove east on Thatcher Road after leaving 39 Highway, and came to a stop at the little bridge that crossed the Alafia. Randy, Felicia, and Jake all came to the rear of Patrick's car. Patrick was the first to speak.

"Felicia, this is the South Fork of the Alafia, and I think we'll find Morgan somewhere near here. It'd be best if you're nearby when we find her. I don't know what her condition will be, but I'm sure the face of a trusted friend will be helpful in any case. So, I want you to stay with me. That okay with you?"

"Sure, just don't walk too fast. I'll try to keep up."

"Randy, I want you to help Jake any way you can. You can take my portable radio and drive for him. That way if he gets off in the bushes you can drive to pick him up."

Automatically, Jake handed his spare key to Randy. "Lieutenant, I'm gonna get Thor out and see what we can pick up."

Jake attached the thirty foot lead before releasing Thor out of the back of the Blazer. Thor jumped out, urinating on the first bush he found to identify it as his territory. Jake led him to the bridge and over to the locked wide entry gate. Sniffing the dirt and grass, Thor tried to pick up a scent, but didn't locate anything.

As Jake led Thor around the other three stood on the bridge. It was Felicia that first saw the footprints in the mud just south of the bridge. "Hey, look at that. Someone has been here."

Patrick called out to Jake, "Come over here and look at this."

"Damn," Jake swore. "That's going to be hard to get to. Let me get my rubber boots out of the car." He walked over to the Blazer and got his knee high boots out, and pulled them over his everyday boots.

Jake trudged through the mud and under-brush to get over to the place Felicia had seen the footprints. Sure enough they looked fairly recent, but already there was water standing in the deep indentations made by someone's attempt to walk. It was easy to tell that who ever had made them was a small person, and had quickly doubled back to the river, probably unable to walk in the mire. He didn't need Thor to know the trail ended there.

"Nothing to track Lieutenant," Jake shouted. "We'll have to try further down-river. There's no way for me to follow this shoreline. This way is too overgrown with weeds, and the ground is totally soaked. That cold front that came through this morning re-ally dropped the rain out here."

They all got in the vehicles, leaving Randy's parked on the side of the bridge. Randy locked it before leaving it, and jumped into the driver's seat of Jake's Blazer. They drove south to the first road on the east side of the road to continue to look for the proverbial needle in the haystack.

THIRTY-THREE

Chuck parked his Firebird on the north side of the gas station on 39 Highway across from Thatcher Road. It was closed today. Who knew why? It took him a few minutes to locate the radio channel the lieutenant and Jake were using. They weren't talking much, but after a patient wait of thirty minutes he found them. His AR-15 sat in his lap, he still smelled the gun oil from cleaning it yesterday. He had always been a firm believer in the head shot. It certainly worked on Greg.

"Jake, park at that little cemetery and see if you can make your way to the river from there. I'll go on further south and see what it looks like."

"Ten-four," was all that Jake said.

Chuck started up the Firebird. Maybe it would be a good idea for him to go even further south, see what he could find. As an after thought he jumped out and opened the trunk, removing his scope, and attached it to his gun. He just might need this little jewel if he located Morgan. Although his conscience troubled him a little at the thought, he reminded himself this was only a job, a job just like any other.

No one saw the Firebird as it whizzed past. It was just another vehicle southbound on 39 Highway. The only difference was that it held a deadly assassin, one that was closing in on prey that had been on the run for too long.

Morgan would have loved to sit on the bank of the Alafia for a few hours and nap, but the sun would be setting soon. It was already beginning to get cold. She made her way westward thorough the thick bushes, pulling one branch after the next out of her way. At one juncture she had to break a branch off to clear the web of a very large Banana Spider that had made a huge web across the bushes. She was thankful that there was still enough light to see the spider before she walked into it. From experience she knew their bite could be quite nasty.

After walking a few minutes she noticed that the bushes had begun to thin. She came to a clearing graced by some very old oak trees. The branches were beautiful as they hung thick with Spanish moss. Thrilled and hopeful to finally be nearing civilization, Morgan was revitalize by the prospect of a warm place out of the weather, and some dry clothing.

Noticing an old partially paved, half grass covered road just to the south of the oak trees, Morgan made her way with a new bounce in her step. Her melancholy for Ian seemed to fade for a moment, but not entirely. There were quite a few bushes with thorns on them growing low to the ground. They grabbed Morgan's pants legs as she passed. She hardly noticed them, ripping her pants off the bushes in an effort to walk more quickly.

Just as she was nearing the pavement, Morgan saw a sight that made her heart leap. Driving down the road was a beautiful apparition of a red car, an older sports car. It was driving towards her. She thrilled at the sight, waving her arms as she went, certain she would appear as a raving lunatic to anyone who saw her. But she didn't care what anyone thought.

Without warning the car stopped. She watched as the driver door opened. From out of nowhere, a sudden sense of dread overcame her. Telling herself she was only being paranoid, she continued to wave.

The driver reached into the vehicle and

took something out. Maybe he had a pair of binoculars and wanted to see who she was. After all she might be trespassing on someone's property. Hurrying forward, Morgan twisted her ankle in a small hole in the field. Not to worry, it was only a little bit hurt. She rubbed her ankle looking toward the vehicle, too far to see well in the fading evening sun.

It was then that she heard the shot ring out. Confused for an instant, she wasn't sure where it came from. A burning pain struck her left shoulder, high, near the collar bone. She looked down automatically, only to see her blood cascading down her T-shirt.

Still in disbelief, and in seeming slow motion, she looked toward the road, only to see the red vehicle backing out. She shook her head, placing her right hand over the wound. For an instant, she thought she would be able to continue walking. It was then that consciousness fled away, the dizzy lightheaded feeling of passing out preceding her fall. She hit the ground like a tree, nothing to break her descent.

Her last thought had been of Ian. If only she had stayed with him. This is what he was trying to protect her from. He would be very angry with her.

The Firebird backed out in a hurry, throwing gravel and mud as it went. Chuck knew he would have no trouble getting out undetected, but he knew that he would have to hurry. The cavalry wasn't far behind.

He swore to himself under his breath. It was stupid not to have taken the head shot. Somehow he couldn't bring himself to shoot that beautiful blond hair. Through his scope he had seen her smile her happy expectant face, mistakenly thinking help was near. Her curls blew in the breeze, the flow of sunset turning them a beautiful shade of golden yellow. So, he had aimed for center body mass. Well, not really center. Chuck was an expert marksman. He knew well he aimed high on purpose. Now it was all up to fate. Morgan was on her own. With any luck she might make it. If she did his career was pretty much over. Maybe he was getting soft in his old age, but somehow he felt just a little bit good about having declined the head shot.

Randy heard a gunshot and knew instantly that Morgan was in trouble. He didn't know how he knew, it was a gut feeling. Debating whether or not to wait for Jake to come back to the Blazer, he got on the radio and called him.

"Jake, this is Randy. Are you there?"

"Ten-four. Go."

"Did you hear that shot?"

"Roger that," Jake replied.

"Randy, this is Moreno. What are you talking about?"

"Lieutenant, there was just a single gunshot, south of here. Can't be more than a half mile away," Jake inserted.

"Okay, let's go," the Lieutenant said as he threw his car into reverse. He was throwing mud and gravel as he tore out of the field and headed back to 39 Highway.

Felicia gripped her seat belt so tightly that her knuckles were turning white, but she never said a word. She had been riding with deputies before and knew better than to get stupid when someone was responding to an emergency. The best thing she could was to hold on and be quiet.

Randy waited for Jake and Thor to get back in the truck. Jake was running, yelling commands at Thor in Yugoslavian as he rushed back to the car. They headed south, looking for some clue that would lead them to where the gunshot came from.

Patrick found a small dirt road to the east side of the highway, but it looked as if no one had been on it for a very long time. The grass and bushes were overgrown and undisturbed.

Jake decided to try on foot along the shoulder of the road way. He took Thor with him as he walked southward. Patrick and Felicia drove further on past them. Patrick was getting concerned because dusk was upon them. The cold front that had gone through that morning would soon send the temperature down rapidly. It was supposed to be in the low forties overnight. Already he was beginning to feel a chill.

Morgan drifted in and out of consciousness. She was grateful for that because the pain was intense when she tried to move. Looking at the ground around her, she could see where her blood had seeped from her body, forming a small pool in which she lay. She had enough sense to realize that movement would only increase the blood loss. Already the sun had gone down, and she was shivering uncontrollably. It was hard to tell if the pain from the wound was worse, or the deep chill that had overtaken her.

Her mind drifted from the conscious to sub-conscious modes of thinking. Her thoughts were a curious mixture of Greg and Ian, but predominately they were of Ian. She imagined she was back at the cabin warm water flowing over her body as Ian held her in his strong and safe arms. Morgan always felt safe with him, as though enveloped in the protection of his love. Funny she had never realized how alone she had been before she met him. Now she knew she could never be whole without him. Allowing herself to rest there in the comfort of her delusional thinking, she willed him to come for her before it was too late.

Jake was the first to find the small obscure side road that appeared to have been recently traveled. He got on his radio and signaled the others to his location. Walking further along down the road he found the marks a vehicle had left, obviously driving rather recklessly. There were tire marks deep in the mud; someone had been in a big hurry when they took off out of there. The width of the tire tracks suggested it was a car and not a truck.

Patrick and Randy parked the cars on the side of the tire tracks, in case they might be part of a future investigation. After all, they had no idea what they would find. But as for Morgan, if she didn't turn up soon she was going to be a very cold young woman. Patrick got his spare jacket out of the back of his car and offered it to Felicia. She accepted grate- fully, as she had not dressed expecting to be out in the evening chill.

Jake worked Thor back and forth across the road in a grid pattern, overlapping and crossing the road frequently. This was a pains- takingly slow process, but the sun was now fully down, and it was dark.

There wasn't even a moon to help with visibility, but the stars were brilliant. They always were far from the lights of the city. The only sound was the occasional passing car on the highway, and even that was infrequent. Jake thought it was a damned shame it got dark so early this time of year.

Randy felt helpless, standing by the Blazer watching Jake search the area. For the life of him he couldn't figure out how Morgan could have become involved in something as bizarre as this whole situation. He kept think- ing over and over that this kind of thing didn't happen to people you know. Walking over to Felicia, he put his arm around her in an uncharacteristic display of affection. She refrained from making a smart remark, instead she took comfort in his kindness.

ANN BAKER

THIRTY-FOUR

Ian woke up from his sleep feeling totally refreshed and more fulfilled than he had ever remembered feeling. The first thing that came to mind was Morgan. Slowly he allowed his mind to replay every delicious detail of the morning's events.

Dear God, he thought to himself. *I am totally lost to that woman. She was all I had imagined she would be, and I know she felt the same way.*

Suddenly it occurred to him that Morgan was not there with him. He jumped up and threw on his jeans, not bothering with underwear and went to the living room. The house was too quiet. Something was wrong. Sure enough, Morgan was nowhere to be found. He went outside and yelled for her, but there was no answer. Deep in his gut he knew something was bad wrong.

Ian grabbed his keys from the hook he kept them on by the front door, and flipping on the hall light he searched for the key to his bedroom door. Something caught his eye on the white tiles of the hall floor. There on the floor were two small pieces of plastic, a brownish red in color. He was a meticulous house keeper; in fact it was almost an obsession with him. Bending to pick up the objects, he immediately knew exactly what they were. They were the tips to a bobby pin. It didn't take him long to figure out what the rest of the story was.

Ian unlocked his bedroom door and entered. It didn't look is if anyone had been in there, but he knew as sure as he was standing there, Morgan had seen his little collection

210

of photographs and other things he had collected pertaining to her.

Great, just great, you stupid idiot. How could you have been so dumb to leave this for her to find? Now she's probably run off, and if anything happens to her you will be to blame for the rest of your life.

Ian threw on a sweat shirt and some boots and ran to his car. He unlocked the rear and got his cell phone out. Immediately he called Lieutenant Moreno, but there was no answer at his home. He paged him, hoping he would call back right away. Perhaps he could be of some help. Ian certainly didn't know where else to turn.

As Patrick stood watching Jake, his pager went off. He debated with himself whether to return the call. Having nothing else to occupy his time with, he got his phone from the Jeep, and punched in Ian's number.

"Moreno," he said.

"Lieutenant, this is Ian. Morgan has disappeared."

"Yes, I know," he responded. "Where are you?"

"I'm at my cabin on Thatcher Road near 39 Highway. How do you know she's missing?"

"That's not important right now. I'm just south of you about two miles, on a little dirt road on the east side of 39. Get down here. I'll meet you at the highway."

"I'll be there in less than five minutes." He hung up the phone now more confused than ever. Somehow he just knew Morgan was in big trouble. All he had done to protect her had not helped. He had allowed himself to get too comfortable, too careless, and now she was in trouble.

It only took him a couple of minutes to reach the dirt road, but it seemed much longer.

He followed the Lieutenant down the road to where Jake's Blazer was parked.

"What in the hell is going on?" he yelled as he jumped out of his car.

"Morgan's missing. She called Felicia here to tell her she had escaped from you. Were you holding this woman against her will?" Patrick was livid.

"Hell, no! I told you everything. I think she found photographs I had of her. That might have scared her."

"I can understand why it would!"

"How did you know to look here," Ian asked.

"It wasn't too hard. She called Felicia saying she was somewhere along the Alafia. Knowing that she was with you it wasn't a far jump to locate the property you own here."

"Thank God. She must be all right if she was able to get to a phone."

"She was on a cell phone, but the battery went dead, so no one knows where she is, and that was several hours ago. I called Jake here to help look for her, but as we were searching the area, we heard a gunshot. He said it sounded like a high-powered rifle."

"Oh, that's just great. Fucking great," Ian always swore when he felt helpless, and that was exactly what he was feeling now. "How long has it been since she called?"

"A few hours now," Felicia inserted.

"Why don't we get aviation out here?" Ian asked.

"I thought of that, but I didn't want to get a full blown thing going. The media will be crawling all over this place as soon as that chopper takes off."

"Who gives a damn? Let's get them over here."

Just as the words came out of his mouth Jake came up on the radio. "Lieutenant, the dog's alerted to something. Why don't you come down here."

Chuck James had been monitoring the radio since he left the area. He had driven about three miles away and parked, wanting to hear the results of his little attack of conscience as soon as possible. For the better part of the last hour he had been sitting impatiently going over the whole thing in his mind.

Major Crawford was going to be majorly pissed off at him if she made it. How that would play with his future was yet to be seen. He wasn't sure how he was going to live with himself if he had been successful. It was one thing to hit a target you knew nothing about, but when it was someone you knew, it was another thing altogether.

He jumped when he heard Jake on the radio saying he had found her. Lieutenant Moreno told him to shine his flashlight so he could find him easier. That was the last transmission on that channel. Chuck switched from the main channel to monitor the radio traffic knowing he would hear the call for assistance when it came.

Patrick was the first to reach Jake, who was bending over Morgan, looking for a pulse. Thor sat by watching, panting as he rested with a look of satisfaction on his face. He knew he had performed well.

"Is she alive?" he asked impatiently.

"There's barely a pulse. Get the Medi-Vac chopper 51, 10-18."

Jake hadn't had to tell Patrick what to do next. He was already selecting a channel to call Communications. "Ten-forty-six," he stated.

"C4 to the unit with 46 traffic. Go ahead."

"This is unit 7342, Moreno. I need a Medi-vac chopper to respond to 39 Highway, about two to three miles south of Thatcher Road, emergency status. I am 10-25 with a shooting victim. She appears to be hypothermic and is unresponsive."

"Ten-twenty-six, 10-4."

"And advise of a 10-52."

It seemed an eternity before the dispatcher finally came back. "They said they'll be there within twenty-five minutes sir."

Patrick cursed under his breath, "Damn, twenty-five minutes could be way too long," but there was no other option. "Also, I'm going to need crime scene to respond out here and a persons detective, also notify the duty major, shift commander, and the on call homicide detective," he barked at the dispatcher.

"Ten-twenty-six."

Now that everyone was on the way he could go back to the business at hand. While Patrick had been on the radio, Ian had made his way to Morgan. He was pitiful to look at as he tried to help Morgan. He took his jacket off and placed it over Morgan's lifeless body. Her lips were blue and her skin was pale. She had a thin pulse and her breathing was shallow. It was hard for Ian - always the one in charge, the one with the answers - to stand by and wait for help. Any time a cop responded to a medical emergency the wait for medical services seemed eternal, but this was much worse for him. Bending down Ian touched her hand, picked it up and held it in his. It was cold, her fingertips were blue. He whispered the closest thing to a prayer that he had in years.

Morgan's squad was working in when they found Morgan. At first no one knew who had been shot. Even so there was a great deal of urgency as with any shooting incident.

Mollie was at the command position and

began calling all the people who were to be notified. Supervisor Johnson got on the supervisor's channel with Lieutenant Moreno, and as soon as he found out who the victim was, he called Sheriff Stockdale at home.

"Sheriff Stockdale, this is Bill Johnson from Communications. I need to advise you that Morgan McGhee has been located. She's been shot and is being transported by helicopter to Tampa General Hospital."

"Thank you for the information. I'll be on my way to the hospital. I want you to keep me informed of any significant details as they become available. Do we have any idea who shot her?" Sheriff Stockdale asked.

"No, sir, not at this time. Lieutenant Moreno is on the scene, and details haven't been provided yet. Apparently it occurred a while ago."

"Any word on her condition?"

"It doesn't look very good, sir. It looks like there is a very good chance she won't make it."

"All right, let's do what we can to keep the press calm until we can find out what happened."

"Yes, sir."

Supervisor Johnson hesitated before he sent out the message advising all personal in the Comm. Center and the units on the street of what had taken place. Yet, he knew everyone always wanted to know right away when someone in law enforcement was injured.

Dispatcher Morgan McGhee has been located. She is the victim of a signal 33 and is being transported to Tampa General Hospital by Medi-vac helicopter.

DO NOT VOICE THIS INFORMATION ON THE RADIO

Immediately after sending the message he

heard gasps all around the room from dispatchers. One young girl on the phones ran out
crying. The questions flew at him non-stop.
He finally just held up his hands and said
loudly, "There is nothing else to know right
now. As soon as I know more I'll let you know.
If you happen to be a friend of Morgan's you
might just want to say a prayer for her. It
doesn't look good right now."

The messages from the deputies on the
street poured in and he answered each. Some of
them knew Morgan, but not many. It was like a
family emergency. Even though she wasn't a
cop, she was part of the clan. It is a strange
thing with law enforcement - you might not even
like a person - when the chips are down, everyone closes ranks and protects the wounded.

The Medi-vac Helicopter landed in the
field next to the road. They had a doctor on
board, a rare event. It was only for extreme
circumstances they pulled a doctor from the
emergency room to ride on the helicopter. He
took charge of the scene instantly. Morgan was
barely clinging to life. All of her vital signs
were depressed and her breathing stopped twice,
but her heart never did.

She thought she heard Ian whispering in
her ear, surely she must be dreaming. He was
saying he loved her and couldn't live without
her. Death had come for her, and and he was
all she could think of.

Morgan opened her eyes, she could hardly
believe it. It was Ian standing over her. She
must be dreaming again. He looked so hero-like
standing there. It would not have been a
surprise to see a red super-hero cape swirling
around him.

In her mind she imagined she heard a song
that had been playing at the Ovo Café the night
Greg had taken her there. What was it the song
said something about a beautiful release? That's
certainly what Ian had been, a beautiful re-

lease. Being in his arms had been like being with an angel. Was it memories that were seeping from her veins, or her life that flowed out with her blood? That song must have been written with her in mind, or maybe some things were universal, but she had never felt good enough. Not until Ian. Ian made her feel good enough, he made her feel complete. Nothing else mattered now - not Greg, not the past. It was only Ian that mattered. She would never leave him again. God must have sent him to find her.

THIRTY-FIVE

It was the Tampa General Hospital Intensive Care Ward where Morgan regained consciousness days later. She was confused and couldn't understand why she was there or what all the tubes that were attached to her were for. She tried to pull herself up to look at the vast array, but never got past lifting her head off the pillow.

There was a beautiful nurse standing by her bedside checking her IV bag. She looked like a fairy in a misty glade, the glow of the soft lighting radiated around her warm brown hair forming a halo.

"Well hello there," she said to Morgan softly. "We've been wondering when you were going to join us."

"I, uh. What day is it?" she asked groggily.

"Honey, its Tuesday. You're at Tampa General Hospital. It would be best if you don't try to move."

"Ian, where's Ian."

"He is right outside in the waiting room. But you aren't allowed visitors."

At this, Morgan became agitated. "No, no, you can't keep him from me. I need to see him. Please," she begged.

"Calm down sweetie. I'll check with your doctor. Maybe he can make a special consideration. You just stay calm and I'll page him."

Morgan tried again to adjust herself, to get into an upright position. When she did, a sharp pain struck her left shoulder. Wincing she almost yelled out with pain, but stopped just before she did. She wasn't the only patient in the room. As best she could tell there were four other people in her immediate area. She was thirsty, her mouth dry and parched. She lifted her hand to look at the site where they had inserted the IV, there were marks of adhesive tape that had been removed. Her skin was reddened across the top of her hand. It was clear she had been there for quite some time.

More than anything she wanted to see Ian. She needed to touch him, nothing else was important.

After what seemed to be a very long time, the beautiful nurse returned. "I've got good news for you. Doctor Oberfeld has agreed to allow this one visitor. You wait just another minute and I'll have him here for you."

Morgan cried softly. *Thank God!* She didn't know what she would have done if the answer had been no.

When Ian came into the room he looked worse than she could have imagined. He had dark circles under his eyes, and his hair had obviously not been washed in a long time. But he looked wonderful to her. He came over to the bed and shook his head. Although he couldn't put his arms around her, he pressed his cheek to hers, his chest to her chest.

"Ahhh," she sighed. "That's better." Feeling complete with him there she began to cry.

"My God, Morgan, you scared the living shit out of me. What in the hell were you thinking to pull such a stupid stunt?"

"Shhh, let's not talk about it. It's all okay now. Just hold me."

Ian stood there until his legs began to shake from standing so long. He shifted his weight and took her hand in his. They just looked at each other, content to be together.

Morgan was the first to speak. "Does TPD still think I killed Greg?"

"Don't you worry about that. A friend of

mine, Lieutenant Moreno, has been looking into the whole deal. You're no longer considered a suspect."

"Oh, really? How did they finally get that into their heads?"

"Well, apparently the fact that someone is trying to kill you gave them a hint. I really don't know all the reasoning behind it, but Lieutenant Moreno said they have started searching other leads."

"Great! And what are the doctors saying?"

"Well, you were shot in the shoulder by a high powered rifle. As you can imagine there is some damage in you muscles, but no bones were hit, miraculously. You lost a lot of blood. They gave you transfusions. Beyond that, you should be fine in a few weeks. You were very lucky."

"Yes, I was. I'm very sorry for running away from you like I did. I was afraid." Morgan began to remember why she had been scared. Unsure of whether to confront him with the issue at the moment, she decided not to speak of it.

Ian was relieved she didn't mention the photographs. Best to just let it go. Everything was fine for now. He didn't ask what had scared her. He knew.

"When can I go home?"

"Slow down there. They aren't even planning to move you to a regular room yet. Everyone has been waiting for you to come to."

"How many days has it been?"

"Well, this is Tuesday. That would make eight days."

"Damn, over a week gone from my life, and I don't even remember. That's a first."

Morgan had begun to tire, her eyelids were becoming heavy. Ian noticed that she was having trouble with her words.

He stood and kissed the top of her head.

220

"You get some sleep."

She became frantic, grabbing his hand. "Don't leave me, Ian. I can't let you go."

"I'm not going anywhere. Just let me pull up a chair."

Still she refused to release his hand, holding it all the tighter, even though her grip was very weak. Ian planted a soft kiss on the back of her hand. It seemed to comfort her, and she closed her eyes and drifted back off to sleep. A hint of a smile now replaced the frown that had been there earlier.

ANN BAKER

THIRTY-SIX

Lieutenant Moreno was about as exhausted as he had ever been. After a very long night explaining things to his captain and making sure all the necessary reports had been made documenting the locating of Ms. McGhee, he had only a few hours of sleep before reporting for roll call.

Already the news had spread. When he entered the district office, one person after another stopped him to talk about the events of the previous night. Ordinarily Patrick would have stopped briefly to discuss the details, but he was in no mood to talk this morning. More than anything he wanted to talk to Mrs. Thompson, and get a check going on the funds that had been dispersed in the name of Harlan Boswell.

The deputies that were gathered in the roll call room picked up on Patrick's shortness right away, and no one bothered to question him any further on the McGhee case. For that he was grateful. As he left the room, he reminded everyone to watch each others' backs, a comment he never failed to make.

Grabbing a cup of black coffee from the break room he headed straight for the solitude of his office. He pulled out the desk drawer, put his feet up, and started making a few notes to help gather his thoughts. There would be one more roll call in an hour and then he would be free for the rest of the day as long as he kept an ear to the radio. It was very fortunate that it wasn't payroll week, or he would be interrupted by a never ending stream of supervisors asking questions about how to make the totals work in the antiquated and complicated payroll program that was integral to the computer system.

He needed to get in contact with Detective Lockwood. When he had seen him at the hospital last night there was no time to discuss the information he had begun to assimilate. Surely, Danny didn't consider Morgan a suspect now, but he would need to clear the case. Patrick was certain it wouldn't be the real shooter that would be implicated.

Somewhere, someone wanted Morgan McGhee dead. Patrick meant to stop him with whatever means possible. Although he didn't have enough political pull to intervene directly, but if he could get enough dirt on the responsible parties, the threat would go away.

He trusted Danny to help him get the job done. Danny was just as disconnected with the powers that be as he was. He had achieved all of the ladder climbing he ever intended to, but he didn't have the luxury of imminent retirement. While he would have to play his cards right to keep from pissing off some very important people, Patrick was sure Danny had all the testicular fortitude to get it done. He had seen Danny in action before. He could wrestle with the big boys and win.

The trick to winning was to never let them know you were the opponent. Danny had mastered the technique, and that was why Patrick admired him so much. In this arena to beat them at their own game, you had to play stupid, all the while gathering intelligence. The key was to be able to offer a viable alternative to placing the blame on the real movers and shakers. As long as they didn't take the fall, or one of their allies, it was business as usual.

Tampa had an odd mixture of political factions. There the members of the old school, largely in partial retirement at this point, the family business now having been handed down to the relatives that were willing to get their hands dirty. The neo-insiders were a different animal altogether. They were sometimes harder to identify, well cloaked in seeming legitimate business ventures. They usually surfaced through lawyers at City Council meetings and the gatherings of the County Commission. All the news reporting agencies in the area acted like they were the Chamber of Commerce. Stories of corruption and vice were never covered as they should have been. The constant slant to the local news and long ago disgusted Patrick. He assumed it was the same in every city of any size, but he never had grown comfortable with it.

Time after time innocent people were slaughtered on the pages of the Bay Area Herald, while the guilty were never mentioned. If there was a way to print something inflammatory about anyone who dared rock the boat, they would find it. It was almost as if there was direct pipe line to the media. In all likelihood they even told them how to report the stories.

The people controlling the newspapers, the radio stations, and the television stations were all the same big money people that controlled the entire area. But crime was fairly well under control, there were jobs, and for the most part people were prosperous. The influx of middle class outsiders kept the graft from being noticed by the unskilled observer.

It would be a delicate operation to remove Morgan McGhee from the tentacles of what ever Greg had gotten into. She was very lucky to have someone like Patrick at bat for her.

THIRTY-SEVEN

Morgan was moved to a private room the next day, and Ian was waiting for her when they brought her from ICU. She still had the IV attached, but all the monitoring devices had been removed. The color had begun to return to her face, but she was still very weak.

"I need to get into the shower," she complained as they brought her in. "How much longer before I can get out of this bed and walk?"

"As soon as I get you settled, I'll be in to help you get up. It'll be slow going at first though. You don't realize how weak you are. It will probably make you dizzy to sit up, but as soon as you have your bearings, I'll help you get cleaned up," the nurse promised.

"Oh, thank God! And food, when are they going to let me have some solid food?" Morgan asked.

"The doctor has ordered a regular diet for your breakfast. It may not be what you would have picked, but I'm sure you will find something on the tray that you'll enjoy."

"Ian, you look horrible! How long has it been since you shaved," Morgan said.

"Well, thank you, young lady. It's good to see you are strong enough to complain. You must be feeling much better."

"Oh, that's not really a complaint. Actually you look quite rugged. You could be filthy and I'd still think you looked good."

"I like the sound of that."

Just then Doctor Oberfeld entered the room. "Well, good morning Miss McGhee. How are we feeling this morning?"

"Pretty good considering. I can't wait

to get out of here."

"Everyone always says that. I can't imagine why," Doctor Oberfeld said smiling.

"I like my cooking much better than hospital food. Not that I don't appreciate Jell-O and apple juice."

"Right you are. The liquid diet is limited, but I'm sure you'll be happier once you've had some solid food," he said turning his attention to Ian. "You look like you could use something to eat yourself. Why don't you go downstairs and get some coffee and give us just a few minutes?"

"Some coffee and a little breakfast would be great. Morgan, I'll just be downstairs. I won't be gone long," he promised.

"Okay, but don't stay gone too long. By the way, Doctor, when can I go home?"

"Sometime this week I'm sure, but I'll have to wait to see how you do when you get out of bed. You may feel strong, but when you get up and around I think you'll find yourself tiring rather easily."

The doctor checked Morgan's vitals and found them satisfactory. Then after listening to her heart tones and breathing, he removed the dressing covering the wound in her upper shoulder. "You don't realize just how lucky you were. This whole situation could have had quite a different outcome if this wound had just been a few centimeters lower. Lucky for you the bullet passed right through. There is amazingly little damage to the muscles and none to any bone."

"I'm very thankful for that. I felt as though I'd never wake up. I was so cold and I was having the strangest dreams."

"Hypothermia will make you think strange things. If you hadn't been so damp, the temperature wouldn't have affected you so quickly. You were very lucky they found you when they did. There really wasn't much time left when you got to the hospital. We gave you transfusions. We also had to put you on a ventilator for a few days. You weren't breathing well on your own. Yes, I'd say you are a very lucky young lady indeed.

"I'll be back to see you in the morning. Hopefully, you'll get some rest and a chance to get back on your feet. I've prescribed some pain relievers to take by mouth, and they'll be removing this IV as soon as you can tolerate food. Try not to take them unless you find it absolutely necessary. They tend to slow your progress moving around."

"Thank God they're removing the IV. My hand is so inflamed. I hate it when they put it in the hand. The arm is so much less painful. Every time I move one of my fingers it hurts."

"Get some rest, I'll see you tomorrow," the doctor said as he left the room.

Just as promised the nurse returned right after the doctor left and helped Morgan out of the bed. They had been so very right. She was immediately dizzy and had to sit on the edge of the bed for a few minutes before attempting to put any weight on her legs. She was glad Ian had left the room. She would have been embarrassed for him to see her in such a weak condition.

It was heavenly to wash her face and brush her teeth. The only thing that kept her from jumping right into the shower was the food being delivered. Damn, if it didn't taste good, even if it was hospital food. Morgan had to stop herself from licking the plate. It had been a long time since she had eaten solid food.

THIRTY-EIGHT

Lieutenant Moreno could hardly wait for his lunch appointment with Mrs. Thompson. While he waited, he talked a few things over with Danny Lockwood on the phone.

Danny had very few new details that he could talk about. Patrick, however, did have some new things to share. He told him about the information he had found on Greg McGhee at the court house. He explained that he thought it very odd that he was given a parcel of land, and just a short time later sold it for much less than it was valued at.

Danny was more than just a little curious about it too. He advised that he had done some checking into McGhee's finances too, and that he seemed to have just a little too much money floating around to fit with his salary. Not an excessive amount, just a little much. He promised to look into Greg's bank accounts and see what he could find.

Danny also advised him that six months prior, Greg McGhee had purchased a life insurance policy valued at $500,000, double indemnity. That meant Morgan was due to receive $1,000,000. No wonder they had considered Morgan as the prime suspect.

Patrick shared what information he had on the tag that Ian had seen on the Camaro the night Greg was murdered. He did leave out where he got the information, just to protect Ian.

Danny seemed very interested in the details and promised Patrick he would check it all out, discreetly. It would take several days and cashing in a few favors owed him, but he would get to the bottom of it. This wasn't the first Tampa underworld scheme he had stumbled across, and wasn't likely to be the last. Stepping on toes had gotten more than one TPD detective killed in the past, and he didn't intend to be another one.

THIRTY-NINE

Doctor Oberfeld was glad to have finally caught Morgan alone in her room. After ten days in the hospital she was beginning to look much beter. The color had begun to return to her ckeeks. She was sitting on the side of the bed brushing her hair when the doctor came through the door.

"Mrs. McGhee, nice to see you up and about. I don't need to ask if you are feeling better."

"Oh, much. Thank you Doctor. Having solid food works wonders. And being able to shower, that's such a luxury you don't realize until it's gone."

"Are you feeling up to going home?"

"Oh, yes! I can hardly wait to get out of here. How soon do you think I can go?"

"How about tomorrow?"

"That's great," she said excitedly.

"There is something I do need to discuss with you, however," he said becoming more somber in tone.

"Really, is there something wrong?"

"Well, as you know, you were in pretty bad shape when you came to us just a few days ago. We ran quite a few tests when you came in, x-rays and some blood work. None of them indicated any illnesses or problems other than one."

Morgan tensed at that statement. All she needed was more bad news. "What was that Doctor?" she asked timidly, almost inaudibly.

"We ran one test that we always run on any female patient before performing any x-rays when they're unconscious. Morgan, your pregnancy test was positive. You were examined by an obstetrician. He estimates that you are in the very early stags of pregnancy. Two weeks along at most."

"Oh my God! That's impossible!" she stammered.

Despite her protest she knew it was possible. She knew all too well from her experience trying to conceive that pregnancy tests were extremely accurate very early along.

"Apparently, it is possible. I know this must be a shock for you, especially considering the recent events."

"Shock doesn't begin to describe it."

"I've been on birth control pills for the last couple of years. My husband and I tried to have children for a long time, but we finally agreed not to have any."

"Did you miss any of your daily dosages?" the doctor asked.

"Well, yes. Ever since my husband was killed, I wasn't at my home, and didn't have them with me."

She stopped abruptly, not wanting to say anymore. Morgan felt an involuntary flush as her face reddened, realizing the implications of her last statement.

"Oh, dear God. How could this have happened? I have to have an abortion, right away."

"I know you feel that way right now, but that's really a decision you should take some time making. You're in shock, reeling from all that's happened. You may reconsider in a few days and feel differently about a decision that is irreversible."

"Oh, no! You don't understand. I could never have this baby. It couldn't possibly be Greg's. As embarrassed as I am to admit to you, it's undoubtedly true. I really have to have an abortion as quickly as possible. Can you do it before I leave the hospital?"

Doctor Oberfeld spoke slowly, kindly,

"Morgan, I'm afraid that's out of the question. You're in no condition to go through such a procedure. An abortion would not be advisable for at least six weeks."

"Six weeks! You mean I have to let the baby go on growing for six weeks? That's horrible."

"I can sympathize with your feelings, but there's really no way to safely perform the procedure any earlier. You're far too weak; your immune system has been compromised. You need some time to recover."

"Thank you very much, Doctor for your frankness. I don't mean to be rude, but if you don't mind, I'd like to be alone to think things over."

"I understand. If you have any questions, just have the nurse page me. I'll be happy to talk to you, or if you'd like a second opinion, I'll recommend another doctor." With that he excused himself and left the room.

As he left the room Ian came in. He smiled and shook Doctor Oberfeld's hand thanking him for taking care of Morgan.

Without warning, Morgan's anger flared. Ian's timing couldn't have been worse. She had never been any good at hiding her feelings, and this would be an academy award winning performance if she were able to pull it off. What she really wanted was some time to think about the bomb that had just been dropped in her lap.

"Hello, my lady. Aren't you looking lovely today?"

"Ian, you shaved. You know how I loved that rugged look."

"My apologies ma'am. I had no idea that you'd have preferred that scruffy looking beard to this baby smooth skin." He brushed his cheek against hers, kissing her lightly on her ear.

In spite of herself she felt herself responding to him, it was involuntary. Her head turned towards him, with a will of its own.   She didn't resist as he kissed her deeply, savoring the taste of him. *Damned, if he wasn't impossible to resist.*

"When do I get to take you home?"

"The doctor said I would be able to be released tomorrow, if it isn't any trouble for you to pick me up."

"Trouble?   You aren't any trouble.   I wouldn't miss taking you home for the world."

He stayed for the better part of two hours. Morgan was on pins and needles waiting for him to leave. When he finally did leave she breathed a sigh of relief. At last she was free to think.

FORTY

Lieutenant Moreno paged Danny right after having lunch with Mrs. Thompson. She had been a source of very good information. Apparently, there were many cases of people, just like Harlan that were being used to embezzle money from the Florida Retirement system. Mrs. Thompson wasn't sure of how many, but she had come across nearly a dozen in her limited research.

"Danny, it's Moreno. I need you to check into a few things for me. I really need to know where the money is going from some retirement payments by the state."

"What's up with that, Pattie?"

"I've stumbled across something pretty interesting. What are the chances of you checking it out on the sly? If I do it, it'll be sure to raise more than a few eyebrows," he explained.

"Sure. What ya got?"

"I want to know who holds a specific account with the Tropical Bank of Central Florida, and who extracts funds from the account. I can fax you the account number and copies of a couple of checks that have cleared that account."

"Okay, you want my fax number? Danny asked.

"No, on second thought, I'll just bring it by to you. How long are you going to be there?"

"About another hour and a half. This must be pretty important," he ventured.

"I think it is. I'll be there within the hour."

"You want to meet me somewhere else?"

"That probably wouldn't be a bad idea."

"How about The Green Iguana in Ybor?"

"Better not. I'd rather not run into anyone from the office. Let's make it the Village Inn by 275. That's on your way home, isn't it?"

"Not anymore, but that'll work. I'm walking out the door."

Patrick wondered just how quickly he could get the information. It would be much easier if they had someone inside to slip them the information instead of going through the whole subpoena process. The weekend was coming up fast, and he hoped to have something back before the banks closed on Friday.

FORTY-ONE

Ian was right on time to take Morgan home from the hospital. All of the papers had been signed for her release, and all of her few meager belongings were packed up. He had been thoughtful enough to bring her some clothes to wear home. As usual, he had thought of everything she would need. He remembered underwear, socks and shoes. She reminded herself that she should be grateful he was so very thoughtful. If it had been Greg, she would have been lucky to have just a pair of jeans to wear home.

The nurse took her to the front door in a wheel chair. Morgan held the flowers that the Comm. Center had sent. There was also a nice dish garden from Sheriff Stockdale himself.

There had been no flowers or cards from Greg's mother, not even a phone call. Either she was still in shock over the whole thing, or she blamed Morgan. That certainly would not be surprising since she had resented their relationship from the beginning. He was the youngest child from a family of two. Greg's sister had died as an infant before she reached six months of age. That gave Betty all the more excuse to baby Greg.

Ian pulled up in his Rodeo, and jumped out to open the door for Morgan. First he put the flowers and plant in the back, then helped her get in. He reached around her fastening the seat belt. As he did she thought of the baby that she carried, his baby.

After all the years of wanting a child, she marveled at how easy it was for her to despise the timing of the one she now carried. Small as it was, it was a symbol of her stupidity, her lack of self control. How ashamed she would be when everyone found out. Surely they would guess that it was not Greg's.

As they left Tampa General Hospital, Ian headed north on Bayshore Boulevard. "Hey, where are we going?" Morgan asked.

"Well, home, of course," Ian said, smiling and squeezing her hand.

"I want to go to my home," Morgan insisted.

"I thought you wouldn't want to go back there," he said defensively.

"Well, you assumed wrong." Morgan's tone was harsh and abrupt. Almost immediately, she regretted having been so rude.

"Ian, I'm sorry. It's just that I have a lot of issues to deal with. Running away won't make them go disappear. The sooner I go home and face things, the quicker I will be free from all of that."

Hesitantly he agreed, and took her to the location he knew all too well. Funny thing, she never said a word in the way of directions, and he made no explanation for having known the way. After all, they both knew how he happened to be there that evening just a short time ago, even though they had not discussed it.

Ian helped Morgan into the house. Morgan thought she saw the curtains of her neighbor move. Certainly they were all curious about where she had been and how she was doing.

The house was exactly as she had left it. Not a thing out of place, except for the unmade bed. The sheets were gone as was the bed spread. Undoubtedly they were taken by the police as evidence. It seemed very odd to be back there again, almost as if years had passed.

Ian wanted to stay as long as Morgan needed him, but he felt very uncomfortable being in her home. There was a presence of Greg there, one he could not compete with.

"Morgan, do you mind if I go? I mean, I'll certainly stay if you need me, but I don't want to intrude on your privacy."

"No, not at all," she replied, leaning against his shoulder for support. "This all seems so very strange. I can't believe I ever lived here."

"You will call me if you need me, won't you?" He lifted her chin to see into her eyes more clearly, and seeing nothing to worry him, was satisfied that she would be fine.

"Only if you give me you number. This seems so wierd, so surreal. I'll get a paper for you to write it down."

On the kitchen counter, there was a card with a case number. Officer Blakeman, Tampa Police Department, it said. Morgan threw it in the drawer by the refrigerator and took out her address book.

She wrote his number in the book, stalling for time, for she really didn't want to be alone. "Ian, I can't tell you how much it meant for you to take care of me they way you have. You've been so very good to me. I could never repay you."

"There's no need for you to feel obligated. I was actually very happy to have done it." He was obviously uncomfortable, scanning the room, paying close attention to every detail. "Your house is very nice. I like the way you have it decorated. It's very bright and open."

"Yes, it was a major battle with Greg on every decision. We agreed on very little when it came to the house. Mostly he just let me win because he got tired of arguing about it. It was the only real thing I took a stand on. "Seems very strange to be back here again after having been gone for so long. The roses sure need some work, and the dust in this place must be an inch thick."

"I wouldn't worry too much about getting

things done right away. You've been through an
awful lot. You should just take it easy. I
really think you should come with me and take
some time to think," Ian offered.

"No, no, I really need to be here and
sort through things. There are so many people
to call, and things to be taken care of. I
can't think when I'm with you, and I want to go
to the cemetery to see where Greg is buried,"
Morgan almost started to cry, but had vowed to
herself to remain strong.

Ian sensed her vulnerability and put his
arms around her, pulling her head to his chest.
It would have been easy for her to melt right
there, allowing herself to be pulled into the
refuge of his protection, shielded by his overpowering presence. His scent was nearly irresistible.

She really wanted to stay there, to never
leave. But what would be his reaction if he
knew she was carrying his child? Would he want
to own her, or would he discard her like
yesterday's dirty laundry? Either way, she
was sure she didn't want to find out.

"Ian," she said pushing away, "I think
you'd better go now. I really need to be
alone."

"Okay, I'll go. But I want you to promise to call me it things get too bad, if you
need someone to talk to. I told you I would
always be here for you, and I meant it."

"Thank you. I promise if I need you, I
won't hesitate to call you."

He left, reluctantly, feeling very much
like a large part of himself was being left
behind. Morgan closed the door behind him, and
stood with her back to the door, looking around
the house. Memories of her past life, flodded
her mind.

Shaking herself out of deep reflection,
she went to check the refrigerator. Surely
there would be some wonderful science experi-

ments growing there. To her surprise, someone had cleaned out the entire refrigerator. It must have been Greg's mother, she had her own key to the house.

Thinking it would be good to get out; Morgan decided to run to the grocery store. She grabbed the extra set of keys to the Lexus, no need to drive her old Toyota anymore. Greg's car sat in the garage, just where they had left it such a short time ago. So many things were just the same, so many vastly different.

It was comforting to have a familiar activity to do, some mundane chore to take her mind off things. She had to remind herself she was only shopping for one now. Being hungry she found her basket piled high with all of her favorite foods.

At the check out counter, Morgan began stacking her purchases on the conveyor belt as the cashier advanced it at warp speed. For some unknown reason she found herself trying to keep up with the groceries as they sped off, but she was unable to. Preoccupied, she didn't notice Bobbie from work as she came in the store, but Bobbie spotted her right off.

"Hey! How are you?" Bobbie asked.

"Oh, hi there, I'm... I'm just doing a little shopping," Morgan stammered.

"God, you look great! I would have expected you to look bad after all you've been through."

"Well, truth is, I feel better, considering. But, I am still pretty weak. Thanks for the compliment though. I really need it."

"When are you coming back to work? Everyone's talking about you. I can't believe you got shot."

"I'm not sure when I'll be back. I guess I should really call the Lieutenant and talk to her. She probably wonders what I'm doing too.

"Lieutenant Blendale was very concerned about you. I saw her in the Comm. Center more than once talking to Supervisor Johnson about you. I'm sure she'll be anxious to hear what's going on."

"Truth is, Bobbie, I really haven't wanted to talk to anyone yet. There are so many questions people will ask. I really don't know all of the answers myself," Morgan admitted.

"Well, you don't have to worry about me asking you any questions. But, if you should need anyone to talk to just call me."

The cashier had by then finished with Morgan's order and was giving her the total. She was obviously very interested in the conversation, hanging on every word.

"I gotta run now," Morgan said. "It really was good seeing you. I feel like I am really out of touch with everything. I don't think I'm ready to go back to work just yet though."

"I'm sorry about your husband. If there is anything I can do, be sure to let me know."

"Thanks," Morgan said hanging her head. She hadn't expected to be confronted with Greg's death this morning. So far, she had coped well by not thinking of it.

Bobbie gave Morgan a hug. Morgan suddenly felt like crying. It was nice to have someone female to hold on to, however briefly.

"I'll see you soon. Don't be surprised if I take you up on your offer and call you. I appreciate it."

Morgan took her groceries to the car. *Whew, one down and about a hundred or so to go*, Morgan thought to herself. *Certainly the rest would not be so easily satisfied or as understanding as Bobbie had been.*

ANN BAKER

FORTY-TWO

It was very unusual for Danny to suggest meeting at Patrick's home, but Patrick was certain he had some well founded reason for not wanting to meet in a public place. He had hurried home, not wanting Danny to have to wait. He was very anxious to hear what he had to say. Patrick hoped he had some information on the checks he had given to him.

The wait wasn't long. Punctual as always, Danny's white Ford Taurus appeared in the driveway at exactly 12:00. Patrick waited for him to ring the bell.

"Come on in, Bud. You always were the prompt one; never one minute before, and not one minute after. I think you must circle the block if you get somewhere early," Patrick mused.

"You know me too well, old man."

"Have a seat in the living room. I'll get you something to drink. What would you like?"

"Make it orange juice if you have it. I need the vitamin C."

"Just happen to have some. I'll be right there."

As he waited Danny spread the papers he had brought along on the glass coffee table. He noticed it was sparkling clean, not a finger print or speck of dust. Some things never changed. Patrick had always been obsesive about being clean.

Setting the orange juice in the center of a coaster, Patrick took a seat on the couch next to Danny.

"My friend, those checks you gave me were dynamite."

"How so?" Patrick asked impatiently.

242

Danny got right to the point. "Well, it seems that Harlan's check was deposited in an account belonging to JSBMA, Inc. The only address is a P.O. Box, and all of the officers of the company are fictitious, as far as I can tell."

"No shit! Well, that's not shocking."

"Hang on, my man. After the money was deposited it went through two more corporations just like JSBMA. Then it gets real interesting. There is a little local real estate development company called Gennesett, Inc. The company also dabbles in investments mostly in bonds. The officers of this corporation are quite well known. Here, take a look at the list. I put the place of employment of each of those that I could locate."

Patrick took the document, shocked as he scanned the page.

GENNESSETTE, INC.

CHAIRMAN: Jerry Casmeyr-Property Appraiser's Office
VICE PRESIDENT: Douglas Crawford-Sheriff's Office
VICE PRESIDENT: Harold Wilson-Tropical Bank of Central Florida-Branch MGR
VICE PRESIDENT: Martin Bunch-Supervisor of Elections
TREASURER: George Sweeny-County Administrator
SECRETARY: Charles Jaros-Bay Area Herald-Reporter

MAJOR STOCKHOLDERS

Cebellaro, Marcus	County Judge
Rodman, David	Corporal, Tampa Police
Goddette, Thurman	County Judge
James, Chuck	Deputy Sheriff
McGhee, Gregory	Tax Collector's Office Morrison,
Thomas	Lakeside Development, Inc.
Palmer, Robert	Florida Retirement System
Parillo, Timothy	Lakeside Development, Inc.
Peaslye, Roger	Lieutenant, Tampa Police

"Damn!" Patrick exclaimed. It's like a who's who of Tampa."

"You're right my friend. Did you happen to notice the name of our little dead pal there."

"Oh, yes! I did. How very coincidental."

"One thing I don't believe in, Pattie boy, is coincidence. There is no such thing."

"Agreed on that. So what in the hell is going on here? Does this have something to do with why he was murdered?"

"Bingo. Sure did. I've done some discrete inquiring and have found more than just a little was going on with this company.

"Here's the whole story as close as I can tell. Major Douglas Crawford, your old buddy was friends with Greg McGhee's father.   In 1987 Greg got a little DUI arrest. The Major pulled a few strings, which was easier to do at that time, and the officer that stopped Greg just didn't happen to show up to court."

"Wonder if he got suspended for that little trick?" Patrick asked.

"No, as a matter of fact, he didn't. And the reason for that is cute too. He's retired now, but I did call him and ask about it.   I told him that I needed to know as part of the murder investigation."

"Seems that he was an instructor at the local police academy at the time. The night before he was to appear in court they had him do a little demonstration for the class for the effects of intoxication."

"Oh, yeah. I remember from my academy. They get a guy real drunk over a period of a couple of hours and do field sobriety tests. That was a fun class."

"Yep, that's the one I'm talking about. Well, this was a night class, and apparently they got Officer Bradford real good and drunk. Another instructor drove him home, but when he woke up the next morning, he was still too drunk to drive to court. I'm thinking the whole thing was a little too convenient. Officer Bradford did remember that the class was out of sequence from the schedule he had been given."

"Sweet!" Patrick added.

"So, I'm figuring this is how the Major got to know Greg just a little better. As time went on he seems to have recruited him for a little project he and some of his local buds had going on. They were the ones listed on the Gennessett paper there, and probably a few others. They've used their connections to get people placed, or otherwise recruit partners from every important government entity in the county."

"Damn, it's bigger than I'd thought."

"More widespread than I had imagined too," Danny said. "This list is only the ones I've been able to uncover so far.

"So it seems that there is a certain county commissioner that felt there was far too much money being sucked from the Florida Retirement System, and it needed to come to an end. Whether or not he is wise to the little scheme that is going on is unclear.

"Anyway, McGhee was scheduled to be in some rather high-level meetings in Tallahassee to discuss ways to reduce the amount of expenditures for retiring employees. It is a nonfunded item, so the taxes collected don't begin to cover the ever escalating cost."

Patrick mulled over the deluge of information before answering. "I'll just bet that McGhee didn't have the stomach to pull it off. Did he?"

"Apparently not, so, to cover their asses, they had him shot. I doubt we'll ever be able to pin down exactly who it was.

"And there is one other little detail. McGhee has stock valued at approximately a half a million as of yesterday. Our little Morgan is a comfortably wealthy woman, and she well may not know it."

"I wonder what would happen to her assets if she were to meet an untimely demise?" Patrick ventured.

"That my friend, I can't say. There's no telling."

"There are a few things I found that I couldn't explain."

"What's that Pattie."

"Well, I looked at the records at the courthouse and I saw some property given to Greg, and then sold again rather quickly, at lower than market value."

"Ahh, well that's easy. It was Greg's initiation fee into the group. His father helped him by giving him some property shortly before he died of cancer, kind of a passing of the torch of corruption from father to son."

"Danny, all I want to be sure of is that Morgan won't be a target of these sharks anymore. I could'nt give a shit less about Tampa politics. This is nothing more than organized crime on a smaller than usual scale for this area."

"Right you are. I can assure you that we don't consider Morgan as a suspect. I've been instructed to close this case as a random drive-by shooting, by the powers that be. So, as of today, I'm no longer working this case."

"Damn, the more things change, the more things stay the same," Patrick said.

"True that, buddy. People are people and that you can't change."

"Thanks for sharing all this information. You can be sure it'll go no further. But, I am gonna have a little conversation with the Major."

"Have at it, and good luck." With that

Danny left.

Patrick picked up the phone. "Is Major Crawford in this afternoon?"

"Yes, sir," was the reply.

"Thank you," Patrick said as he hung up the phone.

FORTY-THREE

The black Ford sedan rolled to a stop in front of the McGhee residence. Chuck knew he was taking a big chance coming here, but he just had to see her. He wasn't sure why after all these years of being such a hard ass he had suddenly become soft, but what the hell. Getting out of the car was a struggle, he was a big guy. He ambled toward the door, half way hoping she wouldn't be home. He noticed his hand tremble a little as he rang the bell. *Nice roses*, he thought as he waited for an answer.

He was about to leave when the door opened. It was Morgan.

"Hey, there. I'm shocked to see the likes of you at my door. Come on in."

Morgan was actually glad to see him. He wouldn't be full of stupid questions, and she knew he wouldn't be condescending or judgmental.

"I wanted to see how you were getting along," he stammered. "I guess I should have brought you some flowers or something."

"Yes, you should have. But then, if you were to develop good manners at this point in life, you'd probably cause more than a few heart attacks."

Chuck grinned. He had never been very good at small talk with women. "I heard about you getting shot. I tried to visit you at the hospital, but there was this big blond guy hovering around you."

"Oh, that's Ian. He was wonderful to me."

"I'm glad to see you're up and about so quickly. Are they giving you any police protection, TPD that is?"

"No. Why? Do you think they should be?" she asked, a little surprised.

"It wouldn't be a bad idea. You should call the detective working on the case and see what he can do."

"I only met him the one time at the hospital. I'm sure I have his number somewhere in my things that I brought home. Maybe I will."

"Can't hurt. At least you would sleep better. When you going back to work?"

"I don't know. I haven't even called them. Somehow, I just know they're going to all have a barrage of questions for me, none of which I feel inclined to answer."

"Don't blame you for that. It's none of their business. You should just tell them so," Chuck offered.

"I'm sure that's exactly how you would handle it, but I try to have just a little more tact than that."

"Well, you look great. Here's my number if you need anything," Chuck said extending a business card to her. Unexpectedly, he hugged her. He wasn't sure whether he made the gesture to comfort her or himself. All he knew was that he was glad she was going to recover, and that he had come to see her.

As Morgan said her good-byes to Chuck at the door, the mailman arrived. "Hey there Mrs. McGhee, good to see you home. I've been holding your mail for you. I know I'm not supposed to, but seeing how..." he stopped there not wanting to continue.

"Thanks, Larry."

He was one of the most talkative mailmen she had ever met. Finally, he went on his way and she watched as he drove up the street.

Thinking how lonely she was in her big

house by herself, she threw the mail on the kitchen counter. Before she finished the thought, the phone rang.

"Hello," Morgan said.

"Hello, my lady."

It was Ian. She noticed the phone was shaking in her hand. God, how she missed him.

"What you been up to?" he asked.

"Just a little grocery shopping and I've been trying to clean this house up."

"How about a little dinner? I could come by and pick you up."

Morgan hesitated. She really didn't want to see him just yet. Neither did she want to be alone. "What time?"

"You name it. I'll be there."

"How about five? That way we can beat the crowd."

"Then five it is, see you then."

She smiled in spite of herself as she hung up the phone. No sense in trying to lie to herself. She couldn't wait to see him.

FORTY-FOUR

Lieutenant Moreno breezed through the front door and past the secretary's desk, which happened to be empty. Major Crawford sat behind his desk, glasses on, scanning some paperwork. The portable radio he wore on his belt was turned on and the steady stream of transmissions that poured from it seemed to have mesmerized him. He took no notice of Patrick standing in the door, so he cleared his throat.

Immediately he looked up from his work. "What in the hell do you want?"

"Nice to see nothing has changed since I last saw you," Patrick said smiling.

"I repeat. What in the hell do you want?"

"Just a few minutes of your time," Patrick said as he stepped into the office, closing the door behind him.

"And why the hell should I give you that?" he said insolently.

"Oh, I think you'll want to hear what I have to say. Patience has never been your strong suit, neither has being gracious to guests," Patrick was playing with him now.

"Sit your ass down, or don't, but spit out what ever you came to say," he was becoming angry now.

"Okay, I only have a couple of things to say. First, I want Morgan McGhee safe."

"And what in the hell gives you the idea that I could accomplish or influence that in any way."

"The little involvement you have in a certain 'business' relationship with her recently deceased husband."

The major didn't respond right away. Weighing the full impact of the revelation he had just been given. What the hell did he care about her? He didn't. So conceding to her safety was no big thing. On the other hand, Moreno having knowledge of his business was.

Before he could speak Patrick continued, "Furthermore, I have documentation of your involvement in the embezzlement of funds from the Florida Retirement System."

"Okay, big shot. What's your price? I know you too well to think you just came here for a little conversation," he paused, waiting for Patrick to make the next move.

"It's your lucky day, you son-of-a-bitch. First, how much do you think it's worth?"

"I can arrange a one time lump sum payment. Don't even get ideas about milking this for a few years."

"I don't want any of your dirty money. I'm sure you're relieved to hear that. There's only one thing I want. That is Mrs. McGhee's continued safety, and an article in the Bay Area Herald; a large article, declaring her innocence in any involvement with her husband's murder."

"Well, it looks like you're the lucky son-of-a-bitch today. That I can do. It's just like the little pansy you are to play the knight in shining armor, high morals, never a compromise."

"Unlike yourself," Patrick smirked. "I knew you were dirty, but I never could put a handle on it. And now that I have, trust me to keep all the documentation in a safe place, just in case there should be some need in the future."

"Just like the weasel you are. I guess you're just beside yourself with joy for having something to hold over my head."

"Believe it or not, Major, it doesn't make me happy to have found dirt on you. But, you're safe. I don't want anything from you. I'll be retiring soon and moving out of town. Just make sure when I call down here, nothing squirrelly is going on. And just in case anything happens to me, I've got a lawyer who'll have all the information I have on you, just in case anything happens to me, or Mrs. McGhee." He shot the last comment over his shoulder as he exited the door. "So long, asshole."

ANN BAKER

FORTY-FIVE

Morgan took her time getting ready to go. It had been years since she had been on a real date. Even though she knew Ian pretty well she couldn't help being nervous.

She pulled several dresses out of her closet, trying on each, before deciding on just the right one. It was a calf length red dress that flowed over her like a breeze. She always commanded attention whenever she wore it. The buttons that went all the way down the front were easy to get undone too. She scolded at herself for having such a thought. She picked her prettiest set of red panties and bra from her drawer, and a pair of nude thigh-high stockings. One more thing, a pair of spaghetti strap, beige sandals with heels. Perfect.

She was just finished putting on her make-up when a knock came at the door. Glancing at her watch, she swore under her breath, "Damn, it's only four-thirty, I said five. Taking her time getting to the door, there was another knock. This one was more insistent, more authoritative. She laughed to herself, *just like a cop, banging with authority.*

Morgan stopped to check herself in the big mirror next to the coat rack by the door; she looked pretty good if she did say so herself. She tossed her blond curls over her shoulder, and took a look through the peephole.

"Lieutenant Moreno, come in, please," she said nervously.

She had never gotten over her fear of him. When she had been in training, he always came up on the radio, barking commands. Lately when she worked the radio, he had been silent.

She took it to mean he was satisfied with her job performance. It was something felt proud of.

"Sorry to drop in unannounced. And might I say you are looking quite lovely."

She blushed. "Thank you, sir."

"No 'sir' needed. Please call me Patrick," he offered.

"Thanks. I appreciate that."

"I bet you're wondering what I'm doing here."

"Yes, as a matter of fact, I am."

"Just came to give you a bit of news. Some you will be glad to hear, I think."

"Really, and what is that?"

"I can't offer any details, but I just want you to know, you're no longer in any danger. The people responsible for this whole ordeal have agreed to back off."

"That is good news. Of course, I can think of a million questions, but I won't ask."

"And I wouldn't be able to answer anyway. Suffice it to say that you are no longer a suspect, and better yet, no longer a target." He placed a hand on her shoulder as they stood in the foyer.

"That's good news. Is there anything you can tell me Lieutenant that would make this clearer?" she asked.

"Nothing more than this, you're in a very comfortable position. Your husband was involved in something he shouldn't have been. I suggest you hire an attorney as soon as possible."

"That's scary. Greg, involved in something bad? I can't imagine that. He was always such a goody two shoes."

"Well, apparently, that didn't always hold true. I hate to be the one to have to tell you that, but you did ask."

"Yes, I did, and I appreciate your candor."

Morgan paused as the full weight of what he said sunk in. "What do you mean, comfortable?"

"Your husband has left behind a rather large amount in stock in a local corporation."

"How much is large?"

"An estimate is a half a million, maybe more."

At this she was taken aback. "I feel so stupid standing here. Please come in and have a seat."

Patrick followed her into the living room. There were two couches, all white leather. The curtains were white too, hanging in huge billows over black wrought-iron rods with roses decorating the extremities. Black marble surrounded the fireplace and alabaster statues adorned the mantle. He got the impression of class, taste and money combined.

"Can I get you something to drink, Lieutenant?"

"No thank you, ma'am, I really can't be staying very long. Really, I just wanted to tell you what I've already said. But, there is one more thing. I'm sure when you look through your husband's papers you will find the information you need. I would advise you, however, to liquidate what ever stock he has quickly."

"I appreciate that advice. Your opinion is widely respected Lieutenant, and I assure you I will move quickly."

"Well, then, I really don't want to take up any more of your time. Thank you for seeing me unannounced."

"Not a problem. I'm the one that should be thanking you, and I do. Not just for coming over today, but for looking out for me all along. Ian mentioned to me your involvement in this whole mess. I don't know what would have happened without you."

"Very welcome, ma'am," he blushed. "That Ian, he does cherish the ground you walk on. I know he has a strange way of showing it."

She smiled, "Yes, he's made that rather apparent."

Ian was just pulling up in his Rodeo as Patrick stepped out the door. "Speak of the devil..." he said.

"Appropriately said," Morgan laughed.

Ian and Patrick shook hands coming up the walk and exchanged a few words. With that Patrick was off.

"Dang, don't you look nice," Morgan said.

"Why, thank you ma'am," Ian said.

He was wearing starched light blue jeans that fit like a glove. His shirt was a button-down chambray. She knew what he would smell like before he got close enough to tell. The things he did to her were indescribable.

"Come on in. I'll get you a glass of wine."

"Trying to get me intoxicated are you? Think you can have your way with me?" he joked.

"I certainly am not!" she protested.

"Too bad," he said grinning. "Have you decided where you want to eat?"

"What do you think of the Colonnade?"

"Excellent choice. I love that place."

"Do you mind if I drive?" Morgan asked.

"Not at all. I love a woman that takes charge."

"You're a brave man."

The Colonnade was a part of Tampa history. Having been established in 1935, they had never forgotten the importance of fresh-ness and quality when it came to seafood. It was a favorite of all the old-time Tampanians.

The drive took less that fifteen min-utes, even with Morgan taking her time as they drove south on Bayshore. Funny just about three weeks ago, he was following her as she went to dinner with Greg, headed in the other direc-tion. How things had changed.

When they arrived, Morgan requested a

front window seat table. It would be a few minutes wait, but it was well worth it. They waited in the bar.

Morgan ordered a virgin frozen margarita, Ian had the same.

"Afraid I'll get you drunk?" he asked.

"Very much so. I'm afraid that one glass of wine I had is my limit. I can't tolerate much alcohol."

"Fine by me, I'm not a drinker myself. So, what did Lieutenant Moreno want?"

"Oh, not much, he wanted to let me know that I'm not a suspect any more. That I knew already. But he did say that I shouldn't be afraid, that I wasn't in danger anymore."

"Well, that's comforting. If he said it, I believe it. He's a good man."

"Yes, he certainly was a guardian angel to me."

"More than you know."

Their table was ready, and Morgan pinched Ian on the thigh as they walked to the table.

"Don't rub the lamp if you don't want the genie to come out," Ian mused.

"Oh, my, I don't believe I've ever heard it put quite that way before." Morgan laughed, blushing as she did.

The view of the bay was spectacular. The runners along Bayshore Boulevard were out in full force, as the sky turned a beautiful dark pink and purple. Ian ordered alligator appetizer and coffee for them both.

"Coffee should keep you awake. I don't want you passing out on me again."

She put her hand to her mouth, "Oh my, you're really bad bringing that up."

"I must say I've never seen anyone else so lovely with their mouth agape."

"Ian," she scolded, "that's not polite. You shouldn't tease me like that."

"Okay, I'm sorry. Let's change the subject to something more pleasant. Would you like to see my home in Northdale when we finish eating?"

"Sir," she protested, "you wouldn't be trying to lure me there for some inappropriate conduct, would you?"

"Yes, of course, I would," he replied.

"Well then, by all means, yes," she surprised herself with the boldness of her reply.

"Ian, there's something I need to tell you," she said turning serious.

"Why is it you always change the subject just when the conversation gets interesting?"

"Come on. Just listen for a minute. You don't always have to be in control."

"Go ahead. I'm all ears."

"This is hard for me to say, so please just let me finish before you go off."

"Ill try my best."

"I want you to know that I've been in love with you since the very first time I saw you. And that scares the shit out of me."

"My, my, what a potty mouth you are becoming."

"Shhh, listen for a minute.

"I've been thinking things over, and I realize that the beginning of the end of my relationship with Greg was when I first met you. Since the first time I saw you, I couldn't stand being with him. I was always thinking about you, even though I didn't know you at all.

"That night when Greg got shot, I was really thinking of telling him I wanted a divorce. I just hadn't worked up the courage yet."

"Are you saying I ruined your marriage?"

"Not at all. Ironically you had nothing to do with it. When I met you, I realized what I'd been missing. The love between us had long since died, and I hadn't even really noticed it."

"Kind of like that frog in the pot of

water. As long as the heat is turned up slowly and gradually, the frog doesn't jump out."

"Precisely, so now, I've become rather cynical in my view of relationships. I'm not ready for any kind of commitment. I have been married a very long time, and frankly I don't believe in forever anymore."

"Really? You did at one time didn't you?"

"I'm sure I must have, but right now I really don't remember very well why I did. It seems like if you find someone you really want to be with there is always some reason you can't be with that person."

"Yeah. That's the truth."

"Even though I have very strong feelings for you, I'm not going to allow emotions to control my life, now or ever.

"And I've got to tell you I'm terrified of trusting my own judgment. From what Lieutenant Moreno told me, Greg wasn't even the man I thought he was. I lived with him for years, never knowing what he was involved in. It almost got me killed. So you have to realize that I'm very skeptical of how I feel about you."

"I guess I can understand that. Now can we please change the subject back to something more appetizing?"

"Sure, but please, just remember what I told you. Sometimes I think you hear me, but then it seems like you haven't really heard a thing I have said."

"I swear, I'll never forget," he promised.

They both ordered the crispy grouper. It was superb as usual. The Colonnade only purchased fresh Gulf grouper, and the cornflake and almond breading was marvelous. Having eaten their fill, they drove to Ian's house. It was a rare man that would allow a woman to chauffer him.

Morgan felt like a schoolgirl on a first date. She was so nervous it was hard to keep from prattling on about silly things. Choosing instead silence, Ian turned on some music. He chose a saxophone instrumental CD. The sultry sounds melted Morgan into the seat and her mind strayed, thinking of all the possibilities the evening held.

FORTY-SIX

The garage door closed slowly behind them as she turned off the car. She slipped the keys into her purse. Clumsy silence filled the space they occupied with expectation punctuated with desire.

"Stay right there a minute," he said, with his usual authoritative way.

"I can do that," she smiled agreeably. "God, I do love a bossy man."

"Are you suggesting that I am bossy?" he grinned as he opened her door for her.

That grin, it wasn't his usual. He was definitely missing his customary air of confidence that invariably kept her off guard. It was good to see that he felt as uncomfortable as she did. She took note of it, and decided to pass on the opportunity to make use of her advantage.

Taking her hand, he pulled her along gently towards the door leading into the main house. Just as she thought he would open the door, he turned instead, and pressed the back of her hand he still held to his lips. Turning it over he began to lick gently the tips of each of her fingers.

Succumbing to his seduction, she braced herself against the car, as if it could provide some refuge, some power that she did not find within herself to resist him. But none was to be found. She pulled him down to her, as he kissed her mouth with an intensity that spoke of his need.

She still hadn't gotten used to his style of kissing. She hoped she never would. It would be a shame to take such a wonderful thing for granted. His insistent style made her temperature rise without any effort.

Unable to wait any longer she pulled him closer, tugging at his pants pockets to the point of tearing. Her hand reached around to the back of his head, urging him on. At the same time he changed the pace, becoming tender. She never knew what to expect with him, and she loved the feeling. It was a total rush.

She had struggled to categorize her feelings for him before, never able to come to a fitting conclusion. It didn't matter now. The only important thing was that he was here, and he was kissing her. She had been dreaming of this for days.

Before she knew what was happening, she was begging him for what she had sworn to herself just days before she would never do again.

"I want you now."

He gave her that familiar confident grin. "Don't you even want to go inside?"

When no answer came, he persisted. "What do you want?"

"Please," she pleaded. "Let's not talk."

"You know me better than that."

There was a pause, she answered. "No, I don't want to go inside."

"I knew you would be a wild woman."

"Only for you, baby," she said. She couldn't believe these words were coming from her mouth. But he made her do so many things she would never have done before.

Incited by her verbal permission he now felt free to push ahead. "Can you feel what you do to me?"

He pressed his more than ready hardness against her warmth as she felt herself slowly melting into him.

"Please, shhhh" she requested, all the while hoping he would go on.

"Now what kind of way is that to talk?"

he teased.

"Don't play games. I'm not any good at this."

"Oh yes, you are, and you'll get better. Before long you will do whatever I say."

Fear chilled her soul, because she knew he was right. She would do anything for him. There was nothing she could do to overcome her wanting for him.

"Won't you?" he persisted.

He was running his fingers through her blond curls, examining them with great scrutiny; but paused momentarily, both surprised and slightly irritated. She wasn't answering him. He tightened the grip on the handful of hair he held, pulling her head back and forcing her to look at him. The look on his face frightened her. To her amazement, she found it utterly salacious, the thrill exciting her even more.

He was like no other man she had ever known. Willing to be macho with no apologies, his ego was bigger than Texas. On most men it would have seemed pathetic and appalling, but he pulled it off with polish and dignity.

Growing impatient with her reluctance to answer he pulled her against him roughly, still holding the fist full of hair that held her captive to his will. His eyes searched hers relentlessly, watching her like a cat, waiting for her to falter.

His scrutiny was more than she could bear. "Yes, yes, I'll do anything you say," she said in surrender.

Satisfied now, he eased her back onto the hood of the car. He lifted the skirt of her dress by the hem. The tops of her stockings were just as he had imagined all evening. The lace tops contrasting with her creamy white skin drove him wild.

"Oh, yeah, stockings. I love them," he fairly purred.

Things she held secret from everyone else were just known by him instinctively. There was no purpose in trying to hide from him. She looked into his eyes, which he reluctantly diverted from her stockings. Unfastening his belt, she noticed his shirt becoming damp across his chest. Was it just the normal Tampa humidity and the warmth of the garage, or the heat of the moment causing it?

She unzipped his pants, and having trouble with the button, she yanked at the waist of his pants. The button went skipping across the garage floor.

"My, I guess I don't know my own strength," she mused.

"Oh, I don't mind, as long as you sew it on for me right after breakfast."

"I haven't a clue what to do with a needle and thread," she confessed.

"I'm sure you have other talents to compensate."

Tiring of the banter, he began unbuttoning the little buttons that held the front of her dress. When he got to the waist, she began helping him and slid the dress from her shoulders, dropping it to the floor around her heels.

Ian stood back to look at her and she blushed in spite of herself.

"You are so fucking fine," he whispered, sucking in his breath.

She hung her head covering her eyes with one hand.

"Look at me," he demanded.

Morgan acquiesced, having suddenly lost all her nerve.

"Am I making you uncomfortable?" he asked.

"Yes," she managed to whisper.

"Good, I like that."

He slid a thumb inside each of the cups of her red lace bra and slowly peeled back each, revealing her pink tipped breasts. They were the same creamy white as her thighs. Al-

ternating one to the other he suckled like an
infant would.

He took her hand and guided it to his
crotch. She could feel his pulse racing wildly
in her hand as she squeezed him aching to have
him, all of him.

"See what you do to me baby," he whispered.

It was too much, Morgan could wait no
longer. "Please, Ian, do it. I can't stand
this anymore."

"That's just what I wanted to hear you
say."

He didn't bother removing her matching
red lace panties. She had made the effort to
look pretty for him, remembering his favorite
color. It was much too nice to waste. Instead
he slid them to the side and paused rubbing
himself against her, reveling in her warm suc-
culence. Pants still around his thighs, he
slipped off his shoes and tossed them aside and
following them were his pants and boxers.

"Oh, nice," Morgan said. "The car is
still warm."

They both laughed a little, glad to have
a momentary diversion. Things were moving so
very fast. Ian forced himself to go slow,
deliciously, savoring each sensation. He wanted
her to beg him to be rough with her, and he
didn't have to wait long.

He yanked her off the car and turning her
around he gave her what she had been wanting.
Morgan looked to see his strong hands gripping
her hips. They seemed to belong there. The
intensity was just what she had been craving
and although she knew she should feel guilty,
she did not. It was wonderful, raw, and totally primeval.

Ian grabbed her hair that hung down her
back and pulled her head back as he leaned
forward to whisper in her ear. "I want you to
always remember what this feels like. You're

266

mine and you always will be. This is what you were meant for."

Morgan felt a shudder rush through her entire body. Was it the peak of their sex, or the realization that he was right? Fear and lust were powerful partners.

Ian must have known. He emptied himself into the deepest part of her being. Pulling her back to him by the shoulders he held her back against him and the sound that came from him was somewhere between a growl and moan. Morgan shuddered again.

Ian showed Morgan through the house, and left her in the bathroom to fix her hair. He threw her his robe from the back of the door, and went to retrieve their clothes from the garage floor.

After that romp on the hood of her car her dress looked pretty rough. She laughed to herself, never before had she done anything so crazy, but had to admit it had been fun. In fact, she couldn't remember having more fun. He was a great lover, the best ever by far. She was shocked at herself having sex on the hood of her car, and she having been the one to suggest it. She was changing way too quickly to keep up with.

"Damn, I'm sorry about your dress," he said truthfully. "If you like, I'll buy you another one."

"Don't even think of it. After all, what can a man do when a woman begs him?" she laughed.

"I try to be accommodating," he grinned, almost blushing.

"So, if I beg will you give me what ever I ask for"

"Sure," he volunteered.

"Then come here and let me hold you, just for a minute."

"Huh? That's all you want?"

"That's it. I think I am way too easy to please, don't you?"

"If that's what you want."

They stood there a long time. The fragrance he wore mixed with his own was etched in her memory permanently. She rubbed her cheek against the fine golden hairs of his chest. It felt like heaven.

"You're welcome to stay if you like."

"How long?" she teased.

"Forever if you like," Ian said, but this time he wasn't smiling. There wasn't a hint of jest in his eyes.

"Thank you, I really do appreciate that. But I feel more comfortable with my own things."

"Understood, just say the word and we'll go back."

"How about now? I think I'd better pass on the wine."

"Your wish is my command. I didn't hurt you did I."

She blushed and shook her head, "No."

Morgan was thankful that he did not pressure her to stay any further. She needed to be alone, to think. Maybe she shouldn't have come here, allowed things to go as far as they had. It was clear he wanted forever, and she needed time before she thought about that.

Ian didn't have to ask, Morgan threw the keys to him as they walked to the car. They were quiet on the drive back to Hyde Park, both numb from the romp in the garage.

Ian was the first to speak as they neared her house. "I want you to think about coming to stay with me. You may have thought I was just kidding before, but I wasn't."

"You mean like moving in?" she asked, incredulous.

"Exactly, it's not good for you to be in that house alone. I know it's premature to mention it; Morgan, I'd like you to think about marrying me."

"Yes, you're right that is very premature to say the least. It might be good to let the grass start to grow on my husband's grave before I buy the wedding dress."

He glanced over at her as he drove. "Now I've done it. I shouldn't have said anything."

"Probably not," she agreed.

"There is one thing I want you to know though."

"What's that?"

"If you do decide to be with me, it'll always be my way."

Now she looked at him. "What does that mean, precisely?" she asked trying not to sound harsh.

"I mean, I have to be the man. I like things my way."

"Well, as long as your ways are my ways that shouldn't be a problem," she said haughtily.

He just laughed. *Women... Who can understand them?*

Ian escorted her into the house, checking the rooms to be sure no one was inside. "You really should stay with me. I don't feel safe leaving you here."

"I feel safe staying here, and it's my decision. At least I think I can still make my own decisions."

"Relax," Ian responded. "I didn't mean to make you mad."

"Me? Mad? Never... What ever gave you that idea? I appreciate your honesty. It makes it easier to make decisions when you know what's really going on."

"I feel the same way. Now don't you go running off on me again," he said. "I don't think I could take losing you again."

Morgan said nothing but kissed him, holding him closely. Funny, she hated kissing Greg, but with Ian, she could go on for hours. She held him there for a long time before she released him.

"Good night you gorgeous man."

He smiled that mischievous grin of his and left. She closed the door behind him and watched out the window as the Rodeo made its way up the street.

It was sad watching him go. He was so childlike and trusting. In so many ways he had never grown up, but in so many others he was more of a man than anyone she had ever known.

Everything was like that with him. Just when you thought you could fit him into some category or identify him with some character quality, you found just the opposite equally as true. She wondered if she would ever be able to put the whole thing into some sort of perspective. Probably not, she had to admit.

FORTY-SEVEN

Sleep came easily that night. Morgan's mind was made up. She knew what she had to do. It wasn't like her to make a snap decision. However, she had done so many things recently that she had never done before, like having sex on the hood of a car, or being head over heels in love with a man she hardly knew, and of course there was being pregnant. All these firsts coming so close together had her emotions running away with her. It was time to stop the spinning in her head and bring things back to some manageable level.

The first thing the next morning, she made herself some coffee, and got her address book from the drawer in the kitchen. She dialed Aunt Alisa's number, and waited as it rang several times. At last there was an answer.

"Hello."

It was her. Instantly a flood of feelings overtook Morgan and she began to sob uncontrollably.

"Who is this?" Aunt Alisa asked concerned.

"It's Morgan."

"Child, what's the matter?"

"Oh, God, Aunt Alisa. Everything is wrong. I don't know where to start."

"Honey, you just take your time. I have all day. You want me to come down there?"

"I actually called because I want to come up there. Do you have room for a wayward niece?"

"If I didn't have room, I'd make room. How soon can you come?"

"I'm going to call the airline this morning. Can you pick me up at the airport?"

"You just say when. I'll be there."

"Thank God. I'll call you right back."

"You going to be okay, honey? You are scaring me."

"I'll be fine now. Don't mind me. I just needed a good cry. We will talk all about it as soon as I can get there."

"Don't forget to pack your long john's sweetie. This Tennessee weather has turned cold already."

"Yes ma'am," Morgan agreed.

Aunt Alisa had always been Morgan's favorite relative. She could remember when she was small and visiting her grandmother's house, Aunt Alisa had made her hot dogs one afternoon. They were boiled, the best she ever had. She served her meal with a Grapette soda. Morgan could still remember the taste.

The first time she had ever seen snow was with Aunt Alisa. She had turned on the light that night and sat by the big bay window of Grandmother's house with her, a big bowl of popcorn, and a raging fire behind them. They must have sat there for hours.

Aunt Alisa had never married, and there were speculations that she might not have been of the more commonly accepted sexual persuasion. Morgan didn't care what she was, it wasn't her business. All she knew is that she had been kind to her after her parent's divorce, when all the rest of the family had only offered a cold shoulder.

Morgan wondered if she could keep her dirty little secret from them while she was there. It didn't matter to them that it was the nineties. They would still find it shocking if they found out that Morgan was pregnant by a man other than her husband. The speculation would be endless with her husband so soon in the grave. They would never think that the baby was Greg's. Of course, that had been the focus of conversation concerning the McGhee's ever since their marriage. Certainly some vigilant, tongue-waging busybody would figure it out in no time.

The only way to keep her secret was to only tell Aunt Alisa. She had enough experience of her own with them to ever reveal anything. Of course, she only had to keep it quiet for six weeks. Surely that wouldn't be difficult. She wouldn't be showing, and there was no way anyone could know.

Reservations made, Morgan arranged for the neighbors to watch the house. She could have her mail forwarded when she got to Knoxville, and the answering machine could be accessed from there also. She fertilized her roses and watered them, cleaned the refrigerator, and made all the necessary phone calls.

Supervisor Johnson was very understanding. He told her that he was certain there would be no problem with a leave of absence considering the circumstances. After swearing him to secrecy, Morgan gave him the phone number where she could be reached.

The last thing she needed to do was pack her bags. As instructed, she included the warmest clothing she owned. She didn't pack many things, but it was only for six weeks. If Lieutenant Moreno had been correct, she didn't have to worry about money. She could buy what ever she needed when she got there.

As she called a taxi to take her to the airport, Morgan felt remorseful for not having the courage to call Ian and tell him she would be gone. She knew he would never understand.

The comment he had made the night before on the way home had helped her tremendously in making up her mind. It was the one about how if she were to be with him it would always be his way.

She loved him, more than she had ever loved anything or anyone. But, she had been down a similar road before. As much as she hated to admit it, she was glad to be free of Greg's control. Not that she was happy that he was dead, not at all. The truth was she just wasn't ready to belong to another controlling man.

The love she had for Greg couldn't be compared to the ravenous hunger she felt for Ian. On the one hand there was an easy security that eventually bred contempt. On the other was a blazing passion that could quickly consume all but the most vigilant of souls foolish enough to trust it's seductive call. The two were totally different. One more insideous in it's danger than the other.

Maybe she was one of those people that were destined to be alone. Being alone wasn't the worst thing that could happen to someone. She reasoned it must have been something about her that attracted men that like to be in charge. Somehow, she must be to blame. Admittedly, she didn't have much respect for men that let women run their lives either.

Whatever the reasoning, she knew one thing for sure. If Ian knew about the baby, she would never know if he loved her, or felt only obligation. As much as she had always wanted a child, and as much as she had always deplored the very idea of abortion, she was not going to jump from the frying pan into the fire. It seemed there was only one option.

Ian had been able to protect her from others, but now she needed protection from herself and the consequences of what they had done. The only thing that terrified her more than leaving was the thought of staying.

She knew Ian would be mad when he couldn't find her. He'd go crazy when he realized she had gone. Eventually though, he would get over it, or maybe he wouldn't. That was his problem now.

COMING SOON
from Avanti Books

TIMING IS EVERYTHING
A Morgan McGhee Novel
by Ann Baker

Morgan finds a new career and a new life in the exciting field of law enforcement. Ian is back in her life, but can they make it work? The law enforcement academy wasn't what she expected and the job proves to be more than she could have ever imagined. Tampa's underworld is more apparent than ever. Will she find a way to escape it's tenacles?

Morgan had arranged to meet Felecia Langston for lunch at La Tropicana in Ybor City. It was close to the Sheriff's Operations Center, where the Communications Center was located. Felecia wouldn't have long to eat, and the service was fast. Not to mention, the pork sandwiches were without equal. Morgan could barely wait to enjoy some female conversation and the great food.

Seated near the back door, Morgan watched Felecia walking up the street. She still looked the same, as trim and fit as ever. The creases in her uniform shirt sleeves were knife sharp. Morgan smiled as she notices more than just a few males watching her in appreciation.

Standing to greet her greatly missed friend, the two women hugged like sisters. Morgan fought back tears.

Felecia was like the warm evening breeze coming off the bay, bringing memories back that had long been swept aside.

"My God girl, you look great, Felecia said, standing back to have a good look at the mystery girl. I can't believe you took off like that; although, I don't blame you."

As they took their seats, Felecia grabbed Morgan by the hand, and looked at her closely, as if to see if there was some falseness to be detected. "How are you? I mean really? With all that you have been through, I would expect to be a total wreck. Looking at you, I can't see a hint of the past."

"Well, Morgan began, I'm doing... Actually, I feel like such a bad person. I really should have grieved for Greg, but as it is, I'm still having a hard time realizing he is gone."

"Hey, I think you are doing great, considering the shock. How many women have that happen right in front of their eyes? Then you getting shot, it's a wonder you lived at all."

"The thing is, well, what I really am confused about is Ian. I tried my best to be rid of him. I didn't ever want to see him again. You know he was stalking me, don't you?" Morgan shook her head as she spoke the words. Hearing it spoken made it sound even more preposterous.

"I remember you mentioning something about that. Doesn't that scare the hell out of you?"

"Oh, yes it does. But what scares me even more is that I still am so totally taken with him. I don't see how I will ever live without him, stalker or not."

"Have you seen him? Felecia asked as she tilted her head in inquiry."

"Yes. Oh God, yes. It was the very first thing I did."

Felecia hesitated before speaking, measuring her words carefully. "I really don't know whether to tell you this or not. Maybe you have already heard. Hell, maybe he told you himself."

"What?" A sense of foreboding came over Morgan.

"You know I don't like to interfere in other people's business. If it weren't you, I wouldn't even mention it."

"Tell me," Morgan said trying to remain calm.

"Ian got married about four months ago."

"Oh my God! Oh God! No, he couldn't have," Morgan whispered.

"I'm afraid so. Do you mean to tell me that jerk didn't tell you?"

Morgan didn't answer right away. Her head was reeling. The waitress had just arrived to take their order, and suddenly she had no appetite, but instead nausea.

With the greatest of tact, Felecia asked if they could have a few more minutes to decide. The waitress was gone, and she watched in pity as Morgan struggled with this new information.

"He tried to talk to me and I kept telling him to be quiet. I just wanted to be with him so badly. I thought he was trying to talk about the past. Who's to say that wasn't what he wanted to say I wonder when he was going to tell me."

"Honey, you didn't sleep with him, did you?"

"Sleep? No, sleep had nothing to do with it."

"Oh no… You did it. Didn't you?"